"What are you talking about?" Captain Shelby Davis of the Confederate raider, *Georgia*, asked Arthur Adrian as the two men stood together on the Liverpool dock.

"The *war*, Shelby," Adrian said. "It's over! And Lincoln is dead—shot in Washington just six days after Lee's surrender!"

It took several seconds for Davis to absorb the shock.

The South had been defeated—and Abraham Lincoln was dead!

The young captain knew that these shattering events would mean many things for him.

With the war finished, the barrier between him and redhaired Sarah Warren—a Yankee from New England—was lifted. They could marry and lead a normal life. Even now, Sarah was off to get a room at the St. George Hotel, where he was to meet her.

"You'd better cancel shore leave for your crew," Adrian said, breaking into Shelby Davis' reverie. "They'll be arrested."

"Why?" Davis demanded.

"The Yankees are furious about the assassination, and they're out for vengeance. They say you and your entire crew are pirates because you fought on for six weeks after the surrender. They intend to hang you!"

Suddenly, Shelby Davis' dream was turning into a nightmare. It was a miracle that the war had brought him together with Sarah, but now, by an ironic twist of fate, he would have to leave behind him the only woman he'd ever loved.

And where could the *Georgia* and its fugitive crew go?

Shelby Davis remembered a place—a paradise of islands with a fine climate and damn few Yankees.

The Caribbean! That's where his destiny lay!

He wondered if he would ever see Sarah Warren again. . . .

The Making of America Series

THE WILDERNESS SEEKERS
THE MOUNTAIN BREED
THE CONESTOGA PEOPLE
THE FORTY-NINERS
HEARTS DIVIDED
THE BUILDERS
THE LAND RUSHERS
THE WILD AND THE WAYWARD
THE TEXANS
THE ALASKANS
THE GOLDEN STATERS
THE RIVER PEOPLE
THE LANDGRABBERS
THE RANCHERS
THE HOMESTEADERS
THE FRONTIER HEALERS
THE BUFFALO PEOPLE
THE BORDER BREED
THE FAR ISLANDERS
THE BOOMERS
THE WILDCATTERS
THE GUNFIGHTERS
THE CAJUNS
THE DONNER PEOPLE
THE CREOLES
THE NIGHTRIDERS
THE SOONERS
THE EXPRESS RIDERS
THE VIGILANTES
THE SOLDIERS OF FORTUNE
THE WRANGLERS
THE BAJA PEOPLE
THE YUKON BREED
THE SMUGGLERS
THE VOYAGEURS
THE BARBARY COASTERS
THE WHALERS
THE CANADIANS
THE PROPHET'S PEOPLE
THE LAWMEN
THE COPPER KINGS
THE CARIBBEANS

THE CARIBBEANS

Lee Davis Willoughby

A James A. Bryans Book
from Dell/Emerald

Published by
Dell Publishing Co., Inc.
1 Dag Hammarskjold Plaza
New York, New York, 10017

ISBN: 0-440-01081-0

Printed in the United States of America

First printing—September 1983

Chapter One

As he rode slowly through the crowded Richmond streets, Captain Shelby Davis heard the distant rumble and wondered. Was it thunder or the sound of massed Union cannon pounding the Southern defense perimeter only nineteen miles away? Federal guns and infantry had been hammering those lines for months.

This wasn't the first major Yankee effort to seize the Confederate capital, Davis thought grimly. Would it be the last? Many of the outnumbered and outgunned defenders were sick or undernourished. Even more were barefoot, and this was mid-November. After more than three years of fierce and bloody battle on half a dozen fronts, how much longer could they hold?

The foe had suffered too, the handsome blond Georgian reflected as his stallion cantered past the three-story brick building that was Libby Prison. Once a tobacco warehouse, it now held thousands of Union captives. Many more had been in the huge stockade in Andersonville. Minié balls and grapeshot, bayonets and disease had taken a terrible toll on both sides. The dead and maimed ran into hundreds of thousands, and still this bitter War Between the States dragged on.

There—directly ahead—was the white-columned naval headquarters. Davis smiled in an automatic surge of pride as he looked up at the Stars-and-Bars flag fluttering in the autumn breeze, but he winced when he saw the sentries at the entrance to the building. At twenty-seven, Shelby Davis was the youngest officer to command a Confederate warship. One of these guards was nearly a dozen years younger, sixteen at most. The other had a gray patch over his left eye socket and a pinned-up right sleeve. The strong arm that once filled it was buried with a mound of other severed limbs near a Pennsylvania town named Gettysburg.

The younger sentry's open farm-boy face lit up as he watched Davis dismount. It was hardly surprising that the beaming teenager recognized him. After all, Shelby Davis of the *C.S.S. Georgia* and Raphael Semmes of the *C.S.S. Alabama* were the Confederate States of America's greatest and most decorated naval heroes. The *Alabama* had been sunk off the French coast five months earlier by a Union cruiser that Semmes might have smashed—if some of his shells had not been defective. Now rear admiral commanding the James River Squadron that protected Richmond from Union gunboats and waterborne invasion, dynamic Raphael Semmes was among Davis' closest friends.

It could hardly be otherwise. Though twenty-eight

years separated them, they were of the same special breed. The hunger for action and adventure was in their patrician blood. Both were of prominent families. Both were intrepid sea hawks who had taken or destroyed scores of Union ships—imaginative and daring raiders who had ranged far across the Atlantic and Pacific with dazzling success. Unlike ordinary men, they feared neither life nor death. With all this, it was almost unfair that they should be so decent and good-looking as well.

Their comrades in arms trusted and admired them. Millions of Southerners prayed for them. Single and married women in a dozen states dreamt of them as lovers and sighed in the night in secret fantasies. Neither Shelby Davis nor Semmes sought this, but that didn't matter. As Confederate Navy Secretary Stephen Mallory had shrewdly pointed out to President Jefferson Davis, "A nation at war *needs* heroes, and these two are the stuff that legends are made of."

"I hope you haven't told Shelby that," the tall, thin Chief of State had replied.

"Certainly not, Mr. President. I wouldn't want your nephew to get a swelled head. Matter of fact," the bearded Floridian had confided, "I wouldn't want him to change at all."

Mallory, who had learned a lot about sea power while chairman of the U.S. Senate Naval Affairs Committee before his state left the Union, knew men as well as he knew ships. Aware of what jealousy could do to the small Confederate fleet that he'd built from nothing, he was careful to treat Shelby Davis just as he did other senior officers. When the young raider captain entered Mallory's office at four p.m. on that cloudy November afternoon, the Secretary of the Navy of the embattled Confederate States of America was briskly correct and businesslike. He showed none of the awe that the young sentry downstairs had displayed three minutes earlier.

"Come in, Captain. I believe you know Admiral Semmes."

"We've met," Davis replied, and the two hero-friends smiled at each other in silent greeting.

"Then we can get right to the point. Don't bother to sit down," Mallory said. "We don't have time. Come over here to the chart."

The three men walked to the large world map that covered half a wall.

"That Yankee general, Sherman, says war is hell. He's wrong," Mallory declared. "War is *numbers*. We've beaten off the enemy for forty-three months, but the Union has nearly three times the population and ten times as many armaments factories. Those numbers are beginning to tell."

His right index finger stabbed at the map.

"Federal troops and gunboats now control the Mississippi, practically cutting the South in two," he said grimly. "Union armies hold Nashville and New Orleans. Half of Florida and Georgia are in Yankee hands. Sherman took Atlanta in September, and we have no idea where and when he'll strike next."

He paused for breath.

"There are fifty thousand Union soldiers beseiging Petersburg—less than twenty miles from where we stand— *right now*."

Mallory's finger suddenly swung to the Atlantic coast.

"It's time to hit back. That's why you're here, Captain," he announced.

Shelby Davis smiled as he leaned forward in anticipation. He was going to sea again. The very thought made his eyes glow.

"It's time for the Confederate Navy to hurt *them* for a change," Mallory said, "to sweep the oceans clean of their shipping. Capture their merchantmen if you can. If you can't, sink them wherever you find them."

"I'll find them," Davis vowed.

Mallory barely suppressed a grin. Shelby Davis was like a young tiger—strong, hungry, confident.

"I'm sure that you will, Captain," the Secretary of the Navy replied dryly. "You always have."

"Wish I could be out there with you," Semmes said.

"So do I," Davis answered.

The problem was ships. There simply wasn't another Confederate fighting craft available for ocean raiding duty. The South did not have the industrial shipyards to build combat vessels, and persistent Union diplomats in London had hounded the British government into blocking any more sales. Laird Ironworks near Liverpool had produced the 1,040-ton *Georgia*, the *Alabama* and the *Florida* for the Confederate battle fleet before the ban, but that source was now sealed off.

"Your first problem will be to get out through the Union blockade," Mallory reminded. "Admiral Semmes knows that situation best."

"We're ready to sail," Davis announced impatiently.

"Good. You'll leave just after midnight. There'll be hardly any moon this evening, and we'll provide a diversion so both ships can slip out without detection," Semmes said.

"Both?"

"The *Caroline*'s going out with you, Shelby," Semmes explained.

Davis nodded. He remembered the *Caroline,* a privately owned blockade runner. He turned his attention to the detailed chart of the local coast that Semmes unrolled. They went over each point of Semmes' crafty scheme twice before the two naval officers nodded in silent compact.

"This is the most important mission you've ever had, Captain," Mallory said gravely. "We need victories, and we need them *now*. General Lee is regrouping for a whole series of counterattacks, but his men are weary. Morale is a critical problem. Go out and smash those Yankee ships so we can be proud. Bring us some victories!"

"You have my word," Shelby Davis pledged.

Then Davis and Semmes left to return to the harbor where the *Georgia* and the James River Squadron were anchored. As they walked from the building, Davis saw a familiar gray mare and recognized the splendid animal immediately. She was Traveler, the personal mount of the greatest Confederate commander of them all.

There he was—his beard and mustache white, but his eyes still flashing strength.

Everyone—even the lanky Yankee president—agreed that this Virginian was the most brilliant strategist of the war. Northerners called this conflict the Civil War. Southerners spoke of it as the War Between the States. One of the few things both sides agreed upon was that this remarkable West Pointer was the finest general of all.

Robert E. Lee—son of "Light Horse Harry" Lee of Revolutionary War fame and a military genius in his own right—strode towards them, and the naval officers saluted at once.

"Admiral . . . Shelby . . . Just saw your uncle," Lee said in a tone as troubled as the look in his eyes. The expression on the face of his aide was equally somber. Colonel Raymond Duval had been much cheerier six years earlier when Shelby Davis briefly courted one of his pretty daughters. Louise? No, she was the younger one, just a child. It had been voluptuous *Annette*, one of the most beautiful women in all Louisiana.

Now the distant rumble sounded again.

"Sounds like a storm," Semmes speculated.

Lee shook his head.

"The men call it 'Grant's thunder.' That's Union artillery," he said. "How are things with you, Shelby?"

"I sail tonight."

"Then we'll pray for good weather," the deeply religious general told him.

"Bad would be better, sir," Semmes volunteered.

"Of course—the blockade. Well, good hunting."

For a moment Shelby Davis considered asking him for battle news from Georgia. He had a sister who'd been caught in Atlanta with her four children when Sherman's Federal columns steamrollered into that city. He decided that it wouldn't be right to bother the Commander-in-Chief with his personal concerns, so he merely saluted and watched Lee and Duval stride into naval headquarters.

Davis and Semmes went over the break-out plan again as they rode their horses to the fleet anchorage. When they got there, a blond twenty-year-old lieutenant attached to the James River Squadron had the answers to the questions that Davis had been too courteous to ask.

"Just had word, Admiral. Sherman's on the march again. Moved out of Atlanta in three columns the day before yesterday. More than sixty thousand troops, they say."

"Which way is he going?" Semmes asked.

"Looks like he's marching to the coast—right for Savannah."

"At least that should ease things for your sister in Atlanta, Shelby," Semmes offered.

The lieutenant shook his head.

"Afraid not, Admiral. Seems that Sherman's making an example of Atlanta. Cleaned out every chicken and blanket, every food store and warehouse in town. That's not the worst of it either. They say you can see the smoke for fifteen miles."

"What are you talking about?" Shelby Davis demanded.

"I *told* you, Captain. The Yankees set more'n one hundred fires before they left. Atlanta is burning!"

Chapter Two

"There's nothing you can do, Shelby," Semmes sympathized.

"I can sink a lot of ships," Davis replied fiercely and rode off towards his raider. The *Georgia* was tied up at a dock just a mile down the river, facing a 190-foot craft that looked like a blockade runner. It was new, sleek, and had a low silhouette that would make it difficult to spot on the horizon. A smokestack amidships indicated that this vessel was steam powered and fast. It would need every knot of steam power it had to outrun the Union ironclads and cruisers.

Shelby Davis paid little attention to the other ship. His mind was on his own 220-footer and its eighteen cannon that hurled sixty-four-pound shells. As his white stallion—the horse his father had given him the week before this savage war began—trotted towards the

Georgia, the young captain went over his mental checklist again.

The raider had plenty of fuel.

Ammunition lockers were full.

The entire crew was healthy and aboard.

He had some seven hours to top off the food supplies and fill the water casks, and then the *Georgia* could put to sea. One hundred fires in Atlanta? He'd match that. He'd light up the oceans with the burning hulks of one hundred enemy merchant ships. His head told him that Sherman's devastation might make military sense by denying supplies to the South, but his heart wasn't listening.

As he neared the dock, he heard the sounds of a horse in pain and the voices of men. One of them was loud and furious. It was an obese white man—at least two hundred and sixty pounds and six feet tall—who was shouting curses. He had a riding crop in his left hand. He was beating an old dray horse that had crumpled between the poles of the wagon it had been pulling.

"Get up! Get up, you lazy bitch!" he roared at the fallen mare as he cut at her again and again.

"Don't hit her! Please don't hit her!" a shabbily dressed black man of about fifty pleaded. "She be sick, Master."

The fat man whipped the horse again and again, drawing blood. The animal screamed and thrashed in agony, and now the slave rushed forward to protect the poor creature from the vicious barrage. Suddenly, the man with the riding crop turned from the mare to rain blows on him instead.

The fat man was at least fifteen years younger and

ninety pounds heavier than his victim. He had the riding crop plus a pistol in his belt, while the slave was empty-handed. To make it even more unfair, the black man did not dare to resist, since the penalty for a slave who fought his master was extreme. It might even be mutilation or death in those states where slaves were still considered property not unlike chairs or pigs.

Shelby Davis was no lawyer, but he knew that this awful beating could not be tolerated. Whatever right the fat man had to deal with his slave property, this brutality was wrong. Without hesitating, the young naval officer jumped down from his steed.

"You there! Stop that!" he shouted.

The beefy man in the glossy black leather boots looked up for a moment, sneered, and then resumed his assault on the bleeding slave.

"Stop beating that man!" Davis ordered.

"That's no man. That's an animal—*my* animal. Stay out of my business, Mister."

He raised the riding crop again. Davis stepped forward, ripped it from his grasp and hurled it into the river.

"You're the animal," he told the fat man.

"And you're the fool," the livid sadist snarled as he reached for his pistol. Davis was in dress uniform for the visit to naval headquarters, so he was wearing his sword. He drew it in a flash. Before the fat man could realize what was happening, the blade whistled through the air and the pistol went flying.

"You're lucky I didn't kill you," Davis told him truthfully. "Don't ever draw a gun on a Confederate naval officer unless you're ready to die."

Then Davis slid the sword back into its scabbard, and

the fat man, screaming obscenities, rushed at him. He was big, but clumsy. First Davis punched him squarely on the jaw, then drilled a fist into his right eye. When the yowling man raised his hands to his hurting head, Davis slammed four hard blows to his midriff. He watched his adversary gasp, gag, reel back and sag to the dock like a deflating balloon.

"It's animals like you who give the whole South a bad name," Davis told the moaning, wheezing hulk. "No wonder people up North—even people in Europe—think we're barbarians."

"I . . . I'll get you for this," the fat man threatened in a hoarse voice. The young raider captain shook his head and turned towards his ship.

"Nobody does this to me! Nobody! I'll find you—wherever you go! Whoever you are, you'll pay!"

Davis stared down at him coldly.

"I'll make it easy for you," he offered. "My name is Shelby Davis. I'm the captain of the *Georgia*. You can find me on her anytime."

The beefy man was still cursing as Davis remounted and rode on to his vessel. He had neither the time nor the interest to reflect on the ugly incident. There was a great deal to do. There was a warship to put to sea. He couldn't even think of his sister, or write a farewell letter to his mother in Savannah whom he missed so much.

Within minutes after he was aboard, men swarmed across the deck of the *Georgia* carrying out a dozen of his orders. There were so many things to be double-checked, so many final details for a long, lonely journey. The supply wagons that Semmes had promised arrived with additional food and medicine shortly before six o'clock. Even as these were being unloaded, teams of sailors Davis had sent ashore returned to the raider with casks of fresh water—enough for a sixty-day voyage.

They obeyed Davis without question.

No member of the crew knew where the ship might be heading.

Not one of them asked.

It was safer not to know such things. There might be Northern spies anywhere. Only last week a "friendly" barmaid at a tavern barely a mile from the port had been seized as a Yankee agent.

"Keep those barrels moving, Lieutenant Fitzgerald," Davis called out sharply.

"Aye, aye, sir," the broad shouldered first mate replied in a voice tinged with a Dublin brogue. Fitzgerald's family had migrated to America after the devastating potato famine. Pink-faced and dark-haired, he was a "Black Irishman" and an excellent officer who'd served on a coastal freighter between Savannah and Baltimore before this war.

"Get your backs into it, me boyos," Patrick Fitzgerald bellowed at the loading team. "You're movin' like a bunch of bloody English gentlemen."

Familiar with his hostility towards all things British, the sailors laughed. They liked his earthy speech, his fine baritone voice—and the fact that he never shirked either work or responsibility. The casks began to roll up the gangway more rapidly. By nine p.m. the loading was completed. The lines were cast off twenty minutes later after a final check, and the *Georgia* steamed slowly down the James River towards Chesapeake Bay and the sea.

There was not a light showing on the raider.

When men spoke, they kept their voices low, hushed.

There were Union ironclads waiting on blockade just a few miles ahead. Shelby Davis looked up at the heavens and nodded in satisfaction. Semmes had been right. There was barely a glimmer of moonlight to betray them, and the thick dark clouds seemed to promise the even greater protection of rain.

The danger lay directly ahead.

Within twelve or thirteen minutes the *Georgia* would steam from the safety of the James River out into the broad bay where a dozen Union warships were waiting to blow her out of the water. A single mistake now would be disastrous.

Would the rain come in time?

Again Davis looked around the raider's deck, to make sure that the blackout was complete. It was. A moment later he turned his head to peer back into the inky blackness for the *Caroline*. He saw nothing. If the blockade runner had fallen behind, she'd have to run the gauntlet on her own later. Shelby Davis could not wait for a merchantman or anything else.

Now Fitzgerald pointed back at a thin spume of smoke.

"No need to worry about the *Caroline*," the first mate said softly. "Captain Beecher sails better than he fights."

"Don't know the man, Paddy," Davis replied, as he swiveled to peer ahead at the twisting river, "but I'll take your word for it."

"Begging the captain's pardon, but you met him on the dock this very afternoon."

A jagged flash of lightning zigzagged across the horizon.

"The only person I ran into . . . You can't mean *him*. That fat thug commands the *Caroline*?"

"Commands and owns her, they say. I hear that he's killed more'n one slave with his bare hands," Fitzgerald said solemnly. "Word is, Bart Beecher's done other things too. Things to young girls—some only fourteen or fifteen—things I wouldn't want to talk about, sir."

Another jagged bolt of lightning slashed through the sky, and Davis saw Chesapeake Bay only a mile down the river.

It was time for Semmes to distract the foe.

Suddenly a light glowed off to the left. Then it swelled into a fire, and Shelby Davis nodded in satisfaction. The admiral had promised to divert the attention of the Yankees with a blazing hulk, and there she was. The plan to ignite an old Chesapeake Bay oyster dredger had sounded fine, but would it work? If it didn't, the *Georgia* would have to fight her way out to the Atlantic.

"Stand by, gun crews," Davis called out.

The men had been at their cannon for nearly an hour.

Aware that their shells could do little against ironclads, they were ready for battle.

Now the boom of Union guns echoed from across the bay. Davis and his crew braced for the impact, rigid and resolute. But the foe was firing at the burning decoy. The Union armada was hurrying to engage the burning hulk. The trick had worked.

Three and a half minutes later, the noise of Yankee cannon was drowned out by a massive barrage of thunder. The skies split open, and heavy blinding sheets of rain poured down to shield the Confederate vessels. Half-soaked, but happy, Davis turned to his mate.

"Full speed ahead!" he ordered.

The *Georgia* knifed through the choppy bay like a hunting dog that had been unleashed as it raced through the storm for the open sea. For one moment Shelby Davis found himself remembering a passionate young brunette whose appetites included making love outdoors in the rain. She had laughed and gasped in joy as the water poured down on her glistening white flesh. That had been the year before this war began.

No time for such memories now.

Even if there were, it would be a mistake to yield to them. He would be at sea for many weeks. It would probably be months before he even saw a woman. Davis shook his head, took the wheel and concentrated on getting the raider out beyond the enemy fleet. The *Georgia* heaved and shook in the storm for some eighteen or twenty minutes before the downpour began to subside.

Brushing the water from his blond hair, Shelby Davis raised his telescope to sweep the horizon. There was no ship of any kind between the *Georgia* and the open Atlantic. They had broken free.

"*Caroline* four points off the starboard bow, sir," called Fitzgerald.

Davis looked at the blockade runner half a mile

away. She'd be heading for Bermuda, where many Confederate ships picked up cargoes of British products that the South urgently needed. Some three hundred thousand Enfield rifles in the hands of General Lee's stubborn infantry had been smuggled in from Bermuda and other ports. Some of the blockade runners had greedily chosen to bring in luxury goods like fancy liquor and clothes, ignoring the Confederacy's essential military requirements. Efforts to force these money-crazed men to put their nation ahead of huge profits had been only partially successful. It wasn't merely a Southern crisis of morality. Semmes had spoken of avaricious Yankee traders who sold guns and other military supplies to the South—indifferent to the fact that it was used to kill their own cousins and brothers. This was an ugly war in so many ways, Davis thought grimly.

"*Caroline* changing course, Captain."

Southeast. Straight to Bermuda.

Beecher would pick up his cargo in four or five days, and within a week after that he'd be counting his profits back in Richmond. The very thought of that pig growing fatter on this bitter war made Davis' eyes flame in anger. There probably wasn't any point in wasting time on hating Bart Beecher, Davis told himself. The odds were that they'd never meet out on this vast sea.

The Atlantic was immense, and the regions where the raider was to scourge Union shipping were far from Bermuda or the balmy sea lanes favored by blockade runners. A chill November wind whipping in across the deck made Shelby Davis shiver. He was cold and wet, and the dangers awaiting the *Georgia* were awesome. Dozens of Union warships ranged the Atlantic in their hunt for the few Confederate raiders, and Federal spies lurked in every South American, African or European port where the *Georgia* might put in for food and water.

Davis was not afraid.

He had defied the odds before. He would do it again. He knew his crew and his craft, and he knew the ways of the sea. This was his natural habitat. Even soaked and chilled by the night wind, he felt free and strong out here. He was a bold man of the open water, a mariner no farm or office could ever hold.

"Reduce speed one-third and tell the gun crews to stand down," he ordered.

He looked up contentedly at the heavens and searched for a break in the clouds so he might find the stars. As if on command, the solid overcast broke open and there they were. Within a fortnight the *Georgia* would be in the South Atlantic, ravaging Union shipping.

It was no mere plan.

Shelby Davis realized that Secretary of the Navy Mallory, Semmes, Jefferson Davis and General Robert E. Lee himself were all counting on him. This next great counterattack might be Lee's last—Dixie's final chance.

Davis had given his promise as a naval officer, a Confederate patriot and a Southern gentleman.

Whatever the cost, he would keep his word.

Chapter Three

The *Georgia* steamed east out into the open Atlantic.

The route that Davis had plotted took them from the normal shipping lanes. There was little likelihood that the warship would run across any other vessel out in these choppy waters, he thought as he stared ahead. With any luck, it would be weeks before the foe discovered that the South's most respected naval commander was at sea again.

He was much too exhilarated to sleep.

It was nearly five a.m. now, and dawn was not far.

He should have been yawning, been bone-tired like the others still on duty. He wasn't. He was on his way to fight again. He would need his wits and imagination every minute, for his war was a strange and special crusade.

It was also an exciting one.

He couldn't have slept now, even had he wanted to. His mind was much too busy, and the briny smell of the sea stimulated him like the perfume of a beautiful woman. As his gaze wandered over the horizon, he considered how he'd strike the foe.

Stealth and surprise.

Hit and run.

Those were the crucial rules for a Southern raider in the year of our Lord 1864.

Shelby Davis knew them well, and nobody applied them better. He would devastate Union merchant vessels in areas where no one expected Confederate warships. Then he'd race the *Georgia* away to some other sector of peaceful ocean before the Union cruisers arrived, and start all over again.

And again.

Adding extra smokestacks and changing the *Georgia's* silhouette in other ways, he'd make her appear and vanish in a dozen disguises. At some point he'd double back to waters that the *Georgia* had swept through earlier and sink four or five more Northern cargo craft before disappearing out to mid-Atlantic again.

Speed and timing meant life or death. Whenever the raider put into some neutral harbor to resupply, it could not linger. Staying anywhere for longer than forty-eight hours would be dangerous. Double that period could be utter disaster, as Semmes discovered when the *Alabama* was caught in the French port of Cherbourg. At every moment of the day and night, Union cruisers with heavier guns would be hunting Shelby Davis and his ship. Davis and his men would never have an hour to relax, let alone an entire day to escape from the pressure.

Cat and mouse.

That was the name of the game.

Not all naval officers—Confederate or Union—could play it. Seamanship and bravery were not enough. Cunning counted as much as courage in this strange game—a fantastic nautical chess match in which each move covered five hundred to one thousand five hundred miles. This was not a struggle for little men with small minds, Davis knew. He was glad for it too; it made the game worth playing.

Now the sun rose—a dull burnished glow in the November morning. Davis peered at the distant light, and then looked up to see how much smoke was rising from the *Georgia*. Even though the raider's coal bins were filled with almost smokeless anthracite, he was the wary sort who checked anyway. Another raider captain named Harper hadn't, and his vessel had been spotted and blown out of the water.

So far, so good.

The engine was burning "clean," and there was no black column to betray them to other vessels out of sight on the horizon. The problem would come in a few weeks when the *Georgia* had used up the anthracite and had to refuel in some foreign port with other types of coal. Now his attention was distracted by the smell of coffee, and Davis turned to face his first mate, who held a steaming mug.

"Didn't know you drank coffee, Paddy."

"Indeed I don't," Fitzgerald replied indignantly, "though it's a hard thing to get a decent cup of *tay* on this vessel. The coffee's for you, Captain—unless you'd be good enough to take a few hours sleep."

"*Good* enough?" Davis asked with a grin.

"*Bad* for a ship to have a commander who's red-eyed exhausted," the first mate answered in that lush brogue. Shelby Davis nodded. Fitzgerald was right. It would be stupid to deplete his physical resources at the beginning of this long cruise. He'd need all his strength later, when the fighting began. Reminding Fitzgerald to keep the lookouts alert, Davis descended to his cabin to sleep.

Six hours later, Davis' mental clock awoke him.

"Not a ship in sight, sir," Fitzgerald said as the Captain returned to the bridge looking alert and rested.

"Let's hope it stays that way, Paddy."

It did for the three days that the raider steamed east. Then Shelby Davis gave the order that the whole crew had been awaiting. They had been speculating and arguing—even betting—on which way the *Georgia* would turn. Some said north to the busy sea lanes to Britain. Others confidently predicted that they'd continue east. They were all wrong.

"Due south," Davis ordered and everyone within earshot gulped. When he gave Fitzgerald the precise course, they all understood. He was guiding the *Georgia* to waters off the northern coast of Brazil, an area where no one would expect a Confederate raider to operate. Once again, Shelby Davis would catch the enemy by surprise. Eight more days passed before a lookout spotted a distant craft.

"Sail, ho!"

It was a slow-moving, old Portuguese freighter, a neutral vessel that was no target for the *Georgia's* cannon. Her guns did not boom for another forty hours.

Then they hurled explosive shells at a Union grain ship out of Boston, punching half a dozen holes in her hull before the captain surrendered. Davis put a skeleton crew of armed men aboard, to make sure that the captured vessel followed the raider south.

The next Nothern merchantman tried to outrun the *Georgia* when they met on December the first. It didn't. It couldn't, for the warship was at least five knots faster. When the first shells did not persuade the Union captain to yield, Davis did what he had to do. Four salvos opened holes that left the ship dead in the water, taking in hundreds of gallons of the chilly South Atlantic every minute. Then the *Georgia's* skipper saw a distant puff of smoke, and he knew that he could leave the sinking ship with some confidence that the survivors would be picked up soon.

The *Georgia* devastated nine other Northern vessels during the next three weeks before Davis took the raider and the captured grain ship into the harbor of Recife on the northern coast of Brazil. He had chosen this city quite deliberately. There'd be U.S. diplomats and spies down in Rio de Janeiro, but no one official here to rush word to the U.S. fleet. After he'd unloaded and sold the wheat, he used the money to resupply the *Georgia's* food lockers. Only then did he disembark the prisoners. Then the two vessels headed swiftly out to sea and the Yankee craft was burned as soon as they were out of sight of land.

Shelby Davis watched the flames silently.

Some of his crew joked. A few even cheered at the sight of an enemy craft being destroyed.

The young captain of the *Georgia* merely shook his head.

"It's not a pretty thing to see a ship die, is it?" he said

"That's a *Union* vessel, sir," Fitzgerald reminded.

"I know—and we'll sink a lot more of them. I'll do my duty to the final minute of the last day of this war, but I can't enjoy watching *any* ship die. They're not just wood and metal to me. They're living things!"

"Yes, sir," replied the first mate, who'd long been aware of his commander's private passion. Davis had not spoken of it openly until now, but Fitzgerald had seen that pain in his eyes before when ships were destroyed.

"A ship has a character and a life of its own, Paddy," the handsome skipper of the *Georgia* continued. "It's a sea creature, and I don't enjoy killing them . . . Do I sound like a romantic, Paddy?"

"Not to me, sir. But I'm Irish, and we're a romantic lot. Farmers, soldiers, poets and women so pretty they'd hurt your eyes—all romantic and full of mad notions," Fitzgerald boasted with a grin. "Will I ever forget me mother's tales of magic leprechauns and spirits living in trees and rocks? Live ships, you say? The divvil take me, Captain, but I'd wager you're at least part-Irish yourself."

Davis nodded. His father's mother had been the daughter of a Belfast teacher. The Irish probably had a lot in common with America's proud and independent Southerners. Both were agricultural people who loved their land and wanted to rule themselves. Indeed, Ireland's secret Fenian Brotherhood—covertly preparing to cast out the British army of occupation—had already approached the Confederacy to lend combat veterans to train Hibernian patriots for battle. But at the same time, Davis remembered, many Irish immigrants who'd fled from grinding hunger to the U.S.A. were fighting in the Union forces.

"And there are probably other Irishmen on those Yankee cruisers out to sink us," he reminded Fitzgerald.

"We're not a people to shun a fight," the first mate defended indignantly, "and this is the best one there is right now.".

"Then let's get back to it," Davis said and announced the new course.

Southeast.

Fitzgerald computed swiftly.

The western coast of Africa, an area rarely patrolled by Yankee warships. With her coal bunkers refilled in Recife, the *Georgia* should be three quarters of the way to the Dark Continent before federal cruisers reached Brazilian waters. While they'd be searching, the *Georgia* would hunting more than one thousand five hundred miles away.

It worked out exactly as Shelby Davis had planned. Five Yankee vessels went to the bottom off the South African coast. Now it was January of 1865, the start of a new year. Lee would be launching his counterattacks any day now, Davis thought on the morning of the seventeenth. Then he told Fitzgerald to head northwest.

"We're doing pretty well here, Captain. It's like shootin' fish in a barrel," the first mate said.

"It'll be a rather crowded barrel in two or three

weeks, when those federal heavy cruisers get down here," Davis reminded. "Let's go whaling up north."

The Yankee whaling fleet off the Azores Islands was a prime target. The oil that those ships pressed from the blubber of the slaughtered sea giants was burned in lanterns in many Northern cities, and it was used by Yankee armies as well. These days, whale oil was considered strategic material.

The whalers were taken completely by surprise. Their crews gaped when the *Georgia* suddenly swept down upon them with her guns blazing. Between February thirteenth and twenty-second, five Northern whaling ships were sunk—four within sight of the Azores shores. Davis put into Ponta Delgada for coal, food, fresh water and news of the war back home.

"We have heard nothing from *Norte America* for more than a month," the rotund mayor of Ponta Delgada said—and then politely asked when the *Georgia* would leave. The Portuguese were neutral in this strange conflict between the States, and they didn't want any naval battles in their peaceful territorial waters.

Next, the *Georgia* swooped up to attack Yankee merchantmen east of Ireland en route to British and French ports. By the end of March the raider was in Bermuda. There was news. It was not good. Lee's offensive was moving slowly, and the Confederate troops that had struck to within sight of the U.S. capital in a daring raid had been forced to retreat before they could enter Washington. Sherman's legions were grinding up from Georgia and devastating South Carolina with fire and cannon.

"Of course, the tide will turn soon," predicted David Benjamin. The diplomatic agent of the Confederacy in Bermuda was the brother of Judah P. Benjamin—the South's Secretary of State—and a confirmed optimist.

"You're certainly doing your share," he complimented the raider captain. "Everybody back home is talking about your victories. It's definitely helping morale."

"We're doing our best," Davis answered and turned to go.

"One more thing, Shelby," Benjamin said. "We've had word there are Yankee cruisers patrolling northwest of here. The *Caroline* outran one just four days ago."

So the thug was still in business.

Benjamin noticed the flicker of fury in Shelby Davis' eyes and wondered what it meant. Before he could ask, the raider captain thanked him for the information and hurried back to his vessel. As he strode aboard, he noticed a man, a Caucasian, fishing from a nearby dock.

It seemed unlikely that there would be fish here in the busy harbor. The man's pale skin showed that he was a recent arrival, and his shoes were much too costly for any waterfront ne'er-do-well.

"Union spy," Davis told his first mate on the deck of the raider a minute later.

"They're thick as fleas, Captain. Less than three hours ago, a buxom black lass in that smoky grog shop up the street was being terribly *friendly*. Asked as wather I might be lonely—and when we might be shipping out."

Fitzgerald's face was one huge mischievous grin.

"Exactly *how* friendly was she?" Davis tested.

"Didn't want to hurt the dear girl's feelings. Marvelous mass of female she was. At least one hundred fifty pounds, and not an ounce in the wrong place. Ah yes, Captain . . . Very friendly she was, indeed. *Twice*. She insisted. You know, fond of sailors and all that."

"And what did you tell her?"

"Tell her? The truth, of course! My sweet mother raised me never to lie to a woman, Captain. I said I didn't know when we sailed."

Shelby Davis managed not to laugh. He was amused by the mate's pious cunning. There were some on the *Georgia* who didn't realize how shrewd Fitzgerald was behind his deadpan acting, but the captain wasn't one of them.

"And she asked you to come back tonight, Paddy?"

"Indeed she did, sir. How did you know?"

"Just a guess. Probably your good looks. Go back, and be *friendly* again. Have some more rum if she suggests it."

"If that's your order, sir," the ex-Dubliner replied in a fine parody of reluctance.

"And tell her we're heading north tomorrow night—running the blockade back into Chesapeake Bay and up the James River to get home."

The first mate squared his shoulders resolutely.

"Fitzgerald will do his duty," he pledged.

"And be on board by half past ten!"

Fitzgerald returned to the ship at 10:27, and four hours later the *Georgia* slipped out to sea. As dawn broke, Davis had a dozen crewmen putting up an additional smoke stack—a dummy that would give the ship a very different silhouette. The raider steamed south, sank three more Union ships off Florida and then turned out into the wide Atlantic. Now Yankee admirals would be hunting another Confederate raider that didn't exist—and spreading their pursuing cruiser force thinner.

That might buy the *Georgia* weeks, Davis calculated—maybe even months.

If Lee's genius and his armies' counteroffensive succeeded by then, the North would have to recognize that it could never conquer the Confederacy. After four years of inconclusive bloodletting, the Yankees must be tired too. The long-time dream of the Southern leaders—a negotiated peace and an independent South—would become a reality. All the slaughter and destruction would not have been in vain.

It was a life-and-death race, Davis thought grimly.

Would Lee prevail before those Yankee cruisers hunted down the *Georgia*?

Time would tell, and soon.

Chapter Four

In various disguises, the *Georgia* swung north in a wide arc to catch enemy merchantmen moving cargo from Philadelphia and New York to Europe. On April fifth, the raider steamed by within a mile of a Union warship whose gullible skipper thought he saw a French freighter. The *Georgia* had a wide assortment of national flags for such crises. Three days later, another Yankee cargo ship was sunk eighty miles off Cape Cod.

Davis wondered how long his skills and luck would hold out against the odds. On April tenth he had his answer. The *Georgia* was steaming east again, and it was almost dusk when the lookout up topside called out loudly.

"Yankee cruiser off the starboard bow!"

It was the thirty-two-gun warship *New Jersey*, and her captain was not fooled by an extra smokestack or the French flag.

"Closing fast!" the lookout shouted.

"You think he's recognized us, sir?" Fitzgerald asked.

Davis ordered his gun crews to man their weapons and peered again through his telescope. As he opened his mouth to answer the mate's question, a cannon on the *New Jersey* thundered.

Two more boomed seconds later.

"There's your reply. Forward guns . . . Open fire!"

The battle was joined. Three salvos were exchanged. The *Georgia's* gunners were better. Perhaps it was the extra drills and training Davis had ordered. Maybe it was their country-boy eyes and shooting experience. Only a single Yankee shell hit the zigzagging Confederate raider, but four rounds from the *Georgia* damaged the cruiser. Both ships were blasting away furiously at a range of barely half a mile. Suddenly two more shells struck the raider. Men began to shout.

"Fire party! Fire party! Water to aft deck!"

Davis watched his men fight the blaze for half a minute, but then he had to refocus on the artillery duel. It would be foolish to stay and slug it out with the more powerfully armed Union warship, he decided. Even if the *Georgia's* skilled gunners eventually prevailed, the raider would be so badly battered that it could no longer function as a combat craft.

"Even if I win, I lose," he thought aloud as he yelled to his gun crews to concentrate on the enemy's steering gear. A scant three minutes later the *New Jersey* was drifting out of control, with her rudder disabled and her crippled stern power system spouting steam. Unable to bring more than two guns to bear on the fast and agile raider, the Yankee officers cursed and raged in frustration as they watched the *Georgia* race away at top speed.

"Damage report," Davis demanded twenty minutes later, when the last flickering flames had been extinguished.

"One dead, three men burned—not too badly. One gun out of action, but the chief thinks he can get it working again, sir," Fitzgerald announced.

"Who's dead?"

"Young Atwood. Could have been a lot worse, Captain."

"Tell that to Atwood."

The eighteen-year old sailor from Florida was buried at sea at eight the next morning. The *Georgia's* crew—including the bandaged men who'd been burned—lined the rail to say farewell to their fallen shipmate. It was a cold, foggy morn on the North Atlantic, and the men shivered as Captain Shelby Davis read the traditional last rites from the leather bound prayer book his mother had given him fifteen years earlier.

When Davis had concluded the ceremony, the body was offered to the sea. Then, suddenly, the lookout began to shout.

Less than three hundred yards away, a long, lean ship was moving swiftly out of a mass of mist. She was under full sail in the strong wind, and the flag that fluttered atop her main mast was that of the United States of America. For a moment, something warm surged in Shelby Davis in instinctive response. Though this was the banner of his foe, it still wasn't easy to hate that red, white and blue ensign. He'd loved it for the first twenty-four years of his life. He could never forget that. Changing loyalties did not come easily to this man.

"Yankee whaler!" Fitzgerald identified.

"Gun crews to action stations!" ordered Davis.

He loved these sleek whaling craft even more than other ships, but he could make no exception. He would do what he had to do.

Less than two hundred yards now separated the vessels.

"I don't think she's seen us," Fitzgerald said incredulously.

Soon, though, there were men moving, running on the deck of the whaler. They'd spotted the *Georgia*. At this distance they had to notice the gun ports and the Confederate flag, which had been run up to give young Atwood a proper funeral. Yes, the Yankee captain would twist his wheel sharply at any second in a desperate attempt to escape in the fog.

But he didn't.

He did something even more desperate.

Aware that the raider's cannon could smash his wood-hulled craft to kindling before the whaler could get out of range, the Yankee skipper pointed his vessel's prow directly at the *Georgia's* stern. Davis understood immediately. He began to run.

"He's going to ram us!" a young ensign shouted.

Davis reached the raider's wheel, spun it with all his strength and prayed that he was in time. He didn't rely entirely on divine assistance, however. He was too much of a combat commander for that.

"All guns, OPEN FIRE!"

If the whaler should succeed in injuring the *Georgia*,

it would not escape unscathed itself, Davis swore to himself.

The *Georgia's* steering controls groaned under the strain.

Eighty feet now. Maybe less.

The raider began to turn slowly.

Fifty feet.

Two guns fired. At this range they could hardly miss. They didn't.

Thirty feet. For a second, Davis thought he caught a glimpse of a woman—a red-haired woman—on the whaler's deck. That was impossible, of course. Now he saw his crew—all but those at the cannon—grabbing on to anything they could to prepare for the impact of the collision. He braced himself.

And the whaler slid by.

Only by five or six feet did it miss the *Georgia*.

As it passed, two Yankees fired pistols and another hurled a harpoon. It was unbelievable—to throw a spear at a warship! Those Yankees had guts—or were they simply crazed with hate?

"FIRE!" Davis heard himself order.

This time four shells smashed into the whaler. Shelby Davis saw her name painted on the stern. She was the *Simon Grundy* out of New Bedford. She wouldn't be much longer.

"Blow away her masts!" Shelby Davis ordered.

It took nearly twenty minutes to do the job. The canny captain of the whaler slipped out of sight three times in the fog, but each time the faster and more maneuverable steam-powered *Georgia* found her—and the raider's cannon thundered again. Finally, the battered Yankee craft ran up the white flag. With her masts destroyed and her deck half-covered with ruined sails and rigging, the *Simon Grundy* was heeling over as water rushed in.

"Come alongside, Paddy," Davis instructed. "Let's pick up the survivors."

It took half an hour in the heaving waves, but finally forty-six crewmen from the mortally wounded whaler reached the deck of the raider. Now Davis saw that he'd been right. There *was* a woman, astonishingly beautiful with long red hair. She was in her early twenties, wide-hipped and very full-breasted. She was also extremely angry. Seething fury glistened in her large green eyes.

"I'm Captain Davis. Is there anyone still aboard your ship?"

"No one alive," replied a gray-haired survivor in the ruin of an officer's uniform. He spoke with authority in an accent that was pure New England.

The woman's rage seemed to be growing even more extreme. She was panting like an animal in heat. Her lush body was quivering, and she looked as if she might burst out in hysteria at any moment.

"Are you all right, Miss?" Davis asked in concern.

"Murderer! Murderer!" she screamed.

Her right hand was raised high as she ran towards him. It held a saw-tooth edged knife.

"Butcher!" she shrieked in accusation as she neared him.

She was only two strides from Davis when an ensign from North Carolina drew his pistol to stop her.

"No!" the raider captain ordered.

A split second later, Fitzgerald caught her with a grunt and wrenched the weapon from her hand. With the same motion he hurled it over the side as the furious redhead struggled to tear loose. She wriggled one hand free and made a wild clawing lunge at the first mate's face. Her nails barely missed his eyes.

"Lady . . . lady," he reproved and dropped her onto the deck with a thud.

"I think she's gone mad," he judged. "Shall I tie her up, Captain?"

Before Davis could reply, she was on her feet again—charging directly at him. This time it was the gray-haired Yankee officer who grabbed her.

"Let me go! Let me kill him!" she demanded urgently. The man who held her shook his head.

"I'm Captain Joshua Warren," he said firmly as the woman strained to wriggle loose, "and this is my daughter, Sarah . . . she is not insane."

Davis nodded. "I can understand her emotion," he assured the Yankee. "After all, the shock and violence of a naval battle, the shelling and the danger, then being rescued in rough seas from a sinking vessel . . . It would unnerve any gentlewoman."

"Let me kill the brute!" she pleaded.

Her father ignored the appeal.

"She is no gentlewoman, and never was," he told Davis bluntly. "She's what some call a tomboy—a man in a woman's body."

An extraordinary body, Davis thought.

"It is not her mind that my daughter has lost," the old Yankee Captain continued, "but her temper. She has a terrible temper—for which I apologize."

"The sight of men dying, the blood . . . It could panic anyone," Davis said.

Captain Joshua Warren shook his head again.

"I shouldn't have given in to her," he brooded aloud. "A whaler's no place for a woman—not even in peacetime. She has shamed me. We struck our colors, and you believed us. You trusted us to cease fighting, took us aboard. And she tried to kill you."

"Next time *I will,*" she vowed fiercely.

"Her mother died when she was ten," the Yankee said, "and I was away at sea a lot. Maybe that's why she's wild. Always on her own, always fighting with people—not like other girls. I swear I didn't know she had that knife."

Suddenly Fitzgerald pointed off to the starboard.

The battered hulk that had been the *Simon Grundy* was sinking fast. Only the whaler's stern still projected from the surging blue-green waves. Warren and his surviving crewmen stared in grim silence. Shelby Davis could almost feel their hurt.

"Attention!" he ordered, and as his Confederates stood rigid he raised his hand to his forehead in crisp salute to honor the final struggle. A strange creaking sound—almost a wooden groan—sounded across the waters as the oak-hulled vessel disappeared from sight.

"At ease," Davis commanded a moment later.

"Thank you, Captain," Joshua Warren said in a voice choked with gruff sincerity.

"I'm sorry," the Georgian replied. He turned and instructed his second mate to find quarters for the survivors. "They could probably use some hot rum too," he added.

"What about *her*, sir?" the mustachioed Texan asked.

Someone had to protect her. This voluptuous redhead could cause all sorts of problems. The sailors of the *Georgia* were not animals, Davis thought, but why tempt them?

"Captain Warren and his daughter can share my cabin," Davis answered. "Move my things in with Mr. Fitzgerald."

"Why don't you put me in irons, Southern gentleman?" the girl taunted bitterly.

"I'll think about it," he promised good-naturedly.

Her reply was a glare of glowing hatred.

After the survivors had been escorted down below, Fitzgerald noticed that the commander of the *Georgia* was wearing an odd smile. No, it was something more, and the Irish-American recognized it.

It was the man-woman look—the hunger, the animal thing.

"She's a fine figure of a lass," Fitzgerald tested.

Davis nodded in silent agreement.

"But a dangerous one. Begging the captain's pardon, I do believe that she still means to kill you."

"You're probably right, Paddy," the handsome young captain replied, still smiling.

"You know, sir, her idea about the irons wasn't such a bad one," Fitzgerald pressed.

"No, that wouldn't do . . . but I'll keep a very close eye on her."

Jesus, Mary and Joseph, Patrick Fitzgerald thought and swallowed hard. *That* would only make it worse.

* * *

Sarah Warren probably didn't know it herself, but the fuel that fed the fires of her rage had nothing to do with ships, politics or war. It was something much more primeval—something difficult, if not impossible to control. Burning within her, coursing through her very bloodstream, was a woman's passionate need for affection and love.

It was entirely normal and natural to feel this. It was her right.

Alone and proud, unsure but hungering, she had, however, repressed and denied this human truth. Inhibited by the rigors of New England Puritanism, she had distilled her bottled-up need for companionship and completion into fury. By now—at twenty-four—she was capable of almost anything in her hurt and longing.

Yes, she could kill.

It was hardly surprising that the sight of handsome Shelby Davis had ignited her wrath, Fitzgerald told himself. In dreams that she could not dare let herself remember, she had yearned for such a man. Now Fitzgerald wondered how to explain this to his well-bred and gallant captain. He had to warn him that she wanted and needed and feared and hated him desperately and all at the same time.

Beautiful Sarah Warren was a taut and troubled virgin, a woman seething with pent-up passions and living with a hair trigger.

Such women were the most dangerous of all.

The girl remained in Davis' cabin for three days, refusing to come out even to eat. The sailors who brought in her meals reported that she simply glared at them in sullen silence.

Was it fear or hatred, the Captain wondered. He found himself thinking of her frequently—and at the oddest times. He'd look up at the sky, and suddenly a cloud scudding across the horizon reminded him of Sarah Warren.

No, it wasn't *thinking*. Thinking is done with the brain.

He *felt* the absence of the redheaded beauty only ten yards but still so very far away. There could not be anything between them, he realized, but he wanted to see her. It was probably just the loneliness of a mariner who had not been with an attractive woman for months.

Maybe she wasn't well.

"Is your daughter ill?" he asked Joshua Warren on deck one night after supper.

"With pride," the Yankee snapped gruffly. "I told her I'd have done exactly what you did if an enemy craft tried to ram my ship, and I told her she owes you an apology. Didn't even answer me."

"She doesn't owe me any apology," Davis assured.

"She owes the world an apology," Captain Warren fumed as he stamped away to descend to the cabin.

"The Captain was asking about you," he reported to his daughter.

She continued to stare out the porthole.

"How long do you mean to keep up this nonsense, Sarah?"

There was no reply.

"Captain Davis did nothing wrong. In fact, he saved your life," Joshua Warren reminded her. "That ensign would have shot you dead if Davis hadn't stopped him."

Not a word, not a look, not a shrug.

"I've had enough of this and enough of you," the whaler erupted angrily. He slammed the door behind him as he left.

She wasn't the least bit disturbed.

Sarah Warren wanted to be alone in this cabin—*his* cabin. She made her way to the bunk, lay back and closed her eyes to escape into the fantasy again.

She was in *his* bed—half-asleep. These were the sheets on which the handsome, frightening stranger slept. Reality was slipping away as she slid into the daydream. He was tall and strong. It would be impossible to resist such a powerful man. She had no desire to do so.

Gold.

Yes, his hair was golden and she knew that he'd smell clean. Despite his power over her, he would not hurt her. His touch would be gentle and knowing. Now she felt his caress. What was he doing? Her breasts swelled. Her nipples stiffened. She felt dizzy and helpless.

She opened her mouth to protest, but no words emerged. Only a muted, choked sound—barely audible—came from her knotted throat. It was hot in the room again, just as it had been the other times when she had yielded to this consuming dream.

It was too late to cry out. His lips covered her mouth. They were—somehow—gentle and fierce, cool and fiery. The temperature in the cabin was rising. She felt her mouth open under his magical kisses. Her heart was pounding, and she knew that she was lost.

The heat was moving down her body. What was he doing? Her hips began to quiver strangely, and her breaths came in urgent gasps. She tried again to scream for help. She had to stop him. *Someone* had to save her.

But no one did.

How could this happen on a ship filled with people?

Only a low despairing moan came from her clenched throat as she realized that no one heard. No one cared. Hands were at her thighs. What had he done? Her whole body seemed to be on fire. She was grinding her teeth in frantic resistance. Sweat sheeted her face. The flames flickered higher.

The brute was upon her. His body was heavy, his hands ruthless. It was terrible. The dizziness swirled again, and she prayed that she might faint.

Father! Father!

There was a loud knock at the door.

It sounded like a cannon. It was not her father, but a sailor come to collect the dinner dishes. The nightmare was over. She blinked for a moment in confusion. Then she swiftly composed herself, and glared hostilely at the enemy.

What a cold woman, he thought as he left the cabin moments later. He'd seen frigid females before, but none like her. This Sarah Warren must be made of ice.

Chapter Five

The storm broke an hour later.

It seemed to come out of nowhere—sudden and savage.

Weather on the North Atlantic was frequently rough between November and the end of April, but this tempest was something extraordinary. The battering that the raider took was relentless and brutal.

Winds of more than seventy miles-an-hour howled and hammered, twisting the 220-foot warship as if it were a toy in some child's bathtub. Even with full power from the big steam engines, the *Georgia* barely crawled ahead at a few knots. The noise of the screaming winds was almost deafening. Deckhands could barely hear the orders that Shelby Davis shouted from the bridge. It became routine to repeat every command two or three times.

It was impossible to see fifty yards. The rain poured

down in awesome torrents, forming rippling walls of water that seemed almost solid. Drenched and half-blinded by the intense downpour, the crew of the raider cursed the treachery of the sea, the inadequacy of their storm gear, the bucking and nauseating rolling of the ship, the war and anything else they could think of.

Shelby Davis had been at sea since he was eighteen, and these were the biggest waves he'd ever seen. They slammed against the hull like giant fists and sent men reeling under the impact. Those on the deck held on for their very lives. Many were lashed to safety ropes that would keep them from being hurled overboard. Anyone catapulted into those churning waves would have no hope at all. There wasn't the slightest chance he'd be seen, let alone rescued. Estimated life expectancy: three minutes.

The winds grew stronger at dawn. More than eighty-five miles-an-hour.

It was a real hurricane, and it wouldn't stop. By mid-afternoon, the crew of the *Georgia* was nearly exhausted from the unending struggle. Several had been injured, hurled against machinery and deck gear with enough impact to smash teeth and break shoulders.

"How much can the men take?" the raider's pot-bellied medical officer asked as he clung to a rail.

"The question is how much can they *give*, Dr. Preston," Shelby Davis corrected, "and they'll give what's necessary."

"Maybe we can help."

It was a soaked, but determined Joshua Warren. His men's lives were in danger too, and they wanted to volunteer.

"Least we can do is spell some of your weary lads," the whaler captain said. "You have my word—all our words—that we won't try anything improper."

Improper—it was such a righteous New England term.

"I'll take your word," Shelby Davis agreed, and soon Yankee and Rebel were sweating side by side to save the ship. Putting aside all their years of bitter differences and anger, they fought to stay afloat and alive. United, they could. Divided, they were all doomed. It was as simple as that, and every man aboard knew it.

The Atlantic would not surrender. It still meant to have this ship. The storm raged on furiously. Waves rose to moving mountains that swept the deck and clawed for the desperate mariners who were so tired they could hardly blink out the stinging salt water.

More men were hurt. Shortly before midnight, the hurricane tore loose a piece of the *Georgia's* smokestack. It spun through the air like a broken top, struck Captain Joshua Warren in the left leg and snapped it like a dried twig. He dropped, as if felled by a forester's axe.

Only Shelby Davis saw him fall in the blinding rain. He ran from the bridge as the Yankee captain began to slide towards the rail. The *Georgia* was heeling sharply under the impact of the hurricane, and Warren was slipping to his death. His head and shoulders were over the side when Shelby Davis grabbed the ankle of the unbroken right leg.

The ship kept tilting.

Shelby Davis tensed at the lethal embrace of the icy Atlantic.

But the mighty ocean changed its mind. There was

another surge, and the *Georgia* straightened up abruptly. Now Fitzgerald fought his way through the wind and rain to drag them back. Two deckhands loomed out of the hurricane to carry the injured Yankee below for medical treatment. Davis and his first mate inched and battled back to the bridge, both bone weary and dazed. Panting and bruised, they felt as if they'd been in a no-holds-barred fight with some huge bareknuckle champion. It was more than a minute before either of them could speak.

"Bloody . . . damn . . . storm," Fitzgerald gasped.

He was proud—but oddly embarrassed—that he'd saved his captain's life. For all his Irish rhetoric, the first mate of the *Georgia* had a shy streak that he rarely showed.

"Thank you, Paddy," Davis said simply.

Then they returned to the war with the savage sea. At midnight Davis went below to seek two hours of badly needed sleep, leaving word to be awakened so he could take the helm again and someone else might rest. First he made his way to the ship's small surgery to visit the injured men. The pain-killing laudanum had done its job. All but one were unconscious.

"You can tell Miss Warren that her father will be all right," Dr. Gordon announced. "Tough bird—but I suppose all those whalers are. He'll be walking most good as new in six or eight weeks."

"And the others?"

"Adams got a nasty gash. Won't look so pretty, but he never did, anyway. It's Eddy's arm I'm still worried about. Doing my best," the fat little physician reported with a concerned frown.

The other members of the *Georgia's* crew often kidded the portly doctor about his size, age and past. Only five-foot-six and one hundred eighty pounds, he'd been treating the fluttery wives of rich Carolina planters until July 24, 1861. That had been his fifty-eighth birthday—and the day he learned that his youngest son had died on a federal bayonet in the battle of Bull Run some seventy-six hours earlier. Dr. William Cicero Clark had enlisted a week later. He served two years with Lieutenant General Thomas "Stonewall" Jackson's infantry before a bad leg forced reassignment to naval duty.

"Your best is very good," Davis reminded the physician, and started up the passage to give Sarah Warren the news of her father. Buffeted by the brutal storm, the ship was heaving and swaying wildly as he walked and lurched to the cabin door. Bracing himself with one arm to stand upright as the *Georgia* rolled, he rapped twice.

It wasn't going to be easy to tell her.

There was no way to predict how this passionate woman might react, but he had no choice.

"It's Captain Davis," he announced.

There was no response.

Perhaps she hadn't heard the knocks. She could be asleep, or maybe the howling violence of the massive hurricane drowned out the sound of his knuckles. It could also be that the abrupt and extreme movements of the ship in these ferocious winds and seas had made her ill.

He knocked again.

"Captain Davis," he repeated loudly as another blast of thunder sounded.

The door opened—about three inches. All he could see inside was a dramatic billow of that long red hair. Even that small glimpse stirred him.

"What is it?" she asked huskily.

"It's nothing to fear. Everything is under control," he assured. "Your father and most of his crew have been on deck helping us . . . doing a fine job."

"What's wrong?"

"It's not that bad. Could be much worse."

"My father!" she guessed.

Now the door swung open wider.

Even wearing Shelby Davis' nightshirt she looked splendid and exciting.

"He'll be all right," the handsome Georgian said firmly. "His left leg's broken, but Dr. Gordon says he'll be walking in six weeks."

"Where is he?"

"Sleeping like a baby. He's in sick bay. It's no place for a lady. You'll see him in the morning."

The ship swayed, and she grasped at the door jamb.

"Is that the truth?" she demanded uncertainly.

"I don't lie."

They eyed each other for several seconds. Each felt the pull, but neither realized that the other was experiencing the same sense of raw physical attraction. The closeness was disturbing, threatening. Davis opened his mouth to say good night, but she spoke first.

"I'm sorry, Captain. I didn't mean to call you a liar," she told him.

Her eyes were shining, but not with anger.

Her lips were parted, as if she had something more to say. She hesitated . . . And the moment was gone.

"Try to sleep. Good night, Miss Warren."

Then the biggest wave of all struck the *Georgia*. The impact sent her reeling back and swung the cabin door open wide. Another huge wave made the Confederate captain stumble forward. He reached out for some handhold, anything. Before either of them knew what was happening, she was in his arms.

Jarred by the collision, they each gasped.

He was even taller and stronger than she'd dreamt.

She looked up into his wide blue eyes, and the cold sea water that coated his storm gear drenched the nightshirt. The wetness felt good against her warm body. Now she saw the caring in his face—the sweet wanting—and her arms encircled him in instinctive response.

"Yes," she whispered a moment before he kissed her.

It was amazing. It was wonderful.

It was everything she'd fantasized.

His lips, his touch. His strong, but gentle power. And the *fires*: those flames flickering all over her as he kissed her again and burning even higher when he closed the door and began to caress her. His fingers stroked her luxurious tresses as he kissed her eyes, her shoulders, her face.

She was defenseless and utterly unafraid.

"Yes . . . yes," she sighed, and they kissed again. Her eyes were open as he undressed her. She wanted to see everything, to experience every step and instant completely. She shivered as his fingers ran down her spine, and she smiled as he lifted her and carried her to the bunk.

What would he look like naked?

She had never seen a man wholly unclothed before.

He took off his garments, and she saw his male desire. It was extraordinary to the fascinated virgin, who knew nothing of such matters. But her body knew everything, instinctively. There was no fear or uncertainty in her as Shelby Davis kissed and caressed her lovingly. She realized that her body had always known what had to be—and how to be it too.

This was in the fundamental order of things.

One did not learn these needs and ways. A woman accepted them naturally like the seasons when it was time.

This was the man and the time.

It was right.

She felt hot and wet deep inside, and she heard herself making sounds. Slowly, very slowly and gently, he entered her. For a few moments it felt strange to have another person within her. This was the ultimate intimacy, the connection and completion she'd hungered for so long.

It was as if they were one. They began to move at precisely the same moment, in precisely the same rhythm. Coils of heat spun deep within her womb. It was amazing. There was a man on top of her, but he hardly weighed anything. She cried out and shook her head as her virgin's membrane yielded. The pain was over quickly, or did it only seem so? Her hips were churning more urgently now. Yes, they had known for a long time.

"Good . . . that's good . . . that's *so good,*" she said between gasps.

Lightning flashed across the porthole beside them.

Now they were moving faster, and thunder crashed above the ship. It boomed again. The *Georgia* rolled and bounced in the churning waves, but it seemed far away. She heard her lover grunting. The churning was within her body now, and she sensed that *it* would be soon.

It was.

The hurricane outside didn't matter. It hardly compared to the tempest inside them, and the simultaneous bliss that swept over them. She had never felt this relaxed, this complete.

This was the way it should be, Sarah Warren thought. She locked her legs around him and held his shoulders. He was to stay like this, close and warm and heavy upon her. They kissed and talked and touched, and then it started all over again.

This time it was even better.

They dozed with her head on his shoulder for more than an hour before Shelby Davis had to return to the bridge. Half a minute after he locked the door behind him, she floated off serenely into a very deep sleep.

Now she knew it all.

Chapter Six

The great storm raged on for two more days.

It seemed to follow the *Georgia* like some hateful giant, pounding the exhausted men relentlessly until they were literally black-and-blue from the physical struggle. Rebels and Yankees grimly took their shifts, warred with the hurricane, then stumbled below to collapse into sleep.

Shelby Davis put in more hours than anyone else—as the captain should. But when he descended from the deck, he hardly slept. For him a magnificent woman was waiting. She was as demanding as she was beautiful, and quite irresistible. Whenever he was working, she helped tend the injured, but she was always in his cabin waiting—naked and glowing—when he arrived.

This was her man.

Now that she *knew*, she had no time to waste.

They spoke a good deal because they wanted to find out everything about each other—childhood experiences, favorite songs and food, attitudes towards people and sunsets and the sea. They talked about almost everything, except for politics and the war. Neither dared to mention those.

Or what lay ahead next month or year.

Or the day that the Confederate raider reached some neutral port and unloaded the Yankee survivors.

Their bodies and their love were much safer. They explored both like delighted children in the land of a new fairy tale. No matter how or how many times they made love, there was still more to discover, more to know.

Inexperienced and glowing in her first love, Sarah Warren wanted and trusted the handsome young captain—utterly. This was no mere sexual adventure to Shelby Davis either. Though the dashing Georgian had wooed and won more than a few women since he'd turned seventeen, they all paled in comparison to this extraordinary Yankee.

How could it be?

How could he come to care for this redheaded stranger so deeply in so brief a time?

How could he bear her to leave?

How could she possibly stay with him?

The hurricane passed—stealing away suddenly in the black Atlantic night like a thief. The battered warship steamed east in the grey dawn, and then the orange ball appeared overhead. Sailors smiled and pointed to it as if it were some incredible natural wonder, and they appreciated it as never before. Confederate and Yankee alike grinned and hummed as they began to repair the damage.

Then Sarah Warren appeared on deck. Men stared. It wasn't merely because this was the first time she'd been up since her attempt to stab Davis. No, it was her radiance. There was that rosy flush, that total contentment so easy to recognize. Even the way she walked—hips swaying and legs almost leaden—told them what had come to pass. There wasn't a trace of tension or hostility. She was relaxed, fulfilled, pleased.

She was a woman in love.

That was clear.

It was equally obvious that she had made love recently—and totally. She tried not to glow when she saw Shelby Davis, but she couldn't help it. She could not hide the fact that this was her lover. It showed in her eyes, her pink face, her breathing. No trace of the fierce and homicidal enemy who'd come aboard less than six days earlier remained. This woman looked like a benign redheaded angel.

Some of the men on deck exchanged knowing glances, but not one of them said a word about the liaison. The *Georgia's* crew were disciplined naval personnel who wouldn't dare embarrass their commanding officer. The whaling men were "correct" New Englanders who respected their captain's daughter and wouldn't think of discussing her private life. Some were surprised that she'd taken a Rebel into her bed. More were silently pleased at the change it had made in her.

Sarah Warren herself could barely control her delight. When she closed her eyes for a few moments, she could feel his weight again. Now she was filled up once more, and she *had* to smile. It was an effort to suppress that grin. She barely succeeded, and walked on towards the bridge where *he* stood.

He seemed incredibly handsome.

"And how is your father, Miss Warren?" Davis asked courteously.

"Getting better, the doctor says. Please thank him for me, Captain."

Then she lowered her voice so no one else could hear. "And come back to bed," she said mischievously, as she swept by in a swirl of skirts. Fitzgerald reached the bridge seconds later. Seeing his captain beaming, the first mate automatically smiled back.

Could Fitzgerald possibly know, Shelby Davis wondered.

"What are you grinning about?" the Captain challenged.

Feeling obliged to keep up the pretense that he was unaware of the passionate affair, Fitzgerald improvised quickly. "The nearness of my native shore," he lied without hesitation. "We're only two or three days off the Irish coast, sir. I can almost smell the peat fires."

"How about *our* fires, Paddy? Did you check the coal as I asked?"

"Indeed I did, Captain. We used up a terrible great quantity in that bloody storm. There's only a week's supply left."

There was no choice, Davis knew.

The *Georgia* had to put into a neutral port soon.

And then he'd lose Sarah Warren.

But not for good, he vowed.

He began to work on his plan. His attention was

distracted by the realities of battle the next morning when the *Georgia* came across a Yankee merchantman heading west from Glasgow. After four salvos left the Union craft crippled, Davis steamed on. He didn't have any fuel or time to spend on sinking this ruined vessel.

On the twenty-first of May, Davis saw the lights of Liverpool harbor on the horizon. It was nine p.m. when the raider finally glided slowly up the Mersey River estuary to a dock north of Pierhead. This was a great industrial city of more than five hundred thousand, with flour and sugar mills as well as the shipyards where several Confederate iron rams and raiders—including the *Georgia*—had been built. There was also a Confederate "diplomatic agent" here. He'd have funds to pay for coal and other supplies.

Within minutes after the heavy hawsers were secured to the dock, the commander of the *C.S.S. Georgia* summoned the woman he loved to the bridge. His plan was complete.

"After you've taken your father and the others to the Royal Hospital, get a room at the St. George Hotel. I'll join you there in the morning," he promised, "and we'll be married by sunset."

"Please, Shelby. I want to come with you," she pleaded.

"You can't. There's no place for any woman—Northern or Southern—on a warship. But I'll be back when this war ends—*before*, if I can. Meanwhile, we should have a one day honeymoon before the *Georgia* slips out again. Let's not waste a minute of it!"

Now he didn't care who saw. He swept her into his arms, and they locked in a fervent embrace. Fitzgerald and the others watched them kiss intensely. The first mate had to turn away to avoid showing his own emotional response to the moving scene.

It was tender. It was wonderful.

It was something only a romantic such as Shelby Davis could do. Fitzgerald suddenly felt a surge of pride that this man was his captain and comrade-in-arms. Then he turned his attention to the unloading. By 10:05 p.m., all the survivors of the *Simon Grundy* had disembarked—free at last. Within hours the U.S. embassy in London would hear that a Southern raider was resupplying at a Liverpool dock.

"Post sentries at the dock and both fore and aft on the deck, Paddy," Davis told his first mate. "Let half the crew go ashore now. Tell them they must be back by nine in the morning. The rest can take their shore leave when the first group returns."

"Aye, aye, sir."

"I'm afraid you'll have to wait until the second shift," Davis apologized. "I'm going to find Arthur Adrian to get some money for coal."

But it was Arthur Adrian who found Davis. When the commander of the *Georgia* hurried down the dock, he saw the Confederacy's local diplomatic representative emerge from a hansom cab and walk rapidly towards him. Davis had known him for years. It was obvious that the Southern envoy was troubled.

"What's wrong, Arthur?"

Adrian could not answer. He was close to tears.

"It's over," he replied in a choked voice.

"What are you talking about?"

"It's all over. It's *all* over," Arthur Adrian grieved.

"At Appomattox Court House in Virginia. And Lincoln's been shot dead."

"At Appomattox?" a puzzled Shelby Davis tested.

Adrian shook his head.

"In Washington . . . on April 14th . . . six days after Lee surrendered!"

It took several seconds for Davis to absorb the shock.

"The Army of Virginia?" he whispered.

"There is no Army of Virginia! There is no Confederacy! It's *all over*!"

The long war was finished.

All the Southern sacrifices, all the gallant young men who had died on a hundred battlefields, all the ruined farms and plantations, all the cities and towns smashed and burned—none of it had been enough. The better equipped Union armies and munitions factories, the new Federal generals who'd replaced the earlier incompetents, and the tough shrewdness of Yankee commanders the likes of Grant and Sherman had finally prevailed.

The Confederacy's Secretary of the Navy had been right when he'd told Davis and Semmes that "war is numbers." It didn't matter anymore. The slaughter was ended. The War Between the States was now mere history. Maybe scholars would understand it better in a hundred years. At this grim moment, though, Shelby Davis hurt too much to make any sense of it.

Perhaps it had to be.

Maybe it was America's destiny to go on—to rebuild and grow as one great nation, one great country, united forever.

In time the terrible divisions and wounds would heal. Eventually even the scars would fade. There would be many changes. Slavery—which had ripped the nation apart—was dead. Lee had never really believed in it, Shelby Davis remembered. Indeed, the great Southern general had never owned a slave himself. Deep in these thoughts, Davis barely heard the bustle of his crew coming down the gangplank thirty yards away.

Peace meant many things.

The barrier between him and Sarah Warren was lifted. They could marry and live a normal life . . .

Then Arthur Adrian broke into his reverie.

"You'd better stop that shore party. They'll be arrested," he warned.

"Why?"

"The Yankees are furious. The man who killed Lincoln was some wild actor named Booth, a Southern sympathizer in Washington. Shot him dead in a theater there. The Yanks are looking for vengeance, and you fellows are prime targets."

"Us?"

"They say you're *pirates*. You fought on for six weeks *after* the surrender."

"We didn't know," the handsome young Georgian protested.

"They mean to hang you, Shelby. The Yankee ambassador in London said so. Stop that shore party!"

"This is insane," Davis said.

Then he turned and lifted his hand to the approaching sailors. Puzzled, they halted.

"Are you sure, Arthur?" he asked.

"*Dead* sure. I've brought you the last $19,000 I have to buy fuel and supplies. You've got to run, Shelby. They've already applied for arrest warrants. If you're not at sea by mid-morning, you'll all swing from a rope!"

Shelby Davis' dream was turning into a nightmare.

The woman he loved was only a few miles away, and the awful war over—but some crazed actor across the ocean had built a new wall of hate to keep them apart. How many other lives had been ruined by the bullet that took Lincoln's? It had been a miracle that this war had brought Shelby Davis and Sarah Warren together, and now this ironic twist of fate would shatter it.

The commander of the raider had no choice.

He was responsible for the lives of his crew. He could not risk them for his own happiness.

"I've had men at every British port waiting to warn you," Arthur Adrian said. "Come on, Shelby. There's no time to lose. I've already made a deal with a coal merchant. As soon as my friends saw your ship enter the estuary, I told him to get his wagons down here."

Davis nodded.

"Here they come now," Adrian announced and pointed. "I've bought you some food too."

"But I've four injured men in a hospital. You've got to take care of them."

"We will. I'll have them out of the city in a few hours. We'll hide them. Let's load that coal."

The *Georgia's* crew worked all night at top speed, sweating to fill the bunkers with the fuel that meant their survival. Then the food was manhandled aboard and the water barrels replenished. No one had a moment to question or complain. No one wanted to.

It was a race against time—and the hangman.

"Hurry, Shelby. Hurry," Adrian urged as the sun rose over the sprawling industrial city.

Even as he spurred his men on, Davis could not help thinking of the redheaded woman.

Would she believe he'd abandoned her—that he'd never meant to wed her at all?

What would she do?

What could he do?

He'd bring her with him. It didn't matter where they went. All that counted was that they'd be together.

No, he couldn't do that to her. He couldn't risk her life on a ship the whole world might be hunting as a pirate craft.

When the last supplies were aboard at a quarter to nine, Davis sighed and turned to Arthur Adrian.

"There's a woman waiting at the St. George Hotel," he said. "Very beautiful, redheaded. Her name is Sarah Warren. You must give her a message."

Adrian recognized the look of love in the mariner's eyes and understood. She was Shelby Davis' woman.

"Tell me quickly," he appealed.

"Let her know why we had to leave like this. Tell her that I didn't want to . . . that I had to. Say that I'll find her—*wherever she is*—when this is cleared up."

"I'll tell her. *Please*, the police may arrive at any moment."

They shook hands, and the *Georgia* steamed from the dock ten minutes later. It was a mile away when six policemen, an army lieutenant and a score of soldiers carrying Metford .303 rifles swarmed onto the pier. The broad-shouldered sergeant who led the police glanced at the warrant in his hand and put it in his pocket.

"Sorry to have troubled you, sir," he apologized to the Army officer.

"It's those poor devils on that ship who have the trouble," the lieutenant replied. As a military man himself, he sympathized with the fugitives who had done nothing but fight for their country. He didn't mind that these unlucky Americans had escaped.

Their flight wouldn't do them much good, of course. They had no place to go and no hope of surviving more than sixty days.

They were doomed.

Chapter Seven

The crew of the *Georgia* was silent as the vessel slid out of the Mersey River estuary into the choppy waters of the Irish Sea. There was one question on every man's mind, but no one dared speak it aloud.

Where could they find refuge?

They had no friends, no allies. They were men without a country.

The Confederate Stars and Bars fluttering above them was a banner from a dead dream. Without any nation willing to risk Yankee revenge by accepting them, the *Georgia's* men might soon be corpses themselves. Half their ammunition was gone. Much of the storm damage had not been repaired. How could they hope to defend themselves when the Federal battleships tracked them down?

Many of the Southerners found it difficult to absorb

the shock of the sudden change. Overnight they'd become hunted outlaws—criminals and outcasts. It seemed insane and unreal.

Their cause, their hopes, their identities were gone. This vessel wasn't the *C.S.S. Georgia* anymore. C.S.S. stood for Confederate Steam Ship, and the Confederacy didn't exist. All they had left was their ship and their captain. He would have a plan. Shelby Davis had saved them in impossible situations a dozen times before. He'd think of something. He'd have to.

Some of the sailors couldn't accept the report of the surrender. There had to be a mistake. Robert E. Lee was the greatest military genius America had produced. He might lose a skirmish, a battle, perhaps even a campaign, but no Northern general could possibly force the brilliant commander-in-chief of the Confederate armies to hoist the white flag in total submission.

It had to be a lie, a Yankee trick.

The captain would explain that in short order. An hour after the *Georgia* left Liverpool, Davis told Fitzgerald to order all hands to the foreward deck. The first mate relayed the command loudly, and then for a long moment he stared west. Somewhere out there beyond the horizon—perhaps fifty or sixty miles—lay his Dublin home. Would he ever see it again?

Now the tense crew assembled. Before Davis could say a word, the chief gunner burst out in desperate appeal.

"It isn't true, Captain, is it?"

Shelby Davis nodded solemnly.

"What you've heard is fact. Nothing can change it.

The war is over, and so is the Confederacy,'' he announced.

Then he saw tears streaking down the faces of two men in the front row. Someone behind them was sobbing.

''We fought well, and we lost. We have nothing to be ashamed of. I'm proud of every one of you,'' he said, ''and I'm honored to have served with you. Gentlemen, I salute you.''

His hand rose to his brow.As if one man, the entire crew returned the salute.

''Thank you. Now we face a new challenge and a new life,'' Davis said firmly. ''I intend to make it a long one. I mean for it to be a peaceful and decent one. Our consciences are clear and our ship is sound. We must change with the times. The *Georgia* will carry on—not as a man of war—but as a merchant vessel.''

It took several seconds for the men to absorb the startling idea. They looked at each other uncertainly.

''Will the Yankees let us?'' Dr. Preston asked.

Davis shook his head.

''Not if they find us,'' he answered. ''That's why we have to stay away from the major European ports and the busy shipping lanes. We have to find a region where people don't care about politics, where they don't ask questions—and where there are few if any U.S. diplomats to report our presence.''

The one-eyed cook cursed the United States.

''That's over too,'' the handsome Georgian told them. ''We must put our bitterness aside. It's one country again, or it will be in a while. How long that'll take is anybody's guess. But it has to be.''

A low muttering signalled that at least some of the

crew disagreed. Davis realized that there'd be no point in arguing the issue now, when the wounds of four years of war were still raw.

"Right now we face a more immediate question," Davis pointed out. "Where can we be safe until the Yankees come to their senses and the rage over Lincoln subsides? I believe that I know of such a place."

He had a plan.

"It's an area with damn few Yankees and lots of inter-island shipping. I think you'll like the weather too. It's a lot warmer than the North Atlantic. I'm talking about the Caribbean."

A dozen officers and crewmen nodded in approval.

They'd sailed those waters a hundred times during the war. There were scores of islands, large and small. The people who lived there had been friendly to Southern vessels, and many of the inhabitants didn't even speak English. More than two centuries of French, Spanish and Dutch rule had created a relaxed international atmosphere. Even those islands governed by Britain were really just sleepy, sun-baked backwaters, almost indifferent to both Europe and North America. One more cargo ship plying the inter-island routes would hardly be noticed.

"My idea is that we head first to Cuba," Davis continued. "Very few people there understand English, and all North Americans probably seem alike to them."

That was only part of his plan. It was too early to tell them that they'd have to manufacture a new identity and forged papers for the *Georgia*. They weren't yet ready to face up to a new name for the ship—and a new *flag*. That would hurt the most.

"Cuba—that's my plan. What do you say?" Davis asked.

"*You're* the captain," reminded an engine room stoker.

"And there's none better," the mustachioed ensign from Texas added loyally.

"I value your confidence, men," Davis told them, "but now's the time for everyone to say his piece. If anyone has another idea or a question, let's hear it."

No one spoke for ten seconds.

Then the blustery one-eyed cook stepped forward. Hinkley was his name, Davis recalled. Cyrus Hinkley.

"Cuba's a stinkin' jungle so far as how I hear," he challenged loudly, "and I ain't interested in that. I want to go home to Mobile. Those damn Yankees don't scare me!"

"They don't intend to *scare* you," Davis replied. "They mean to *hang* you—and all the rest of us."

"You telling me they'd hang us all if the *Georgia* just steamed into Mobile?" Hinkley argued.

Davis shook his head.

The cook grinned in smug triumph.

"No, they'd blow us out of the water," Davis said. "There are more than a dozen heavy gunboats—mostly ironclads—in the Union squadron based in Mobile. Have been for more than a year. They'd shoot us to pieces before we entered the harbor."

Hinkley scowled in anger.

"Cuba makes sense to me, Captain," the chubby physician declared, and the rest of the crew murmured in agreement.

"Then that's it. You'll get home to Mobile before too long, Hinkley," Davis assured. "We all want to go home—as soon as it's safe. All right, men. Return to your stations.''

The crew dispersed, and Shelby Davis told his first mate to set a course for Cuba.

''Right to Havana,'' Fitzgerald exulted.

''Let's try Guantanamo on the other end of the island. It's much quieter, and a lot less likely to have a U.S. counsul, Paddy.''

Davis was right, as usual. Guantanamo was an excellent deepwater port that served the outer-island trade. It drew only a few ships from the major maritime powers and hardly any North American craft at all.

''I'll have our course for Guantanamo in half an hour,'' the first mate pledged. For several moments after Fitzgerald left the bridge, the captain of the *Georgia* thought about Cyrus Hinkley. They'd have to keep an eye on him. He could be trouble. His record of past disciplinary problems made that more than clear.

It might be better to get rid of him. Perhaps, in six or eight months, the hot-tempered cook could leave the ship and make his own way home from some Caribbean port. His work in the gallery was barely adequate. He wouldn't be missed.

Suddenly Shelby Davis hungered for the woman he'd left behind. It could be months—perhaps longer—before he dared to write to her. He could not risk letting the U.S. authorities know where his ''pirate'' vessel was. Even if he wanted to get in touch with her, he couldn't be sure where she'd be.

She was no longer a virgin, Davis reflected.

Now she *knew*, and she might not easily give it up for a hunted mariner who might never return.

How long could he reasonably expect her to wait? How long could he count on her faithful love?

On the burning hot morning of June 23, 1865, forty men stood on a grassy hill at the edge of Guantanamo City. Thirty-nine of these were armed Spanish soldiers in uniform. Sweating in the humid ninety-degree heat, they were disciplined and silent.

The other man was stripped to the waist.

He was making a great deal of noise.

Each time the bullwhip slashed pain across his already ravaged back, the Cuban screamed. His body jerked violently under the impact of the flailing leather, and when the corporal with the whip skillfully aimed the awful thing to carve off a chunk of the prisoner's right ear, the man chained to the dead tree trunk howled.

But he didn't talk.

He didn't utter a single word.

They could do whatever they wanted to Carlos Paz, but he would not tell *Teniente* Bortelo what he wanted to know. Some fifty brave men and women would end up on the torture rack—or in nearby Santa Anna Cemetery—if Paz betrayed the secrets of the Cuban underground to the ruthless Spanish officer.

There had been many good—and quite a few bad—military officers sent to Cuba since Cristoforo Colombus discovered the island in October of 1492. Not long after the famed explorer claimed the island for the Spanish crown, Madrid shipped in the first wave of troops to conquer the Ciboney and Arawak Indians. In all the decades since then, none of the Spanish officers had been more brutal than Bortelo. *Capitan* Colon of the Third Cavalry was equally cruel. As the *commandants* of the Guantanamo garrison and this whole corner of the island, he encouraged *Teniente* Bortelo and the other lieutenants to use terror tactics.

"Just as we exterminated those stupid Indians nearly two hundred years ago, we must eradicate these subhuman rebels today," Colon told his officers. "Use whatever methods are necessary, and I'll deal with those weaklings in Habana."

So Bortelo gestured one more.

The whip slashed open another oozing gash in the back of the stubborn *insurrecto*. That was what the Spanish authorities called the insurgents. To most of the people of Cuba—the Hispanics, Indians, Blacks and French who'd come from nearby Haiti in flight from slave rebellions—the men and women of the small underground force were not rebels. They were patriots.

The man chained to the tree shrieked in agony.

Then he fainted.

"I think the bastard's passed out, *Teniente*," the expert whipper noted professionally.

He might have been talking about the weather.

"Turn him around and work on his groin," the lieutenant suggested. He'd noticed some movement in the nearby trees. It might be useful to give Carlos Paz's *insurrecto* comrades a frightening lesson in what they could all expect if they did not lay down their arms and submit. A neutered Carlos Paz might be quite impressive to the *macho* Cuban males. It was already standard practice in the Guantanamo command to gang-rape female *insurrectos* as the first step in interrogation. Since virginity was highly prized on this devoutly Catholic island, a woman who'd been ravished by fourteen or fifteen illiterate soldiers became an object of pity or shame rather than desire. After such sexual debasement, even the island's slaves would shun her.

"I'll do whatever you say, *Teniente*," the torturer said, "but we'll have to wake him up first. Be helpful if one of the men got a bucket of water from that stream back in the trees."

As soon as Bortelo gave the order, the barefoot peasant girl who was watching from the nearby underbrush hurried away to safety. Moving warily over little used cattle paths, she made her way to the town. There were soldiers at every gate, in every square. She was careful to avoid their attention, using back alleys as much as she could to zigzag to the rear entrance of the *Farmacia Arias*—one of the two drug stores that this small community had.

José Arias, the pharmacist, and his dramatically lovely sister, Isabella, were waiting.

"He has said nothing," Maria Laredo reported breathlessly. "They have done terrible things, but he does not speak."

"They will do more terrible things," José Arias predicted.

"But Carlos Paz will die before he speaks," the sixteen year old farm girl said. "I saw him suffer. He is very brave."

"And he'll die bravely," the pharmacist declared.

"So will a lot of other Cubans, but for what?" Isabella Arias Garcia asked bitterly. She was the widow of a teacher who'd been shot by the Spanish two years earlier.

"What chance have we to win our freedom without proper weapons, brother? How can we do anything but die so long as the garrisons can laugh at us from inside their forts?" she challenged in a voice filled with emotion.

"She's right," the barefoot farm girl agreed. "We have pistols and machetes—and they have cannon."

"We will get cannon," José Arias promised.

"And men who know how to use them?" the angry widow demanded.

"Perhaps sooner than you think," the head of the local resistance movement told his sister. "The problem has been to smuggle in cannon past the Spanish gunboats patrolling the coasts. I think a solution may be near—down in the harbor right now."

Then he explained to the women that an American vessel named the *Sarah W. Lee* had dropped anchor in Guantanamo Bay at dusk on the previous day. Though it was a merchant ship, it carried a number of cannon as protection from attack by pirates.

"They have at least a dozen guns—and we have gold coins," the pharamcist reasoned. "Perhaps we can buy just two of their cannon. After all, there are few pirates left in these waters—hardly any."

Isabella Arias Garcia looked dubious.

"And we'll pay them to teach us how to shoot the cannon," Arias continued. "Not here, in some small bay down the coast. Then we'll blow those bastards out of their forts—and out of Cuba."

"It could be, Señora," the farm girl said to the skeptical widow. "*Los Americanos* they believe much in freedom. They have just fought a great war for it. They will help us!''

Now Isabella Garcia turned to her brother.

''And if they won't? What if they refuse to sell those guns, brother?''

José Arias hesitated for several seconds before he answered.

''There are maybe sixty—at most, seventy—*Americanos* on that ship. We are hundreds.''

''What are you talking about?'' his sister asked.

At that moment Maria Lardeo understood, and the pious peasant crossed herself devoutly.

''If we can't get the cannon peacefully, we'll take them by force. We can, you know. At three in the morning when they're all sleeping, one hundred desperate Cuban patriots with machetes that make no noise could do it,'' he told them.

''You'd *kill* the *Americanos*?'' Isabella Garcia asked incredulously.

''Only if we must,'' her brother answered as he reached for his straw hat. Then he excused himself and left without saying where he was going.

It had to be the harbor, Isabella Garcia guessed, the ship with the cannon.

She could not let him do this—not even for Cuba. What honor could there be in victories bought with the blood of innocents, the blood of men from a land known for its love of liberty? The only sympathy that Cuba had received came from the *Americanos*, and their compassion would turn to loathing if her foolish brother did this terrible thing. He'd be as bad as that butcher Bortelo.

Perhaps she could persuade the ship captain—or appeal to him in that other way. She was not vain, but Isabella Garcia realized that many men found her desirable.

At the very least, she could stop her brother from committing this atrocity.

She rushed from the *farmacia,* mounted her horse and set off for the harbor. She did not dare ride too swiftly, for that would attract the attention of the police and soldiers. She was already under suspicion as the widow of an *insurrecto.* Wearing a wholly false smile, she cantered slowly through the dusty streets of Guantanamo City.

The midday heat was terrible, but she hardly noticed it. She had more important things on her mind. Poor, heroic Carlos Paz would almost surely be dead within twenty-four hours, another victim of *Teniente* Bortelo's expert torturer. The *Americanos* had a few days more.

How many?

Chapter Eight

Renamed and repainted, with four gunports boarded over so she'd look less like a warship, the newly converted merchant vessel was getting no special attention in the small flotilla anchored in Guantanamo Bay. Glancing around at the other craft, Shelby Davis decided that this port had been an excellent choice. The bay was huge, and nobody appeared to pay any attention to the comings and goings of the various freighters. A single patrol boat seemed to make up the entire Spanish Navy security effort.

No one had shown any curiosity about the *Sarah W. Lee* during Davis' first visit ashore, and the harbor master had barely scanned the forged registry papers that identified the craft as one whose home port was Baltimore. Since that city was at the edge of the South and its residents spoke with a trace of Dixie, the false story was roughly compatible with his crew's accents.

It was clear after three hours along this waterfront that asking questions simply wasn't done here. The Cubans didn't care, and Davis had an idea that a number of Spanish naval and customs officials were paid not to. More than one of the freighters had the sleazy look of smuggling craft. Davis made a mental note to change the spit-and-polish tone of his own ship and crew.

It wouldn't do to stand out in this down-at-the-heels crowd of fishermen, sailors, peddlers, food vendors, ship's chandlers, waterfront laborers, prostitutes and unwashed alcoholics. There was hardly a pimp in sight, for the simple harlots of Guantanamo Bay dealt with their unsophisticated customers directly.

Though this harbor wasn't a quarter as busy as that in Havana at the other end of the island, the men whom Davis saw, bumped into and sometimes stepped over in the streets were a highly diverse group. Most were *mestizos,* mixtures of Hispanic and Indian or Hispanic and Black. Great numbers of slaves had been shipped in from West Africa in the seventeenth and eighteenth centuries to work the sugar, cotton and tobacco fields.

There were haughty "pure" Spaniards from Europe, and equally "pure" upper-class and middle-class Cubans of Castilian lineage who'd been born here. Cuba had been a major base for the Spanish invasion of Mexico, and some of those warriors had come back with Aztec mistresses or wives. There were also French who'd fled bloody uprisings in Haiti, Canadians and

Jamaicans hiding from wives or police, and the descendants of some lesser British and Irish pirates.

All of these assorted males spoke a working brand of Cuban-Spanish with a variety of accents, and they dressed in an equally colorful assortment of clothes, rings and hats. Since stripping sailors of their pants and wallets was a routine occurrence in the local bars and brothels, more men wore daggers or pistols than shoes. None of this worried the handsome Georgian particularly, since these conditions prevailed in many other tropical ports.

The officers and enlisted men of the *Sarah W. Lee*—the last name a tribute to the great Confederate general—had been in places like this before. You went ashore in twos or threes and in larger groups at night. You shunned dark alleys, unfamiliar drinks and other men's females as routinely as you avoided unboiled water. And you never trusted unusually "friendly" strangers, since four out of five of them seemed to travel with marked cards, knockout drops or "sisters" who had highly infectious diseases.

"*Buenas dias, Capitan.*"

The man who spoke to Shelby Davis was in his late thirties, well dressed and wearing gold-rimmed spectacles. He looked like a respectable small businessman. Probably a full-blooded Spaniard, Davis guessed, though there could be a trace of an Indian grandmother in those fine features.

"You are the *capitan* of the *Sarah Lee*, aren't you?" The accent was local.

"*Buenas dias,*" Davis answered noncommitally.

"It is an honor to meet you, *Señor*. Welcome to Guantanamo. Of course, the city itself is a few miles from here. You should see it. It is much more civilized than this waterfront."

What did he want?

"A thousand pardons," the stranger apologized. "I stop a foreign visitor on the street in this boiling sun and I don't even introduce myself. I am José Melendez Fabrega Otero Arias, at your service."

"Nice to meet you."

"And your companion?"

"Mr. Fitzgerald is our first mate."

Despite his outgoing charm, the Cuban was clearly wary. His eyes roved—looking for something or someone. Noticing this, Fitzgerald's left hand inched a bit closer to the derringer in his jacket.

"Ah, the ocean life! How exciting and free!" the Cuban enthused. "How I envy you that freedom!"

Was it mere gush, or was he telling them something?

"I am a pharmacist myself," Arias explained.

"We might need some medical supplies, Captain," Fitzgerald reminded. They'd left Liverpool too quickly to replenish Dr. Clark's locker.

"I am not trying to sell," Arias declared indignantly. "I am here to welcome. Of course, if you should need anything, my *farmacia* is the finest in the province. I would be happy if you would visit."

This was the perfect opportunity, the underground leader calculated. If he could get them alone in the privacy of the drugstore, the risk of being overheard by some government spy would be much less. Yes, he'd play the role of the sly merchant. It was a splendid cover.

"Why don't we have a nice cool drink first?" Arias proposed, "and then we can go on to my shop."

Fitzgerald shook his head—about half an inch. Davis understood immediately. The *farmacia* could be some sort of trap, or armed thieves might ambush them on the way. Davis assured the Cuban that he appreciated his gracious invitation, and thanked him. Then the Georgian proposed that it might be quicker—and more comfortable on such a torrid day—if the pharmacist spoke to Dr. Preston on the nearby ship instead.

"Mr. Fitzgerald could make sure he's aboard—or find him—while you and I have that cool drink," Davis proposed.

The message was clear.

The first mate left immediately to alert the physician and the others that a stranger was coming. Fitzgerald moved quickly through the ship, warning every man that he must be careful not say or do or show anything that could betray them. All Confederate insignia had been removed at sea thirteen days earlier, but extreme caution was still crucial.

"He *says* he's a pharmacist," Fitzgerald reported uneasily.

"I'll find out," the doctor promised.

"Do it on deck. If he should be some bloody spy or thief, there's no sense in lettin' him see the ship's guts, is there?"

The shrewd Irishman was right. A pair of trained eyes might recognize that the interior of this craft was not designed for cargo. When Davis and the Cuban walked down the decrepit dock ten minutes later, the first mate and the physician were waiting at the head of the gangway. After a brief exchange of courtesies, Preston steered the conversation to the vessel's medical supplies.

"You know the pharmacopeia very well," he complimented a few minutes later.

"We have had a fine university in Habana since 1728," Arias replied patriotically. Then he looked startled.

The reason for his surprise was a remarkably pretty woman of twenty-seven, or perhaps thirty, who was coming up the gangplank. Her jet black hair crowned her lovely face like a queen's tiara, matching her regal figure—one that would turn heads anywhere. She had the wide hips of so many women in these islands, a dress far better than any Davis had seen in weeks and a coolly ambiguous smile.

"It is my dear sister," Arias explained weakly.

Fitzgerald could not help staring.

"That glorious lady is your sister?" he blurted.

"I'm a very fortunate man," the underground chieftain replied mechanically.

Beneath his polite exterior José Arias was furious. It was outrageous that she should follow him here. This was a delicate matter—not an affair for a well-meaning widow. Cuban men of the nineteenth century generally considered women to be lesser creatures destined to be mistresses and mothers—with a few "called" to serve God as nuns. Arias realized that his high-spirited sister was hardly convent material, but sometimes he wished she'd consider it.

The look on her face, when she reached the deck, was that of a tigress, Fitzgerald judged. She was utterly attractive in that black dress, radiating both elegance and something animal. *Black?* Could she be a widow?

"What a pleasure to see you, Isabella," the pharmacist forced out grimly.

She smiled in mock sweetness. Arias wanted to hit her. Instead he introduced her. She couldn't help noticing the admiration and appetite in the first mate's boyish face. Then she saw something else—and nodded towards the waterfront.

"Company, brother," she said.

It was a Spanish cavalry patrol—sixteen men led by an officer. The armed detachment was cantering slowly towards the ship. Arias wondered how they'd found him. Shelby Davis tried to calculate whether the *Georgia* had been identified. There was a prearranged signal he'd give if the ex-Confederates had to fight their way out of this harbor.

Should he sound it now?

When the tall, thin officer dismounted on the pier, Davis studied the man's uniform and tried to recall. Yes, those were the insignia of a Spanish Army lieutenant. From the way he swaggered up the gangway, he was not a pleasant one.

"*Buenas dias,*" the officer said.

Somehow he managed to make this routine salutation sound like an insult. Davis noticed that the faces of Arias and his sister were blank masks now. The lieutenant bothered them too.

"*Buenas dias,*" the pharmacist answered. "*Capitan* Shelby, I have the privilege of presenting *Teniente* Bortelo of the noted Third Cavalry. They protect this district."

A number of crewmen were moving towards the rail, ready to rip loose the hawsers. Davis spotted the head of his second mate rising from a hatch. Others had seen the cavalry too. Sharpshooters were almost surely loading their rifles below at this moment.

The soldiers would not take this ship without a fight—a bloody one.

"Welcome aboard, *Teniente,*" Davis greeted. "This is my first mate, Mr. Fitzgerald, and Dr. Preston. I assume you know Señor Arias' sister."

Bortelo bared his teeth in a parody of a smile.

"Señora Garcia and I have met," he confirmed. "I knew her late husband more *intimately.*"

Now the smirking lieutenant paused to take out and light a long, thin cigarillo. Neither the dark beauty nor her brother spoke. Their hatred was too great for mere words.

"*Si,*" Bortelo continued smugly, "I was present at his demise. As a matter of fact, I killed him!"

Bortelo blew a perfect smoke ring before he explained.

"I assure you that it was nothing personal—purely official. Diego Garcia was quite a good mathematics teacher, until he fell in with evil companions. Then this confused fellow turned to violence—because an *insurrecto.*"

"What's that?" Davis asked.

"A rebel, an enemy of Spain. They preach hate against our noble queen, and they spread this filth among the simple peasants. To stop this contagion, we are obliged to exterminate these vermin whenever and wherever we find them."

The lieutenant puffed on his cigar again and looked directly at José Arias.

"Why, if we caught one right here on this ship, we'd shoot him—or her—dead on the spot. I have that authority," Bortelo boasted.

It was more than a statement of power. It was a threat.

Davis saw that his first mate was struggling to control his Irish temper. Then he remembered what Fitzgerald had told him about how ruthlessly the British treated the underground fighters back in Dublin. Execution was not nearly as swift or routine, but the tactics of repression were brutal. It was easy to see why Fitzgerald might identify with the *insurrectos* here.

"You won't find such people on this vessel, Lieutenant," Davis announced calmly, as if he hadn't noticed the threat. "We're a peaceful American merchant ship in to pick up a cargo and move on. Dr. Preston was just ordering some medical supplies from Mr. Arias when you arrived."

"I hope that I didn't interrupt anything," Bortelo said with an arrogance feigning politeness.

"Not at all," the physician answered and told the pharmacist what he wanted to buy. Arias informed him what the purchases would cost. He'd deliver the medicines on the following afternoon.

"Very businesslike—that's the Yankee way," the cavalry officer taunted. "No time to waste. Probably be out of here in a few days, *won't you*?"

Translation: *get out*.

"Sooner if we get a cargo," Davis answered. "You're

sure you wouldn't want a cup of coffee before you go?"

Translation: *Good-by.*

"I have other things to do," Bortelo snapped and left. All but two of his horsemen rode off with him into the town. José Arias was sweating visibly as he started for the gangway. Had Bortelo's spies been following him or his sister? Would the Spanish be watching the *Americano* ship now?

"Thanks again for the drink," Davis said a moment later.

The underground leader glanced at the horsemen again. "My pleasure, *Capitan*. Ah . . . one more thing."

"Yes?"

"That *Teniente* Bortelo, he is truly dangerous."

And vicious, Davis thought. Yes, this nasty lieutenant had a cruel quality that reminded the Georgian of the brutish blockade runner, Bart Beecher. Beecher would get along well with the sadistic cavalryman.

"I'll keep that in mind," Davis replied.

Then he heard Fitzgerald speak to the buxom widow.

"Will *you* come back tomorrow?" the first mate asked.

"If I can. *Adios*," she said and started down to the dock. Her brother followed her down the gangway. The three Southern officers watched them mount up and ride away—with one of Bortelo's cavalrymen following.

"I don't mean to meddle, Paddy," Shelby Davis said warmly, "but that pretty lady you find so interesting could be trouble. She and her brother are being watched right now."

"So are we," Fitzgerald replied.

One of Bortelo's horsemen remained on duty less than seventy yards away, staring directly at the ship. Another soldier replaced him twelve hours later, and a third was on duty when Arias delivered the medicine—alone.

"My sister could not come," he reported, and nodded toward the watching cavalryman. "She sends you her sincere greetings."

Fitzgerald understood. It would be risky—foolish—for the *insurrecto's* widow to come to this foreign ship again—a vessel under open surveillance. Arias saw the disappointment in the first mate's face and made a mental note of it. The Cuban would have no compunction about using Fitzgerald's interest in Isabella for the defeat of the Spaniards.

Cuba Libre—a free Cuba—came above everything.

Now Dr. Preston appeared, inspected the straw and bamboo box and the medicines it contained, then began to count out the money. Arias looked around the deck for the Yankee captain. A chance to negotiate for those big guns was the real reason the *insurrecto* was here.

"Glad you could deliver these today," the physician said as he handed the currency to Arias. "We'll be loading cargo tomorrow, and then we're off."

The freedom fighter winced at the news.

"Where are you going?"

Davis had briefed his crew carefully.

No one must know their routes or destinations. Loose talk could lead to interception by a U.S. warship lying in ambush.

''I think it's Barbados,'' the doctor lied.

''And when may we expect you back?''

The pot-bellied physician shrugged.

''Who knows? Couple of weeks, I guess . . . Why do you ask?'' he tested.

''We'll have a party when you return—a fine barbeque with suckling pig and lots of the best rum,'' Arias improvised.

''Very nice. I'll tell the captain.''

''Let *me* tell him,'' the Cuban urged.

He had to speak to the Yankee *capitan*—as soon as possible. Those cannon could save many Cuban lives. Arias barely managed to maintain his composure when he heard that the man he knew as Captain Shelby was ashore and would not return for hours.

There was no time.

Not enough hours—it might take *days*—to persuade the Yankee commander, or else to organize an attack if that failed.

And the cannon could not be removed so long as this ship was in this harbor, watched by soldiers around the clock.

''We shall miss you,'' José Arias announced and left the *Sarah W. Lee*. The pharmacist nodded respectfully as he rode past the cavalryman a minute later. The young trooper was no more than nineteen or twenty. Probably illiterate and with no ill will towards the Cubans, Arias guessed. The odds were that the soldier would rather be home on his father's little farm near Toledo than sweating on this distant and steamy tropical isle.

Still, the *insurrectos* might have to kill him.

And if the *Americanos* refused the cannon, they would perish too.

Whatever the cost in men or morality, Cuba must be free.

Chapter Nine

Hides from Guantanamo to Kingston on Jamica.

Laborers from Kingston to build roads in Trinidad.

Then a mixed cargo to Martinique, a hilly French-speaking island with a live volcano and cordial native women who managed to communicate with the American sailors via saucy grins, low-cut dresses and the same international body language that worked with men from a dozen other countries.

Martinique to Barbados.

Barbados back to Guadeloupe, where the *Sarah Lee's* crew could show off the twenty words of French learned in Martinique.

There wasn't a huge amount of freight to be hauled within the Caribbean, but there was almost always some cargo for those who'd work cheap and were not choosy. After they transported forty-eight live cows to Antigua, it took nearly a week to scrape the decks and get rid of the lingering stench.

"We take what we can get," Davis told his ex-Confederates frankly, "and we keep moving to avoid being noticed. If we don't stay anywhere more than a couple of days, nobody will even remember we've been through."

Though their craft was no longer a Confederate raider, there wasn't any harbor where they could rest—not yet. Reports from men on other ships and articles in tattered newspapers told that the fires of hate were burning even higher back in the United States now. Grant had told Lee at the surrender that the Confederates should put down their guns and go home, and take their horses with them for spring plowing. The Union general had known that his commander-in-chief, President Abraham Lincoln, was committed to a policy of compassion and reconciliation towards the South. The lanky "country" lawyer from Illinois had made it clear to his cabinet that he meant to heal, not to punish. But Lincoln was dead, and vengeance was the order of the day for the bitter U.S. Congress. They would make the former rebels pay dearly. They would scourge every inch of the South in retaliation.

Lee was going to stand trial for treason.

Jefferson Davis was in leg shackles in Fortress Monroe, Virginia.

Hundreds of others—including the crew of the *C.S.S. Georgia*—were being hunted by determined U.S. authorities. The "pirate" ship had been "seen" near Dakar off West Africa, in a habor in the Philippines and wrecked on a reef south of Rio de Janeiro. The latest word from Washington was that the Secretary of the Navy had asked Congress to vote a $50,000 reward for information leading to the capture of the "pirate" crew.

Reactions among the hunted crew varied drastically.

"We'll *never* get home," the ship's chief engineer lamented.

"Those reports are garbage," sneered the one-eyed cook. "We could probably go back next week with no trouble at all."

"Why don't you swim home yourself, Hinkley?" a stoker suggested, and the bitter cook stalked out of the palm-leaf bar cursing.

He did something worse when the ship was anchored in San Juan harbor. Puerto Rico was ruled by Spain, and Hinkley was deriding "the dumb natives" and "fat ass greasers" as he lurched from a grubby tavern and brothel. Reeling out, he nearly collided with Fitzgerald, who was striding by en route back to their ship.

"Watered rum an' ugly women!" the cook grumbled loudly. "Worst lookin' whores I ever did see."

He was obviously tipsy.

"Take it easy," Fitzgerald ordered.

"This whole island is a sewer!" Hinkley jeered. "Stinks of olive oil an' garlic—makes me sick. What the hell am I doin' here?"

"Making a bloody fool of yourself."

"So the thick Mick doesn't like my talk!"

Fitzgerald's large right hand closed into a fist as he tried to control his temper. It wasn't easy. The news he'd heard ten minutes ago was certain to shock the Captain.

"You're drunk, Hinkley. We'll have to settle this on the ship tomorrow."

"Why not sell that tub?" the cook taunted. "There's a good price on the *Georgia,* I hear."

The sullen sot was risking the life of every member of the crew by mentioning that name.

"We could split up the money," Hinkley continued loudly, "and—"

He didn't finish the thought. He was interrupted by a big Irish fist that smashed into his mouth. Two seconds later it crashed into his jaw, and the stunned cook fell to the street, unconscious. *That* should keep the damn fool quiet for a while, Fitzgerald thought. He saw three other members of his crew leaving a restaurant and told them to carry the cook back to their ship.

Shelby Davis was on deck when they arrived. He stood alone beneath the September moon and sad with longing. He rarely spent much time ashore. The bars and women in these ports held no appeal for him. The only female he cared about was far away. When would he find her? Where?

Davis watched as Hinkley was carried aboard, but said nothing until the sailors had manhandled the troublesome cook below.

"I see he hurt his face again," Davis observed.

"Someone did that for him," Fitzgerald replied, and flexed his bruised knuckles. They were still sore.

"Hurt much, Paddy?"

"Not as much as his face," the first mate reported with visible satisfaction. "I know I'm not supposed to hit crewmen, but I did it for all of us. Had to shut him up, Captain. The idiot was talking about the *Georgia*, sir. I closed his mouth."

Davis shook his head angrily.

"You shouldn't strike him, but I'm glad you did. One bad apple in every barrel. I guess. Keep him below till we leave tomororw."

"Aye, aye, sir."

Davis studied the mate's swollen hand.

"One punch?"

"Two, sir. Getting old, I suppose."

Fitzgerald wondered how to tell him the news.

Davis had a right to know.

"Captain?" he began uncomfortably.

"Yes?"

There had to be some tactful way to say it, but Patrick Fitzgerald couldn't think of any.

"Captain . . . I was down at a little grog shop named Elena's, down near that square with the fountain—the one with the statue of the feller on the horse—I met some lads . . . Maybe they were wrong, sir."

"What is it, Paddy?" Davis asked sympathetically. He'd never seen his first mate like this before.

"It *could* be a mistake."

"What could?"

Fitzgerald swallowed hard before he replied.

"They were from the *Duncan Sneed*—out of New Bedford. It could be they've got it all wrong!"

New Bedford. That was *her* home town.

"Is it news of Captain Warren and his daughter?"

"Aye, sir. I'm sorry. Maybe the rum addled them. They were talking about what a fine skipper he'd been and how terrible it was about the *Mersey Star*."

The Mersey was the river into Liverpool.

"The *Mersey Star* went down in a storm off Newfoundland ten weeks ago," Fitzgerald blurted. "She was on the Liverpool to Boston run. No survivors, sir. Not a one."

"The Warrens?" Davis asked grimly.

The first mate groaned.

"Tell me, Paddy."

"They were aboard, sir. Half of New Bedford's in mourning—or was two months ago. I'm sorry, Captain . . . I'm really sorry."

Davis stood stiff and silent for what seemed to be a long time. He appeared to be staring right past Fitzgerald. After a while, he nodded in farewell and went down to his cabin. He sipped a glass of Barbancourt Rum—the quality kind that Caribbean folk drink in place of cognac. Then he looked out the porthole.

The full yellow moon overhead was huge.

But all he saw was her face and that billowing red hair.

He would never hold her again.

They would never wed.

She could never bear his sons.

Davis emptied his glass and refilled it with the fiery sugar-cane rum-brandy.

It was unfair. The war was over. The dying was supposed to have ended. Why had this happened?

He was utterly helpless. He could defeat a hurricane or an enemy man-of-war, but now he could do nothing. Aware that captains did not cry, he looked at the moon for several minutes. Then he began to weep.

She was gone. His love was gone.

He cried for an hour before sleep came to ease the pain. When he awoke red-eyed at dawn, the hurt was still there and he knew that it would be for a very long time. There were many things for a captain to do, many plans to make and all those lives to protect. But right now he could only think of one thing.

Sarah Warren was dead.

He was alone.

"They're not coming back," José Arias told his sister at 5:10 p.m. the following afternoon.

"The *Americanos*?"

The rebel leader nodded.

"I was a fool to think they would," he said bitterly.

"It's not your fault, José. If you'd ever gotten to ask them, they might have sold us some cannon."

The pharmacist remembered how the first mate had eyed her, and he sighed at the missed opportunity.

"That Fitzgerald would have *given* them to us—or to *you*, Isabella. You charmed him, sister."

She had found the open-faced first mate interesting, but a respectable Hispanic widow could not consider some transient foreigner attractive. He had been sincere and rather pleasant—one might say attentive—but that was all, she told herself primly as she smoothed her skirt.

Then her body told her something else.

It was more than two years since she had loved or made love—twenty-six lonely months of emotional and physical deprivation. This abstinence was unnatural for a woman who had enthusiastically enjoyed eight years of a healthy marriage. Still, Cuban custom required widows to remain celibate, though widowers need not. The men made the rules for their convenience, she reflected.

''Fitzgerald? Oh, the *mate*. I remember him now,'' she fenced in a casual tone. ''There's no point in talking about him or any of the other *Americanos*. We'll have to get our cannon from someone else.''

The sound of hooves echoed in the street outside the *farmacia*. They saw the cavalry clearly through the open window—a full troop with the monster Bortelo in command. With his throat knotted in anger, José Arias could not speak until the hated horsemen were gone.

Then his scowl dissolved abruptly.

''I think I know who that someone else could be,'' he announced.

He explained his plan, and his sister shrugged.

''It's not impossible,'' she judged cautiously.

José Arias found it annoying that his sister was so guarded in her approval. Still, women were often wary, if not fearful. They lacked the *macho* courage and boldness of Cuba's brave men, he reminded himself. War and resolution were hardly women's work anyway, the underground leader reflected. Of course, there were certain non-combat duties that females could handle exceptionally well.

On the nineteenth night of September, a maid who worked in the Officers' Club of the Third Cavalry Headquarters reported that a supply corps lieutenant had mentioned the imminent movement of an artillery battery to the garrison in Miranda—seventy miles inland. At noon two days later, the madam who ran a brothel frequented by Spanish sergeants came to the *farmacia* with word that one of her prostitutes needed some medicine for "the usual" and another had heard that four cannon would leave for the Central Oriente province town on the morning of the twenty-third.

"Catrina says that the soldier was complaining it would be miserably hot in Miranda," the plump madam told Arias as he handed her the medicine.

"He's right," the pharmacist replied, and began to consider what road the military convoy would take. The Spaniards were bound to send at least twenty or thirty soldiers to escort the artillery pieces, Arias estimated. With fifty or sixty intrepid freedom fighters in ambush, he'd make the trip to Miranda a very warm experience indeed.

The underground leader sent word to his men.

He also alerted a clandestine network of young "eyes"—some male and others female—to report on the convoy as it rumbled inland slowly over rutted dirt roads. A journey of seventy miles would take two days for the slow-moving artillery caissons. Yes, the *insurrectos* would strike just this side of the large town named San Luis—roughly half way to Miranda.

"Be careful, José," Isabella Arias Garcia said as he prepared to leave on the evening of the twenty second.

"Is that all you think about?" he grumbled in response. "Have you no faith in our plan and our valor?"

"I have, but . . . Well, go with God, dear brother."

"And justice!" he answered earnestly.

He rode all night to be in position by morning. Before the sun was directly overhead, at 11:50 a.m., a courier brought word to the *insurrectos* that sixty cavalry had left the Guantanamo fort with the cannon but forty-five had split off to patrol north. There were only fifteen horse soldiers protecting the guns.

The situation was perfect.

With three times as many Cuban fighters as Spanish cavalry, the *insurrectos* would win easily.

All afternoon long the reports came in from Arias' "eyes," and each message encouraged the rebels more. The cavalry were dawdling along in the heat and dust. The column had only a single scout out front. This was obviously a routine chore for the Spanish troopers, who were plainly bored with the dreary journey.

At five p.m. the convoy was nine and a half miles from the place Arias had chosen for his attack. It was a bridge over a small river. The Spaniards would almost surely halt there to water their horses, and then the freedom fighters would strike. They'd beat off the guards with a hail of bullets, drive the captured artillery across the wooden bridge, and then set it on fire to halt pursuit. While half of the guerrillas kept the soldiers pinned down with rifle and shotgun fire, the others would escape with the cannon.

At a quarter to seven, Arais saw the pillar of smoke.

That was the signal.

"Get ready," he told his men. "They're just a mile away."

The convoy was moving slowly. It didn't reach the ambush point until five after seven. Exactly as Arias had hoped, the column halted at the edge of the river and the drivers of the artillery carriages got down. In a minute they'd start to water their steeds. In another twelve or fifteen minutes, the rebels would have the cannon they needed so desperately.

José Arias raised his hunting rifle and took aim at a sweaty-faced sergeant.

This was the moment.

He sucked in his breath and fired. Seconds later a volley rattled from the weapons of the other *insurrectos*. They were not expert marksmen, but eight Spaniards fell under the first salvo. The guerrillas were shouting and firing as fast as they could from their positions in the brush. At any second the troopers would panic under this assault by so many more guns, and they'd run.

They didn't.

They were trained soldiers. They knew what to do, and their discipline did not crack. They dropped to the ground or took protected positions beneath the wagons. They returned the fire. They couldn't see their attackers, but they shot back at the flashes, reloaded, and shot again.

"They can't hold out long," Arias told one of his men. "They'll have to fall back to the river, and then we seize the cannon."

In the next five minutes, more than a dozen men—some Spanish and as many Cuban—were hit. Four were killed. Then, exactly as Arias had predicted, the remaining troopers began to crawl back towards the river. He waited until the last one had left the wagons and smiled in triumph.

His plan had worked perfectly.

Now it was time to charge the unprotected wagons and gun carriages.

Soon shells from these cannon could be falling on the enemy. The Spaniards would no longer be safe in their massive stone forts. Those bastions would be blasted, and a tide of revolt would sweep across the island all the way to Habana. Thousands more would join the *insurrectos*. They'd capture more cannon and arms. This was but the beginning of the great offensive.

"We've won, Antonio!" he exulted to the Cuban fighter beside him.

But they had not.

He heard a rumble, and then the sound of a bugle not far away. As he turned to peer through the smoke down the road back to Guantanamo, another bugle called from behind him—somewhere on the other side of the river. The bugles knifed through the twilight twice more before he recognized their message.

It was the call to charge of the Spanish cavalry.

There were enemy horsemen galloping to attack the *insurrectos* from both front and rear.

The ambushers themselves had been ambushed.

It was a trap.

The earth vibrated beneath his feet with a warning that the Spanish riders were very near. Arias shouted to his comrades to take to the nearby woods, then ordered half a dozen to lay down a covering fire as the others fled for their lives. He saw the first wave of cavalry sweep round the curve in the road. The sun glinted on their swords and lances.

And that bastard Bortelo led the charge.

The *insurrectos* ran. Some got away, but more than a score were hacked down by sabres or impaled on those terrible lances as the cavalry rode them down.

A bullet from a Spanish carbine seared Arias' left ear. He stumbled onto the thicket where he'd tied his horse, swung up and galloped away at top speed. The pain in his ear was matched by the hurt and anger that filled his head and his belly.

Bortelo had made a fool of him, and many brave patriots had paid a terrible price. Arias had strolled into the trap like the most gullible schoolboy. Now, with his heart pounding and pride battered, he was riding for his life. Drenched with sweat and panting, he crouched low to present a minimum target.

There was a sour taste in his mouth. He recognized it as fear, and he cursed the enemy fiercely.

Bitter and embarrassed, José Arias led the desperate survivors through the woods until they had lost their pursuers. Then they split up into twos and scattered, each pair taking a different back road or twisting cowpath home.

It was nearly one a.m. by the time Arias saw the lights of Guantanamo. He was tired, dirty and ashamed. He had been degraded by the cunning Spanish *teniente*, who was probably laughing right now as his torturer savaged the *insurrectos* who'd been captured.

Even those who had escaped would not be safe. Spanish patrols would be sweeping through every town and village, looking for exhausted horses or other clues that might help identify those who'd fled from the trap.

Worst of all, the freedom fighters' bloody sacrifice had been in vain. So many courageous men had perished for nothing. Someday streets and parks would be named after those martyrs, but that was of little comfort now. The Spaniards were still secure in their forts. Without those cannon, the rebels were almost helpless—little more than curious children beating at the walls.

How many other Cubans would die before the underground managed to get those big guns?

Madre de dios, why hadn't the Yankee ship come back? Where was it? Would it ever return?

Chapter Ten

Something was wrong.

Every man on the ship knew it, but only two understood why the captain was so sober and distant. This was not the Shelby Davis they'd sailed with for so long. Subdued and often silent for long periods, the handsome Georgian seemed to be far away. Where? Why? Uneasy, but afraid to ask, the crew could only speculate on what the problem might be.

Was he ill? Was there some danger he was hiding from them?

Fitzgerald had the answers, but could not bring himself to betray the captain's private pain.

"I've been watching him," Dr. Preston confided to the first mate on the morning of October 18, "and I've been watching you, too."

"What the divvil are you talking about?" Fitzgerald dodged.

"*You* know," the physician accused.

"What?"

"What's bothering him. It's an odd look he has. Either a tropical fever or a broken heart."

Averting his eyes, Fitzgerald pretended to scan the horizon.

"It isn't a fever. There isn't a trace of the sweats, Paddy. He's cool, too cool. You'd better tell me."

"It's his business, Doctor. I don't pry."

"You don't have to. I'll say it again. You look as grim as he does—and don't tell me it's your stomach."

Fitzgerald patted his abdomen and winced.

"As a matter of fact, Doctor, I had some pork chops that last night we were in San Juan and—"

The physician wasn't the least bit deceived.

"Come on, Paddy," he reproved. "We both know you've got a belly made of solid brass. You could eat horseshoe nails and you wouldn't even belch. Out with it, man. What's tearing at him?"

The first mate hesitated.

"You'll feel better yourself if you tell someone," Preston argued.

Fitzgerald shrugged in surrender.

"Maybe I will," he admitted. "It's been bloody horrible. I was the one who gave him the nasty news. She's dead."

"The redheaded woman?"

"Aye. He loved her something fierce. Mad for her, he was, and she for him. It was so strong between them, so wild and beautiful."

The pot-bellied physician shook his head.

"So you're still the Irish romantic in love with love? Listen, Paddy, I admire that. Well, I respect it anyway. But people do die—every damn day. As a doctor, I've seen a lot of dying, both in peacetime and in war. Those who survive have to come to terms with it—and go on."

"He knows that!" Fitzgerald defended.

"He should. He's seen plenty of dying too."

"You won't say anything about this, Doctor?"

"Not a word," Preston vowed, "but I hope he gets back to normal soon."

"Ah, she was a great beauty. 'Tis normal enough for a man to mourn a smashing female such as that lass."

"For a while and within reason. Let's see how he is in another few weeks."

The days slid by, and the *Sarah W. Lee* steamed on to Guadeloupe, then to Jamaica again and up to the Danish-ruled chain called the Virgin Islands. The cargos changed with each trip, but Shelby Davis didn't. It was weeks since he'd learned of her death, and there was no sign that he'd made his peace with it. Every night he stood on deck staring out to sea.

It was not the cays or waves of the Caribbean that he saw.

It was the redheaded woman from New Bedford.

He hardly ate, barely slept and rarely spoke.

He lost weight. His eyes were haunted and his once powerful voice devoid of strength or authority. It was as if he were dazed, functioning on memories of what a captain was to do.

On November 24, the hunted vessel unloaded a shipment of third-rate wine and iron pipe in the Haitian capital of Port-au-Prince. Shelby Davis did not want to go ashore, but he needed to secure another cargo. Fitzgerald was at his side, as he often was these days. There was little in the way of freight moving from this impoverished young nation that had been a French colony until 1804. Wracked by war, invasion and rebellion repeatedly since then, Haiti was among the very poorest and most primitive islands in the whole Caribbean. Many of the people were gifted wood carvers, weavers or painters. Most of them were illiterate farmers. It was never easy to find a cargo here.

It took Davis and Fitzgerald five hours and visits to a dozen merchants to put together a shipment that would just about pay their expenses for the run to Kingston. Walking back to the dock, the first mate tried to ignore the seductive calls of the harlots crooning invitations from doorways and upstairs windows. His mind was on a Cuban woman whom he'd never touched, a shapely widow whom he could not forget.

Was he a fool to daydream about a female he'd barely met?

Would the ship ever return to Guantanamo?

It could be months or even years. By then, the dark-skinned Isabella Garcia could be wed to another, perhaps even a mother. It was ironic, Fitzgerald thought as he stepped back to avoid an aggressive street peddler. The captain was haunted by a dead woman and the first mate by a voluptuous widow whom he hardly knew.

Then Patrick Fitzgerald forced himself back to reality.

Though nine out of ten Haitians were decent and friendly, this street ran right through the *Zone Rouge*, the red light district. The denizens of this sleazy section would kill a ship's officer for the brass buttons on his coat, which were worth a month's wages in this desperately poor land.

"Careful, Captain. This is a rough lot here," the mate warned. Davis nodded in vague response, leaving Fitzgerald uncertain whether the troubled Georgian had understood a word he'd said.

And then it happened. Very suddenly.

A quartet of burly toughs armed with clubs poured from a foul-smelling alley. Their weapons were raised and their intentions clearly written in the murderous expressions on their thuggish faces. They would batter the white foreigners to a pulp, strip them to their skins and leave them in the garbage-filled street bleeding. Or dead.

"Captain!" Fitzgerald shouted in warning.

Davis responded instantly—and expertly. In a single moment he changed from a star-crossed lover to a fierce fighting machine. It was startling to see how many gutter tactics this elegant Georgia gentleman had mastered.

He had learned his lessons well.

While Fitzgerald was fighting off one two hundred-and forty pounder, Shelby Davis was battling the other three to their knees. He moved with stunning speed, breaking the wrist of one attacker and seizing the hoodlum's club to crash it between the eyes of another.

As the poleaxed thug tottered, Davis turned—a club in each hand now—to confront the third. That man turned too—and ran. He didn't get far. Shelby Davis hurled one of the clubs like a spear. It struck the fleeing tough at the base of his skull, and he staggered against a building wall. He drew an eight-inch knife. Then he lurched forward with an obscene oath to stab the young Georgian.

Shelby Davis spun aside with the speed and grace of a professional athlete. As the groggy hoodlum passed, Davis crouched and swung his remaining club to shatter the bullet-headed attacker's right kneecap. The man fell screaming, still clutching the dagger. He dropped that weapon when Davis' club shattered most of the bones in his hand.

At that moment, Fitzgerald slammed an uppercut to his foe's jaw and then pounded the man's head against the stone wall of *Maison Renée*—a "house" that sheltered seven slim women and was certainly no home. Stone prevailed over bone. The fight was ended.

And Patrick Fitzgerald stared at his commanding officer appraisingly. There had been no hesitation or indifference in the way Davis had responded to the threat. The distant look was gone and the "old" sparkle and alert intelligence shining again.

Was it the survival instinct or something else that had done this? Fitzgerald didn't care. His captain was "back" at last.

"Stop dawdling, Paddy," Davis said crisply. "Time to get back to the ship."

It was the "normal" voice and authority. Fitzgerald found himself smiling broadly as they walked quickly towards the nearby harbor. He could hardly wait to tell Dr. Preston. The rest of the crew would see it for themselves.

Captain Shelby Davis was in full command again.

Though he surely missed her deeply, the ghost of the redheaded woman no longer ruled him.

He wasn't a captive of melancholy or depression anymore.

The haunting was over.

Chapter Eleven

At three p.m. on the twenty-ninth day of November, Patrick Fitzgerald saw the Cuban coast and his heart surged. They'd be in Guantanamo Bay in less than an hour. The ship would only stay long enough to unload and find a new cargo—probably two or three days. That was all the time he had to find her.

"Keep those lookouts alert," Shelby Davis reminded his mate.

The *Sarah W. Lee* had steamed with extra lookouts on duty for the past two weeks, and other freighters plying Caribbean waters were being equally cautious. The British and French frigates assigned to these islands were being reinforced, and everyone knew why. The word was flashing from Trinidad to Nassau and every port between.

There were pirates in the Caribbean again.

No one could say whether it was one ship or more. These criminals did not leave any survivors to describe them or their vessels. In the past four months, some eleven cargo ships had simply disappeared. These ranged from relatively small vessels to craft as big as the *Sarah W. Lee*. Nobody noticed what was happening at first, for in the casual Caribbean there was no organized mmonitoring of ship movements.

The initial three ships had vanished at the start of the hurricane season, so foul play was not suspected. Word traveled slowly about the others. There were no cable or radio communications, only mail or weekly newspapers that moved by ship.

Then the bodies began to appear.

Bloated corpses with bullet wounds and deep gashes that could only be made by cutlasses or machetes floated ashore. Even though some of the bodies had been badly gnawed by sharks or mangled on saw-toothed coral reefs, the evidence of murder was clear.

An ankle bracelet on one body—actually it was closer to half a body—identified it as the remains of the captain of a French inter-island freighter based in Martinique.

The tattooed arm of another was recognized as belonging to a Canadian cook employed on another missing ship.

The severed head that floated onto a Puerto Rican beach was a more difficult problem. Someone had ruined the face in the process of tearing out the dead man's dental work—gold, no doubt.

Of the hundreds of mariners missing, nine corpses

from four of the vanished ships were found. That was enough to sound the alarm. Though the era of such ruthless buccaneers as Lolonois and "Blackbeard" Teach was long gone, there were new brigands sweeping the Caribbean.

And they were butchers—as bad, if not worse than any of their monstrous predecessors. They had to be destroyed. No vessel was safe so long as they roamed free. These nameless thugs posed a special problem—no, threat—to the *Sarah W. Lee*. With so many destroyers and frigates and coastal patrol boats searching and checking, the risk that the ex-Confederate raider might be noticed as a hunted "pirate" vessel itself was suddenly many times greater.

In response to his captain's order, Fitzgerald signalled to the lookout overhead. He watched as the man swept the horizon with his telescope and waved down in the "all clear" gesture.

"Not a ship in sight," the mate reported.

"That's the problem, isn't it?" Davis replied thoughtfully.

"What do you mean, Captain?"

"A ship—*any* ship—can't be invisible, can it?"

Fitzgerald shook his head.

"But this one is, Paddy. It must be fairly large and fast and well-armed—probably with cannon. How can a big armed vessel—a warship—roam through thousands of square miles of Caribbean without anyone seeing it?"

"Can't be done."

"That's right. Putting aside that childish talk about

ghost ships and buccaneers back from the dead, we've got a real vessel that people *must* see. They see it, but they don't *recognize* it."

"It's disguised!"

"That's my guess. We did it in part, but this must be a total job and a very good one. They're probably operating from some little cay that isn't even on the charts. They hit and hide, leaving no trace except an occasional corpse that bobs up a week later."

Fitzgerald considered the implications for several seconds.

"If they're *that* well disguised, Captain, we could steam right up to them and not know it."

The handsome Georgian nodded.

"That's why I've ordered our gun crews to be ready for action at all times. Nobody's going to take *this* ship by surprise," he announced firmly.

It was good to hear the alertness and authority in the captain's voice. Shelby Davis had his mourning—and everything else—under control. He was once more the energetic commander of a fighting ship, and he was ready for anything. Seeing this buoyed the morale and confidence of the crew immensely. Captain Davis was back in full command, and he'd get them home safely before too long. Only Hinkley continued to sulk.

Suddenly the lookout shouted, and pointed eastward.

Davis turned, saw the sun glinting on metal.

It was a ship carrying four cannon.

It was moving fast—right at the *Sarah W. Lee*.

"Those look like small guns, Captain," Fitzgerald estimated. "We could blow them out of the water."

Davis peered through his telescope for another few moments before he handed it to the first mate.

"Why would we sink a Cuban patrol boat, Paddy?" he asked wryly.

Fitzgerald stared through the glass, then winced in embarrassment.

"It's all right," Davis reassured. "Better to be safe than sorry, as my Uncle Jefferson used to say. No harm done."

It was 4:20 by the time the former Confederate warship was tied up at a pier in Guantanamo. The waterfront seemed quiet, with no sign of any laborers who might unload the cargo. Davis could see the eagerness in his first mate's eyes.

"Why don't you come ashore with me, Paddy?" he invited. "I've got to let Carranza know that his shipment's in, or he'll never send us a gang to unload all this cargo."

Señor Enrique Carranza was delighted to hear that his goods had arrived, and he promised that men would be at the dock at eight the next morning—by nine, for sure—to carry the crates ashore.

He gave Davis and Fitzgerald two fat six-inch cigars, made by his cousin's firm and from tobacco rolled against the thighs of virgins. Female virgins, of course. No one knew why, he acknowledged, but cigars rolled by female virgins seemed to be superior.

Then the merchant produced a bottle of aged rum, from his personal stock, made by his Uncle Tomas. After placing three glasses on the desk, he smiled that courteous Cuban smile of sincere hospitality again. When they had each sipped a finger or more of the dark mellow rum, Davis noticed that Fitzgerald's impatience was even more acute.

"Wonderful rum, Señor," Davis complimented. "My profound compliments to your uncle, and to your cousin too. If I may say so, sir, this is one fine cigar."

The Georgian puffed again, then blew a perfect smoke ring.

"My cousin will appreciate your approval, *Capitan*."

"It is well deserved. How relaxing it is to sit here enjoying these good things with you, Señor—and how sad that Mr. Fitzgerald must leave us on ship's business."

The first mate gulped in surprise.

"Try to be on board before the watch changes," Davis said, "if you can."

He didn't wink.

He didn't have to, for Patrick Fitzgerald understood. He managed to express his "profound gratitude" for the "grand hospitality and noble courtesy" extended by the merchant, to compliment the Cuban people in general and their men in particular, to "salute" the cigars and rum—and to still get out the door in eighty seconds.

He reached the *farmacia* at one minute to six, knocked on the door and entered. He had rehearsed exactly what he'd say to José Arias before he gently brought the conversation around to the pharmacist's sister. He never got a chance to do that. When he entered the shop, there was an utter stranger behind the counter.

"Excuse me," the mate said politely, "but I'm looking for Señor Arias. My name's Fitzgerald. Is he here?"

The man in the white jacket eyed him uncertainly

before he replied—in Spanish. Fitzgerald didn't understand much of what this stranger was saying, but he grasped that the man had no English at all. Why was he nodding towards the door to the street now? Did he know where the buxom widow was?

"*Por favor,*" the mate began, using a tenth of his entire Spanish vocabulary, "uh . . . Señora Isabella Garcia?"

"I'm here."

Patrick Fitzgerald was startled to see her framed in a side doorway leading from the shop to some other part of the building. She was even lovelier than he remembered. He swallowed to control his desire before he dared speak.

"And quite glorious you are, too, Ma'am," he told her. She smiled, enjoying the candid, but still tactful admiration.

"I was passing by, and I thought I'd stop in to say hello to your brother," he lied.

She did not answer him. Instead, she spoke rapidly in Spanish to the man behind the counter, who nodded in a way that suggested he was an employee. Whoever he was, he took off the white pharmacist's jacket and hung it on a nail behind him. Then he said something in Spanish and departed.

"It's six o'clock. Closing time, Mr. Fitzgerald," she explained. She was thinking quickly now. This was her chance.

"I'm afraid that my brother's not here, Mr. Fitzgerald. You and I are the only ones in the building."

Was she merely reporting fact, or was she telling him

something more? The Dublin-born mate wished that he knew the Latin mind better. He realized that the women of every class and culture had their own code-words and signals, but he was far from certain about how this sort of Cuban female communicated "stop" or "go ahead."

"Has he gone far?" Fitzgerald tested.

She shrugged, and those ample breasts moved majestically.

"I am not sure, Señor. Nobody knows where he is. The *policia* have had their agents watching the shop for many weeks. There's one out across the street right now."

"Why?"

She shrugged again, and Fitzgerald's lips were dry. Now some scent she was wearing—something subtle and musky—reached him. It wasn't strong, but his body's response to it was. She saw the gleam of desire in his eyes. It pleased her. This *Americano* with the odd accent could be helpful to the *insurrectos*—if handled right.

"I'm told that it may have something to do with *Teniente* Bortelo," she replied smoothly. "He is said to suspect that dear José, a simple pharmacist who wouldn't hurt a mosquito, is involved with a group of rebels. It's ridiculous, of course."

"I wouldn't blame him if he were!" Fitzgerald declared impetuously. "No country's got the right to tyrannize another one. That's why we threw the British out of the States—and why my cousins are fighting to drive them from Ireland today."

He wouldn't be difficult.

"I'm not a political person, Mr. Fitzgerald, and not a very gracious hostess either. Why don't we continue this conversation over a refreshing drink?"

She locked the shop's street door, then led him down a corridor to a large, dimly lit and cool room with stone floors. Within minutes they were sipping from tumblers of a chilled wine and fruit-juice mixture. She told him about how "difficult" it was "for a widow" and how "concerned" she was about her missing brother. Then she gave Fitzgerald a second drink, this one laced heavily with vintage rum.

It didn't take long for the liquor to start to dissolve his inhibitions. Fitzgerald began gallantly by trying to reassure her that the missing pharmacist would probably return "any day now with a perfectly reasonable explanation" for his absence. Almost immediately after the third drink, he moved on to consoling her sympathetically about the plight of a widow without a man to turn to—and she knew that she had him.

Somehow she managed to move nearer to him and squeeze out a few tears.

Then he put his arms around the "frightened lady" to calm her.

Instead, her sultry perfume, her body heat and the pressure of her ample body against his combined with his desire to arouse Patrick Fitzgerald immensely. He was holding and moulding her fleshy curves tight against him, kissing her fiercely as he cast away caution. She was moving against him, returning his kisses with ardor.

Yes, it was working as she'd planned, she thought.

Then she stopped thinking.

It wasn't supposed to happen this way, but she couldn't stop it. She was shuddering and twisting in his embrace, her lips burning against his with as much heat as glowed in her womb. She was gulping and shaking with passion as the dam that had held strong for two years of deprivation simply dissolved.

She wanted as much as he did. No, more.

Now.

She felt his hard need against her, and there was no reason to waste another moment. This was more than mere animal lust, she realized. This was caring for a fine and gentle man, she thought happily. She led him to the large brass bed in the rear room that was hers, and she undressed quickly.

''Beautiful. You're very beautiful,'' Fitzgerald said in that lush brogue as he dropped his shirt on a big chair.

She beamed.

It was good to have a good man appreciate and admire her splendid body again. She had waited too long for this. He would wash away the lewd glances and ugly thoughts of the *macho* smirkers who saw all females as chunks of meat put on this planet for their pleasure.

He had a fine body too, lean and tanned and manly. He was strong. She had felt the power when he'd almost crushed her in his embrace. Now she saw the muscles that gave him such strength. It would be difficult to resist such a man. Looking at his naked desire, she didn't want to.

He was very gentle when they reached the bed, as

she'd known he would be. He kissed her again and again in many places, and he stroked and caressed her tenderly for a long time. Her hips were moving as if they had a life of their own, and she felt the blood coursing through every millimeter of her veins. When he began to kiss her breasts, she moaned. She had never known such a skilled and caring lover. It was as if he loved every cell of her body.

He entered very slowly, almost too slowly. She could not wait. Impatient and imperious, she locked her legs around him and pressed his swollen flesh deep into her. When he began to move, her head twisted urgently from side to side. She had no shred of control. She heard herself making sounds—some guttural and others shrill, almost yelping. She couldn't stop the primitive noises. Her entire middle and loins were molten, throbbing with this man's inexorable rhythms.

It was fortunate that the building had thick stone walls, that this bedroom was in the rear far from the street and that the windows were closed to keep out the heat. When the awesome spasm came, Isabella Arias Garcia screamed . . . and groaned . . . and subsided in a long, long sigh.

It was the same way the second time he made love to her. That was only ten minutes after the first explosion. She had refused to let him escape from her locked legs. As soon as Fitzgerald sensed what she meant, he didn't try to pull away.

The third time she took the initiative and set the direction. *She* made love to *him*, and it was Fitzgerald who made the sounds of uncontrolled passion. Crouching over him, the widow made it last a long time. When they were both replete and lying locked in warm embrace, she didn't feel like a widow anymore. She knew that she never would again.

This stranger in her bed had done this.

It was odd how it had happened, she thought as her fingers stroked his thigh. She had intended to *use* this tender and caring man for The Cause, and now she was halfway to an intense love affair.

It was probably foolish to care deeply about a foreign mariner, but she knew herself well enough to realize that she could not hold back for long. On a physical level alone, the experience had been astonishing. No man had ever made love to her as devotedly and completely as this black-haired Fitzgerald.

Suddenly she realized that she didn't know his first name, and she grinned. It was extremely unladylike to sleep with a man whose Christian name you'd never heard. She touched him gently at the tenderest spot, and he stirred.

''What's your name?''

He sighed vaguely in semi-conscious response.

''Fitzgerald, what's your Christian name?'' she pressed, and kissed his neck.

''Huh . . . Pat . . . Patrick . . . Patrick Fitzgerald,'' he said with a long yawn.

''Patrick Fitzgerald is a nice name,'' she judged, and kissed him again. She wondered whether she could arouse him once more. As she considered it, a delicious languor spread through her body.

It had been so long since she'd felt this wonderfully

relaxed and drowsy. Listening to his regular breathing, she decided that there'd be time for more love when they'd rested. Yes, he was dozing. Content and confident, she cuddled her body against his and kissed his ear softly before she slid off into profound, dreamless sleep.

Chapter Twelve

Maybe it was Fitzgerald's years of fixed watches on the ship.

Perhaps it was his powerful and instinctive sense of duty.

Whatever it was, some inner thing awoke the first mate in time for him to return to the dock a few minutes before midnight. He managed to leave the house by a rear door that led to a winding back alley—something Isabella Garcia insisted on, so he wouldn't be followed by the Spanish agent watching the front of the building. She sent her new lover on his way with a long kiss and a pact that they'd meet at five p.m. the next day at a small restaurant near the edge of the city.

She thought about him all day long. When she closed her eyes, she could feel him again. The texture of his skin, his taste, his adoring black eyes and boyish curly hair were all astonishingly real and present. But even as she pulsed with these sensations, something else intruded into her consciousness.

It was her brother.

Must she choose between them?

Could she?

Teniente Bortelo was also considering the two men, but he had much less difficulty in making his decision. After listening to the *other* agent—the spy who'd followed Fitzgerald back to the ship—he chuckled.

"So the hungry widow has finally filled her bed!" he mocked. "I'll bet he had a good time. Dammit, I was thinking about taking that juicy lady myself. Might be interesting to bounce a woman whose husband you've killed, huh?"

"As you say, *Teniente,*" the uneasy agent agreed.

"I was a bit concerned when the Yankee ship first put in here and that treacherous dog of a pharmacist went aboard," Bortelo recalled. "I feel better that it's just a stupid first mate grinding away with the sister. Would be more to worry about if it was the *capitan* meeting José Arias."

"You believe that this is an affair of the heart, sir?"

Bortelo guffawed and made an obscene gesture.

"Of the groin, dummy. This is simply old-fashioned lust—a horny sailor who's been at sea too long and a steamy widow he caught by luck at the right moment."

"Then we can stop watching him?"

The lieutenant shook his head.

Where did the Army find such dolts for intelligence work?

"Him, *yes*. Her, *no*," Bortelo replied. "She may yet lead us to that bastard brother of hers."

As they spoke, Shelby Davis was walking the *Avenida Toledo* towards the harbormaster's office. In ports such as this, that was always a likely place for information about possible cargos. He was two blocks away when he heard the shouting. He turned to see a teenage boy running towards him at top speed.

Four—no, five—cavalrymen were riding in hot pursuit. They galloped down the narrow street, and pedestrians hurled themselves into doorways to avoid being trampled by the flying hooves. The soldiers were shouting. Two held pistols, the others swords. There was terror in the boy's face as he sprinted desperately for safety.

He was ten feet from Davis when the lead rider fired.

The bullet broke the youth's spine, and the crippled fugitive dropped less than a yard from Shelby Davis' feet.

The boy lay on the cobblestones like a broken doll. Stunned by the unexpected violence, Davis stepped back. Then he looked up as the cavalrymen reined their sweaty steeds and jumped down. Brushing past the handsome Georgian as if he wasn't there, they cursed the maimed youth.

"What did he do?" Davis asked.

They ignored the question. One soldier kicked the boy twice in the stomach. Another slashed at his groin. A third, the biggest of all, raised his sword and hacked away with all his hate and might at the teenager's neck. With his head nearly severed, the lad was dead.

Then a cavalryman spit on the boy.

The others cursed the corpse before they turned to go.

Davis couldn't believe what he'd seen, couldn't accept what they meant to do. They were leaving the body here, in the street, as if it were garbage.

"What did he do?" the Georgian repeated.

A beefy corporal spun angrily and raised his saber, but saw that he faced a foreign naval officer. The braid on that unfamiliar uniform intimidated the soldier, so he froze—weapon up for the kill.

He lowered the saber to point at the corpse.

"*Insurrecto puerco!*" he scorned.

It took Davis several seconds to recall from his limited Spanish vocabulary that *puerco* meant *pig*. By that time the troopers had cantered away, leaving the Georgian alone with the body. Soon other people appeared from doorways, but none of them did more than look. Not one stepped forward, not even to cover the gory corpse with some burlap or cloth. They glanced at the slain youth, sucked in their breath and walked away quickly.

They were all afraid to get involved or be associated in any way with this dead teenager.

The Third Cavalry had them totally scared. This killing was merely another lesson in its brutal educational program. Anyone who opposed Spanish military rule—or showed the slightest sympathy for the rebels—stood an excellent chance of dying publicly and horribly.

Perhaps the Army High Command in Havana was less savage, but raw terror was the order of the day—every day—at this end of the island. Could the queen back in Madrid know what atrocities were being committed in her name here?

A church bell rang. Davis realized that he had to go on to the harbormaster's office, that life had to go on for him and his crew. As he walked along the avenue, he thought how strange it was to see Spain still applying the ruthless tactics used centuries earlier against the Mayans and the Incas in pagan Mexico and Peru.

When he reached the office, the harbormaster reported that an exporter named del Sol had been in to ask about ships heading for the Bahamas. He'd probably be back tomorrow after lunch, at about three o'clock.

"Is there anywhere I could speak to him now?" Davis asked.

It was impossible.

This was the time of siesta, and after his long nap Señor del Sol might visit a "close friend." The harbormaster winked as he spoke those last words, just in case the *Norte Americano* did not understand that the exporter had a mistress.

"If you don't catch him tomorrow, *Capitan*, try noon the following day," the port official suggested casually. The year-round heat and humidity in this region definitely discouraged urgency, Davis thought. It would be foolish not to accept the Cuban tempo and way of life. Of course, New Englanders might have trouble doing that, he reflected, for they were always in a hurry. He must be careful not to act like those impatient Yankees.

Manners and ritual also counted a lot down in these islands—especially those ruled by Spain. Shelby Davis made a point of thanking the harbormaster extravagantly and giving him a small box of good cigars he'd bought for just this purpose. It was a modest token of esteem—nothing at all like a bribe. This was a culture filled with such graceful niceties and useful distinctions, and Georgia-bred Shelby Davis felt quite comfortable among the warm-hearted Cubans.

Making his way back to the ship, Davis sensed that news of the boy slaughtered in the street had spread quickly. He could practically *feel* the fear and bitterness among the Cubans he passed. The terror was almost tangible. People walked stiffly with deliberately blank faces and avoided eye contact, lest it betray their emotions.

"He was only fifteen or sixteen, Paddy," Davis recalled soberly on the deck of the *Sarah W. Lee* as the church bell boomed four o'clock.

"And they just left him there for the birds to pick?"

"That's right. It was meant to frighten people, and it did."

"They've done worse, Captain," reported the first mate. Then Fitzgerald told him about some other atrocities the widow had described. When he was done, he requested and received permission to go ashore "on personal business."

After Fitzgerald had left the ship, Shelby Davis looked past the dock at the low silhouette of the waterfront warehouses and bars. It seemed like a typical Caribbean panorama—a peaceful, seedy port drowsing in the tropic heat. But only an inch behind that tranquil façade, just below the whitewashed surface, a secret battle was seething.

All his impulses were to help the Cubans in their

struggle for freedom. In his own way, Shelby Davis was just as much a romantic as his first mate. Since childhood, he'd always been willing to fight for justice for the underdog.

"But this isn't *my* fight," he told himself.

It couldn't be, for he was responsible for getting his whole crew home safely. He had no right to ask them to risk their lives again. By skill and luck they had survived four searing years of their own great war, and that was enough.

Like every other people, the Cubans would have to win their own freedom. It was simply a matter of time before the guerrilla struggle erupted into open, bloody war. The *Sarah W. Lee* could not be here for that. Davis made up his mind to start searching for a cargo again early the next morning by rechecking every warehouse and merchant in Guantanamo. He couldn't count on Señor del Sol. He couldn't wait a day longer than necessary.

Loaded or empty, the *Sarah W. Lee* would put to sea in forty-eight hours. Fitzgerald and others might not agree, but there was no question of choice or delay. They had to get out of here before Cuba exploded, and that could happen any day now.

Davis closed his eyes. He saw the boy's mangled corpse again in his mind. First that vision angered him, but then it reinforced his conviction. The sooner the ex-Confederates steamed from this agonized island, the better.

The ship came first.

It had to.

* * *

"*Casa Serena,*" the driver of the horse-drawn taxi announced, and nodded towards the confirming sign on the small restaurant. Fitzgerald paid him and added, a generous tip. The first mate was in an expansive mood. He was meeting her for the first time since they had made love, he and the woman he'd dreamt about for months.

As Fitzgerald walked into the garden, he wondered why she had chosen this public place for their second meeting. He had discovered that her passions and appetites matched his own, and he was disappointed that their rendezvous was not back in the stone house with that brass bed he'd never forget. Perhaps she wanted to show him that her interest was more than physical, he speculated. Whatever her reasons were, Fitzgerald was happy to be seeing her at all.

There she was—glowing with a smile full of female promise.

The high-necked and "proper" black dress seemed to dramatize rather than conceal her voluptuous figure, and the light in her eyes was far from a widow's sadness. It was difficult for Fitzgerald not to sweep her into his arms.

The same wave of wanting washed over her.

Then the uncertainty came again.

How would he take it when she told him?

Would he believe her now? Would he ever trust her after today?

He sat down at the table beside her. The view from the garden was splendid with its grand panorama of the sun-dappled sea. Small sailing craft glided elegantly across the horizon, but Fitzgerald saw none of these natural delights. He had eyes only for this warm woman.

They ordered drinks. They spoke and they smiled and they remembered what they had shared the previous night. When they finished their drinks, she guided him to her straw-topped surrey. She handled the horse well, he noted silently and with admiration. At five minutes after six, she unhitched the gelding in the stable behind the *farmacia*. Ten minutes after that, they were making love.

It was as deep and as uncontrolled as it had been the day before.

But there was a different quality to her passion—something wild and almost desperate. The primitive grunts and gasping sounds had a tone of special urgency—as if she had little time. She seemed to be racing to taste, to try, to do everything in a single hour.

Was she afraid of something?

Was it the awareness that his ship might depart in a few days? Or was it something more immediate and dangerous?

Dizzy with affection and physical completion, they cuddled for only a few minutes before she got up suddenly.

"Come back to bed, darlin'," Fitzgerald pleaded lazily.

"Later. We must wash and dress now. I have something important to show you."

"Can't it wait?"

"I wish that it could," she replied with puzzling force.

She was not looking forward to what she had to do.

"Now what?" Fitzgerald asked amiably as he finished buttoning his shirt.

"*This,*" she replied and kissed him long and passionately.

Then she took his hand. She led him to the storeroom behind the public section of the *farmacia,* stopped a yard from a stone wall lined with shelves of medicines.

"Why are you showing me these bottles?" he wondered.

"Not the bottles."

Then she threw her arms around him and kissed him again. It was as if they were saying good-by. Of course, it couldn't be *that.* Fitzgerald's curiosity turned swiftly to concern.

"What is it? What's wrong, Isabella?" he pleaded.

Afraid that she might choose the wrong words, the anguished widow reached into a space between two blue jars of a low shelf. Taking a deep breath, she pressed her fingers against one of the stone blocks.

The wall began to move.

Fitzgerald watched in amazement as the apparently solid stone barrier opened inward, to expose a secret space behind it.

"Smugglers built this place forty years ago. Please follow me, Pah-treek."

After she'd lit an oil lantern, he trailed her through the opening and found himself at the head of a flight of rough rock stairs. He watched as she closed the secret door behind them. Then she led the way down into the darkness.

A dozen questions rushed through his mind. None

came from his lips. If his woman chose not to explain now, he would wait until she was ready. He trusted her. If she said nothing now, there was a good reason.

At the bottom of the steps was a long corridor, oddly cool in this tropical climate. He shivered under the impact of the temperature difference. The roof of the passage was supported by aged wooden beams. They were eighteen or twenty feet below the surface, Fitzgerald gauged as he followed her along the tunnel and around the turn.

It was not damp or musty in this smuggler's labyrinth. These tunnels had been used recently.

The first mate wondered by whom, but he did not ask. His woman would explain it all very soon.

They were beyond the Arias property now and heading towards the sea. She led him around another corner. A heavy wooden door reinforced with metal strips and studs barred the passage. Patrick Fitzgerald wondered what he'd face when that massive portal opened.

He never found out.

Instead, she pressed on another stone set into the side of the tunnel. A narrow door, one as invisible to the naked eye as that upstairs, creaked open.

Fitzgerald saw something metallic glint ahead of him in the darkness. It could be a gun muzzle, he guessed. He was right. It was a long-barrelled pistol, held by a man prepared to kill.

"It's me—Isabella," she announced and raised the lantern shoulder high.

Now the first mate saw the weapon and its owner clearly.

The man behind the gun was José Arias.

She had said that she didn't know where her brother might be. That was plainly untrue.

Here he was, pistol in hand, and he was pointing it right between Fitzgerald's eyes.

Chapter Thirteen

"That's a fine lookin' weapon, Mr. Arias," Fitzgerald admired, "but would you mind aiming it somewhere else—please?"

The *insurrecto* leader did not move the gun an inch.

"Do as he asks, José," the widow urged.

"Can we trust this foreigner?"

"He is not foreign to me, Brother. I would trust him with my life," she announced simply.

Arias lowered the muzzle reluctantly, still wary of betrayal by the stranger.

"It's cold down here," the pharmacist complained.

"My brother has been hiding in the hills, Pah-treek. I arranged to meet you at that restaurant to draw away the spies from the house. While they followed me, José was able to slip into the secret tunnel by the other trapdoor."

She nodded towards a dark opening behind Arias, the mouth of another subterranean passage that led to some nearby building.

"I am not *hiding,*" Arias disagreed indignantly. "I am avoiding enemy forces until we are ready to launch our attack. That's why I asked my sister to arrange this meeting."

Had she made love only to get him here?

"I give you my word—" she began earnestly.

"You don't have to. I can see the truth in your eyes."

Anyone could. They were aglow with caring.

The radiance of a woman in love was not hard to recognize. José Arias didn't notice it, but his mind was on other things.

"I have a proposition for your captain," Arias announced. "We need cannon to liberate Cuba, and we want to buy four of those on your ship. Gold for iron—a good deal that should appeal to your Yankee business sense."

Fitzgerald wondered what Arias might say if he learned the truth about the ship and its crew.

"Cannon and shells, at least enough to get us started. After we capture the first Spanish fort we'll be using *their* artillery and ammunition," the pharmacist predicted confidently.

It was difficult to determine whether he was cocky or courageous, the first mate thought in the flickering light of the lantern.

"I'm not sure—" Fitzgerald began to reply.

"*I am,*" the *macho* guerrilla leader interrupted. "Now, we'll also need some training in how to fire these guns.

Here's my offer. $6,000 in gold for the four cannon, one hundred shells and the instruction. Take it or leave it. Tell that to your *capitan*."

Fitzgerald nodded in assent. He could not predict what Shelby Davis might decide, but the mate would relay the offer.

"Take it or leave it," Arias repeated aggressively. He probably believed that he had to put on a bold face and act tough in dealing with North Americans, Fitzgerald guessed.

"I'll tell him," the mate promised.

Five minutes later he bade farewell to Isabella Garcia in the pharmacy upstairs. They kissed again and again, reluctant to part. They pressed against each other fiercely, celebrating their nearness, aware that their future was impossible to predict.

Finally, he stepped back to look at her shining face.

"My brother—"

"I understand," Fitzgerald assured her.

"He isn't usually this rude and arbitrary."

"He's afraid," Fitzpatrick observed compassionately. "That's how men who are afraid behave everywhere, not just in Cuba. I'll do my best, darlin'."

He did. Some ninety minutes later he stood alone with Shelby Davis on the stern deck of their ship. He repeated the message carefully, and waited.

"What do *you* think, Paddy?"

Fitzgerald shifted from one foot to the other awkwardly.

"I'm not sure that my opinion would be entirely objective, Captain."

"Not your opinion. Your judgment. I have great respect for your judgment."

"Thank you. I should explain that I am . . . I have a strong affection for Mr. Arias' sister. A deep admiration, you might say."

Irish lovers were as discreet in their language as Southern gentlemen, Davis reflected approvingly.

"And what would you say, Paddy—about this business proposition?"

"Well, sir, we have no cargo and we could use the money. We do have four of our guns we're not using, sir. I reckon that we could defend ourselves from attack by most ships with the other cannon we're showing. We should be able to handle any pirates, I suspect. Can't be sure though. We don't know who they are or what armaments they carry."

"Calculated risk, right?" Davis questioned.

"Exactly, sir. I'd take it."

"So would I," Davis agreed. "We do need the money to get out of here. This whole island's going to explode in open revolution soon, and I want to be somewhere else when it does."

He saw the concern in Fitzgerald's eyes. The very thought of leaving his new love was acutely disturbing. Could he do it? The first mate of the *Sarah W. Lee* would face that ordeal soon.

"I'd also like to do anything that I can—without endangering this ship and its crew—to help the Cubans fight their way to freedom," Davis said sincerely. "God, those Spanish soldiers treat them like animals. No, worse. You don't just kill a horse or a dog because it resists your will. After I saw them butcher that boy in the street. . . .''

He stopped for several seconds, too bitter to continue immediately.

''I believe that he does have the gold, Captain. His sister said so, and she doesn't lie.''

''The gold is not the problem,''Davis replied. ''There are two other issues that must be resolved. First, how and where can we remove those cannon from this vessel and deliver them to the *insurrectos* on shore?''

''Would the second be where can we teach them how to shoot those guns without attracting the bloody Third Cavalry?'' Fitzgerald tested.

''It would,'' Shelby Davis confirmed and explained how he meant to cope with both problems.

Fitzgerald was delighted. The Georgian's plans were simple, imaginative and practical. They stood an excellent chance of working well—if the rebel movement was not infiltrated by Spanish agents. The other good thing about Shelby Davis' program was that it required Patrick Fitzgerald to see José Arias' lush and loving sister the very next morning.

That was the best part of all.

Playing the role of the hungry skipper of a tramp freighter fully, Shelby Davis spent the following day going from exporter to warehouse to merchant to exporter in a dogged effort to find a cargo for his ship. While he was doing this, Fitzgerald and Isabella Garcia were working out the details and timetable for execution of the daring scheme.

It was clever, but it was also dangerous.

Done properly and with tight security to avoid any leak to Spanish Military Intelligence, it ought to work. Davis had asked his first mate to be open—even ostentatious—in his public admiration for the widow. So long as the enemy believed that the relationship was purely a man-woman thing, Fitzgerald could visit her and spend time alone with Isabella Garcia without alarming anyone.

"They'll be there, Captain," Fitzgerald reported that evening.

"Good. I managed to pick up half a shipment today, so it won't look utterly ridiculous when we steam out of here tomorrow at dusk. You can tell the lady we'll arrive shortly after dark."

He was giving Fitzgerald another opportunity to see the woman who meant so much to him. Though the Dublin-bred first mate was an old-fashioned romantic, Shelby Davis had never observed Fitzgerald in such an intense involvement with a woman in the years he'd known him. This was serious—deeply physical but also much more. Even though the cause of a free Cuba was just and important, it would be terrible if she were merely using the starry eyed mate.

Fitzgerald left the ship with the message and spent the night with the widow. He returned at nine the next morning, as Shelby Davis expected. His tired eyes showed that he'd been up most, if not all of the night, but when the longshoremen arrived with the cargo he supervised the loading with his usual efficiency.

The job was done by 4:15 p.m., but Davis stalled the departure. He wanted to reach the rendezvous under cover of darkness. That would make them less easy for Spanish naval patrol craft to spot. The practical Georgian wasn't looking for a fight that might focus attention on his vessel. Even if he won, he'd lose, for then the entire island of Cuba would almost surely be off limits to the *Sarah W. Lee*. It could be years before they could enter any Cuban port if their ship and mission were recognized by Spanish authorities.

The ex-Confederate raider steamed out into Guantanamo Bay at half past six. When it reached the open sea it turned left and headed east for the secret meeting place off the coast near Imias. At ten minutes to ten, Shelby Davis looked towards the beach for the signal light. He saw nothing.

"Let's go in a bit closer. You men with the rifles stand ready," he ordered.

With crews beside the cannon and a score of riflemen prepared to open fire, the ship edged slowly closer to the beach. There was no sign of life on the broad strip of tan sand, no activity visible among the row of trees beyond. If there were *insurrectos* hiding behind that green barrier, they were well-concealed and taking no chances.

Fitzgerald was at the helm. He steered the *Sarah W. Lee* in to a mile and a half from the edge of the beach.

"Do you see them, Paddy?" Davis asked.

"No—but they're here. She gave her word, Captain," the mate insisted.

"Try getting a little closer."

Soon they were within half a mile of the beach. There was still no signal.

"We can't go in further, Paddy," Davis told him. "These are shallow waters, and we can't run the risk."

They steamed parallel to the beach for three minutes, hoping and staring towards the shore in silence.

Nothing. Not a glimmer.

Davis sighed and prepared to give the order Fitzgerald dreaded.

"I guess they couldn't make it, Paddy. Maybe Spanish patrols were out."

The mate shook his head stubbornly.

The young Georgian wondered whether it was hurt or defiance that shone from Fitzgerald's weary eyes.

Suddenly a lookout called a warning.

"Unidentified craft off the starboard bow."

Davis raised his telescope at once.

"Just another few minutes, Captain," the mate pleaded.

"I'm sorry, Paddy. That's a coastal patrol boat. We're out of time."

And then Fitzgerald's index finger stabbed towards the shore.

It was a signal light—bobbing on a low vessel only one hundred and fifty yards from the former raider.

There was another . . . and a third.

Three canoes were twisting through the small waves. They were moving fairly rapidly. The men paddling must be strong and expert.

"Come on! Come on, darlin'!" Fitzgerald appealed softly.

Now Davis could see the paddlers clearly in the balmy moonlight, their arms moving as one to propel their tiny craft forward.

The Spanish patrol boat was veering towards the shore. Had its captain spotted the *Sarah W. Lee*?

The canoes were only fifty yards away. They'd be alongside in two minutes. Did Shelby Davis *have* two minutes to risk?

"Reduce speed to one third. Get those lines over—*now*!" he commanded in an urgent whisper.

The damn patrol boat was but half a mile away. Probably carried a pair of two pounders, Davis estimated. What the hell was taking those paddlers so long?

Then he heard the first bump, and he smiled. He was grinning broadly by the time the third canoe thumped against the hull—and so was Patrick Fitzgerald. The first heads appeared over the rail moments later. The third boarder onto the deck was Isabella Arias Garcia. Her long black hair was wet from the sea, and her sopping cotton dress was plastered to every curve of her splendidly sculpted figure.

The American sailors stared in admiration. They all understood why Fitzgerald wanted her to be his. She might be a proper middle class widow, but right now she appeared ample and animal—the stuff of sailors' dreams.

"They're all aboard," the ensign from Texas called out.

"Then what are you waiting for, Mr. Fitzgerald?" Davis challenged.

With a powerful engine that gave it twice the speed of the patrol boat, the *Sarah W. Lee* pulled away quickly. As it raced off, a helpful mass of dark clouds drifted overhead to block out the moonlight. Within seconds, it was difficult for the Spaniards to see anything more than the silhouette of the escaping freighter—and that only for a few moments.

In accord with Davis' instructions, the mate steered the ship nine miles out to sea and then headed south to open water. Then Fitzgerald gave the helm to a petty officer and took the beautiful widow in his arms. He didn't have orders to do that, but he didn't need them. Davis turned away to give them a minute or two of privacy before they all turned to "business."

"I have half the gold here, *Capitan,*" she announced. She raised her wet skirt to reveal form-fitting short bloomers and just above them a money belt. With no sign of shyness or embarrassment, she reached down to unhook the cloth tube that held the gold. Davis could not help noticing that she had plump and shapely thighs, and how proudly his first mate appreciated them.

"The rest when the guns are ashore, if that's all right with you," she continued.

"Be fine, Ma'am," the Georgian agreed.

Then they set to work training the Cubans how to load, aim and fire the cannon. By the time they got to the actual shooting, the ship was nearly twenty miles away from the nearest land. Here they could fire the sixteen pound shells without much fear of being heard.

Next, the *insurrectos* were taught how to do basic cleaning and repairs, simple maintenance and safety procedures and other practical facts that could help keep these guns booming. Obviously intelligent and alert, the Cubans learned quickly. They asked many questions that touched on a variety of possible problems. Two of them appeared to know a good deal about gunpowder already.

The Americans and the Cubans worked together until after three in the morning. Then the gunnery experts and their students quit for the night. The "course" resumed at nine, with emphasis now on various kinds of ammunition that the Cubans could buy or even fashion themselves.

"Wish we could sell you more than twenty shells per gun," Davis told the widow, "but we have to keep some for our own defense. The pirates, you know."

"We're grateful for what you're doing, *Capitan,*" she assured him warmly.

While the crucial training continued, the ship circled slowly in a wide arc that would bring it back to the Cuban coast a dozen miles west of the mouth of Guantanamo Bay. Shortly after sunset, Davis ordered that the four "spare" cannon be brought up on deck. Then he doubled the number of lookouts.

The most dangerous part of the operation was coming next.

The ship would be most vulnerable during the offloading of the heavy guns.

It would be in near the shore—dead in the water and an almost perfect target.

Whether the plan for getting the cannon ashore would work was far from certain. If there were waves, the guns might be pitched into the sea—perhaps to rust forever.

"It was the best idea I could think of, Señora," Shelby Davis told the guerrilla leader's dynamic sister.

"It will succeed. I know it will," she answered confidently.

Now the Americans rigged the block and tackle and

tested the pulleys. There was no way to be sure that the hawsers would support the weight of the metal cannon—not before they actually tried to swing those big weapons over the side. The ropes were not new. They had never been used to lift such weight.

Ten p.m.—the chosen time.

Plenty of clouds, but a choppy sea.

There was the beach where four lanterns were to beam the "all clear" if it were safe to proceed.

Some fifty men peered into the night, taut with hope.

One . . . two . . . three lights.

Where was the fourth?

"Could be a trap," Dr. Preston warned in a low voice.

But then another light blossomed in the trees behind the beach. A murmur of joy ran through the Cubans on deck. Davis and the widow had each ordered them to keep noise to a minimum. Despite their surge of enthusiasm, they had managed to comply.

Suddenly the sand was alive with men—forty or fifty at the least. Groups of them were carrying logs to the water's edge, where other freedom fighters lashed the lengths of wood together to form rafts. Now teams of horses emerged from the trees, followed by teenage boys dragging coils of rope.

Shelby Davis ordered that a ship's boat be launched, and that it go ahead of the ex-raider to determine the depth of the water here. He wanted to steam the ship in fairly close to shore—without running it aground. The quartet in the ship's boat rowed towards the beach slowly, checking with a weighted line every forty-five seconds to fix the depth.

Ten fathoms . . . eight fathoms . . . seven . . . *six*.

That was it—thirty-six feet. Any closer would be unsafe.

The freighter inched in to where the ship's boat bobbed and dropped anchor. Now swift flight would be difficult. Davis ordered two men to stand by the anchor chain, ready to sever it abruptly if the ship had to leave suddenly.

Other crewmen attached the ropes to the first cannon. Then some thirty Americans and the fifteen Cubans began to strain and grunt as they struggled to pull the gun up from the deck. It would not move.

"Oil," Davis ordered.

This had to work.

If it didn't, all their effort and planning was for nothing.

Grumbling and muttering, the one-eyed cook, Cyrus Hinkley, returned from the galley with a jar of cooking oil. The pulleys were greased carefully, and then the Cubans and their American allies tried once more.

The cannon did not budge. It was too heavy.

They had failed.

"One more try, lads," Fitzgerald pleaded.

This time it moved—an inch.

"That's it!" Davis encouraged.

They tried again, and again, and still once more—but with no success.

On the fourth attempt, the cannon rose a foot from the deck. It hesitated stubbornly for several seconds . . . and then surrendered. It ascended eight inches on one heave, six the next, then a full dozen. The men panted and sweated and struggled, too desperate even to curse their massive metal foe.

Now it was five feet above the deck.

The men paused, gasping for breath and wondering whether the ropes would hold long enough for the raft to get into position. If a hawser snapped, it could maim or kill a man in three seconds. If the heavy gun fell, it might crash right through the deck into the ammunition locker below.

The first raft was moving from the beach. The *insurrectos* handling the crude oars seemed inexperienced. Their efforts to steer the raft out to the ship were barely effective. After about two minutes they appeared to work better together. Slowly but surely, the raft eased across the sea towards the freighter.

Now a hawser creaked under the strain.

Every man on the ship froze and wondered whether it would hold.

They did not relax until the raft bumped alongside.

They remained taut with tension after that too. The process of swinging the cannon over the side and lowering it gently—ever so delicately, as if it were a bomb—onto the raft was also filled with danger. One slip and the big gun would go down in thirty-six feet of Caribbean, probably taking along several freedom fighters with it.

"Easy . . . easy . . . No . . . wait a second . . . *Yes*," Davis instructed.

As soon as the cannon was on the raft, the rebels raced to tie it down before a surge of the sea might send the big gun sliding into the deep water. Even as they worked frantically, the other raft began to move out from the beach. Davis was focused on lifting the second cannon from the freighter's deck. He caught only a glimpse of six horses towing a large wagon out from the water's edge.

Neither the Americans nor the Cubans could rest for a minute.

All four cannon had to be off the beach before 3:30 a.m. if they were to be hidden safely in the hills before daybreak. The guerrillas ruled the night, but with the sun domination of eastern Cuba reverted to the much better armed Third Cavalry and allied Spanish units. The *insurrectos* were soldiers of darkness, shadows who hit and ran. Maybe these sixteen-pound guns and other artillery pieces that José Arias' fighters might capture could change that balance.

In three months.

Or three years.

No one could predict. That there was much bloody fighting ahead was certain, but not much else was. The men straining to get the big guns ashore did not think of such things. They were too busy with the immediate challenge and danger. Staying alive till dawn was as far ahead as they looked.

At 2:10 a.m. they began to load the artillery shells onto a raft. Three of the cannon were already ashore—two off the beach and out of sight. Some of the Cubans on the ship were annoyed by Shelby Davis' decision to send in the shells before the fourth cannon. Isabella Garcia was not.

"The *capitan* is wise, *amigos*," she told them. "None of these guns is of any use without ammunition."

While one raft went back and forth with loads of shells, the other came out for the last cannon. It was

2:55 a.m.—thirty-five minutes before the deadline. The men on the ship and those on the raft felt the pressure. They strained even harder. They knew that they had to hurry.

Maybe that's why it happened.

At 3:08 a.m. the fourth cannon was lowered onto the raft, and the Cubans on that primitive log ferry moved quickly to lash it down. Perhaps it was their hurrying or maybe the wave that spun the raft at just that moment. Whatever it was, the big gun moved—and a rope snapped. The cannon began to roll.

It was grinding slowly towards the edge of the raft.

In five more seconds the precious gun would be in the sea.

Two of the *insurrectos* hurled themselves into the path of the metal juggernaut. They were attempting the impossible. Flesh and will could hardly stop iron. The heavy artillery piece simply crushed one man. The impact killed him, and a smashed corpse fell back into the Caribbean. The other man's shoulder snapped the moment before the big gun pulped the toes of his left foot. He would have screamed, if the shock and pain hadn't rendered him unconscious.

The others hung on to the ropes grimly. Strength and courage slowed the powerful cannon, but nothing could stop it. Another hawser broke. Then there was a rumble as the big gun slid on, inexorably. Those on the ship, the raft and the beach could only stare bitterly as the artillery piece dropped into the Caribbean.

There was neither the time nor the machinery to rescue it now.

The deadline was but twelve minutes away.

Davis sent his first mate ashore with the widow and the other Cubans. He said that it was so Fitzgerald could collect the rest of the gold. That was one reason. Another was to give the lovers a chance to say good-by.

When they climbed from the ship's boat onto the sandy shore, José Arias stepped forward to shake Fitzgerald's hand. Then the Cuban clapped his arms around the mate in a classic Latin *abrazo*—the *macho* hug of approval.

"*Magnifico.* Yes, *muchas gracias,*" Arias said warmly. "You and your friends have earned our appreciation."

"How about the rest of the gold, Brother?" Isabella reminded him.

The pharmacist had a money belt under his shirt. He took off the cloth tube, opened its mouth and began to count out the yellow coins.

"1,900 . . . 1,950 . . . 2,000. Add in the 3,000 she gave you on the ship, and you have 5,000," the rebel leader announced.

"Which isn't 6,000," Fitzgerald pointed out.

"You wouldn't expect me to pay the full price when one cannon never reached us," Arias argued.

"To tell the truth, sir, that I would," the mate replied.

The pharmacist eyed him thoughtfully, wondering whether this American with the odd accent had the nerve to persist in debating money with the brother of a woman he wanted. No, not even a Yankee would risk that vulgar embarrassment.

It would be stupid to give the *Americanos* the last $1,000, Arias told himself. Everyone knew that they were all rich. The *insurrectos*, on the other hand, were always short of money and weapons.

"It was *your* lads who dropped it, sir," the mate pointed out, "so why should we hungry sailors pay for their unfortunate error?"

There was something in his voice that sounded familiar to Arias. It wasn't American at all. It was the tone of a man who might be willing to negotiate—to bargain as Latins did.

"What are you saying?" José Arias tested.

"I'm proposing that we split the difference. Why should good friends waste their time bickering over such a dull thing as money?"

The pharmacist beamed.

"You're right," he ratified. "I'll make it $5,300."

"And two hundred more so the captain won't wring my neck. He's a fierce one, you know."

"Do you think that $5,400 would—"

The mate shook his head. "It *wouldn't*. Could we get on with it, sir?"

Arias counted out the rest of the money, then asked, "You're not *really* American, are you?"

"I was born in Ireland, but America's been my home for seventeen years."

Reassured to find that he'd been right, Arias nodded before he turned to order his men to hurry with the final wagonload of shells. The vehicles and even their wheel ruts must be gone from this beach within five or six minutes.

Fitzgerald and Isabella Garcia walked to the shadows of the trees for privacy. Again they embraced and kissed passionately. They touched and shivered as if possessed by malaria or some other tropical fever.

"*Querida . . . Querida,*" she sighed and kissed him again.

At that moment he realized that he could not leave her.

"I'm coming with you," he told her.

"What? But your ship? Your captain? Your duty?"

"My duty is to be with you, Isabella. The ship can get along without me, but I can't go on without you."

She stepped back to see his whole face and head in the moonlight.

He was by far the handsomest and most caring man she'd ever met. He would make a fine husband, a wonderful father to her unborn children. Something deep in her womb moved in response to that surge of feeling.

"And I can't go on without you," she answered as she stroked his thick black hair, "but I'll have to. And you'll have to survive without me."

"Why?" he challenged.

"Because you cannot go where we are going. We are moving into the hills and then into battle, into many battles. You don't know the country, or the language, or how we must fight to slice away at the Spaniards. You could not survive on our simple food or resist the fevers that our bodies have already met."

"I don't believe you," he resisted firmly.

"You'd be sick in two weeks, dead in two months. And in between you'd be a delay and a hindrance, slowing us down to take care of a sinking patient."

"*No!*"

She stroked his cheek—half mistress and half mother.

"You would hurt our cause and you would die for nothing, my love," she said gently. "I cannot let that happen."

A low whistle sounded in the darkness.

It was the signal.

The *insurrectos* were about to leave.

"I must go now, Pah-treek. So must you. Good-by, *mi amor*."

After several seconds of staring into each other's eyes, they each turned to go. With tears gushing down her cheeks, she was nine or ten steps from him when he cried out.

"I'll be back. You can't stop me. No one can stop me!"

Her knees shook.

It took an effort for her not to fall or to run to him.

"Why don't you come with me?" he appealed.

Her heart jumped, but she too had her duty. It was to a free Cuba and all those who had died—and who would die—for that great cause. Torn between the two powerful impulses, she staggered. She barely caught herself. Somehow, she forced herself to push ahead blindly.

"I'll find you wherever you are!" he shouted the moment before she disappeared into the trees.

"I'll find you!" he repeated into the empty night.

She was gone.

So were all the other Cubans. Only Fitzgerald and four crewmen from the freighter remained on the beach. After nearly a minute, they all climbed into the ship's boat. Fitzgerald looked back grimly as they rowed through the small waves to the *Sarah W. Lee*.

It was 3:50 a.m. when they climbed up on her deck.

Two minutes later, Fitzgerald silently handed the gold to Shelby Davis, who could see that he was in no mood to talk. Davis spoke to a young ensign instead, when he ordered that the anchor be raised immediately so the ship could leave Cuban territorial waters as soon as possible.

Leaning against the stern rail, Patrick Fitzgerald stared back at the Cuban shoreline as the ship steamed east at full speed.

It was 4:17 when the island finally disappeared from view. Though he could see nothing but the open sea behind him, the first mate continued to peer towards the beach and hills beyond the horizon. He did that for a long time. It was not until the first orange rays of the sun appeared that his tired eyes stopped searching.

She was right, he thought wearily.

It was his duty to stay with this ship until sanity had returned to the United States Government and it was safe for this crew to go home.

Then he would come back to Cuba and find her.

No matter where she was or how savagely the war against the Spanish Army of occupation raged, he would make his way to this woman—at any risk, at any cost. Now he felt more deeply than ever before for the tragic loss that Shelby Davis had suffered. The Georgian could never find his woman, for she was wed forever to the Atlantic waves. Death was her mate for all eternity.

He told himself that Isabella Garcia would survive.

Neither bullet nor lance nor sword nor disease would take her life.

She would be waiting when he returned. Some might

say that it would take a miracle for any woman to endure all that. Patrick Fitzgerald might even agree with them. The logic of that chilly analysis did not discourage him a bit. After all, from the age of three Paddy Fitzgerald had believed in miracles. He wasn't about to change now.

Chapter Fourteen

As the American ship steamed away from the Cuban shore, the *insurrectos* struggled to move the cannon and ammunition inland. They had only an hour and a half—perhaps a few minutes more—to get this precious cargo to some place safe.

It had to be somewhere the enemy rarely patrolled and a spot where even informers or spies would not see the armaments.

The wagons could not move rapidly. The weight of the big guns made every yard an effort for the horses. As if that were not enough of a problem, the freedom fighters did not dare jarring or dropping the artillery shells.

If one exploded, it would do more than kill a dozen patriots. The sound would almost surely draw a Spanish patrol, and the entire convoy might be wiped out by the rifles and lances of the hard-riding Third Cavalry. Neither *Teniente* Bortelo nor *Capitan* Colon were fond of taking rebel prisoners.

José Arias had thought out the problem carefully. Though some of the *insurrectos* sometimes joked about his stuffy manner and starchy citified clothes, he had the mind of a soldier. He had planned ahead as a field commander should. His plan was a good one.

"We'll never reach the hills tonight," one rebel worried.

"Only a fool would think we could," Arias replied.

Then he explained that he had picked out four hiding places where the armaments could be concealed under brush. Each secret depot was at least a mile and a half from the others. Some thirty *insurrectos* would ring the area in a loose line of sentries, not to defend the arms but to draw away any Spaniards who might wander too close.

"And what good will the cannon do us out here?" a hot-tempered farmer demanded.

"They won't *stay* here, Manuel," the shrewd pharmacist replied. "We'll move them every other night—only in the darkness. It may take a dozen nights to get them safely into the hills, but time is the only thing we've got plenty of."

Isabella Garcia tried not to dwell on the pain of her lover's departure. She knew that the best way to bear the loss was to hurl herself into the fight to free Cuba—a long struggle that would surely need clever commanders.

Even if she couldn't hack off a Spanish head with a

machete, she could contribute too—as much as her brother. A woman's mind was just as ingenious and ruthless as a man's, whether the local males understood that or not. She too could hate. It would not be difficult to turn the warmth of her shattered love into icy hostility.

This would be her work—and her revenge.

During the weeks that followed, the pharmacist and his sister got to know each other better than ever before. They also learned new things about each other. Each came to respect the other afresh.

It was strange what emerged in the next series of skirmishes. José Arias proved that he was more than cunning. He showed that he was brave.

The *insurrectos* first noticed his courage during the attack on a rural police station on New Year's Day, January 1, 1866. It was José Arias who entered the building in his best clothes and told the semi-hungover constable on duty that he was there to see the senior officer on duty. Intimidated by Arias' tone of authority, the constable took him to the sergeant.

"What can I do for you, sir?" the sleepy-eyed sergeant asked.

"Raise your hands—NOW!"

One glance at the twin derringers he held persuaded them to comply. After he disarmed both men, he signalled through the window and a score of *insurrectos* entered the rear of the building to capture the other police. The raiders left with thirty-six firearms, three thousand bullets and an increased appreciation of Arias' personal courage.

He'd walked in totally alone, and he'd pulled it off perfectly with the cool expertise of a professional bandit.

That took nerve. So did leading the charge against a force of Spanish soldiers on the march near Tiguabos—two platoons of infantry from the Ninth Division. The Spaniards had not broken under the first *insurrecto* assault. Instead, the soldiers had regrouped, fixed their long bayonets and confidently counterattacked.

Some of the Cubans were shaken at the sight of cold steel.

José Arias wasn't.

Not after his sister uttered a single word.

"Cannae!"

He nodded. Then he ordered the guerrillas to split into two groups, leaving a space of some one hundred yards between them. The soldiers trotted through the low scrub to finish off the rebels, but they found only air. Suddenly the Cubans opened up from both flanks with a deadly crossfire. It slew a quarter of the Spaniards within a few minutes and wounded even more—a punishing loss for any combat force.

Now Arias stood up defiantly, raised his rifle and ran directly at the stunned foe. Within minutes the other freedom fighters were charging with him, shouting fiercely and firing as they advanced.

Perhaps José Arias was mad to charge the professional soldiers.

If he was, it was catching. Not one *insurrecto* held back or wavered. Among them was Isabella Garcia, who bore a pistol in each hand, and used them as well as any man.

Shattered and confused, the skirmish line of infantry collapsed and the surviving soldiers ran. Dozens of rifles and other supplies were seized by the jubilant

Cubans that scorching afternoon. They all realized that this booty would never have been theirs if Arias had not led that final charge.

"That was a bold thing, *amigo,*" a grizzled fisherman told him, "and a clever idea to draw them into the trap."

José Arias shook his head and smiled.

"The credit for that should go to Isabella," he corrected.

"And Hannibal," Isabella said. "He used the same tactic against the Romans in the Battle of Cannae two hundred and sixteen years before Christ. And thank Sister Anna, who taught me history at the convent school."

The *insurrectos* were surprised that a woman should understand military strategy. Even Arias looked at her a bit differently, reflecting that an educated woman might be helpful in other ways.

"I commend your knowledge, Sister," he said.

"And?"

"And the fine way you used it. And your quickness," he added.

"Thank you, José. If I can help again . . ."

"I—*we* would all welcome that. I didn't realize you . . . well, it was unusual for a woman . . . it was splendid."

"So were you, José. Our father would have been very proud of you. I am."

They had no more time for compliments or other talk. More Spanish troops could be there at any moment. In fact, it was nearly two hours before half a troop of cavalry reached the scene. By then the rebels had vanished into the hills.

It was to happen like this many times in the next three months. The *insurrectos* would hit, then run. They would slash at some military unit or base and fade away like ghosts. These had been the classic tactics of guerrilla warfare for thousands of years. The ancient Jewish Maccabees had fought this way against Syrian armies, as the Old Testament itself recorded. In a hundred other causes and countries, bands of rebels, all outnumbered by foes, had struck at their enemies in the same ways. Indeed, it was the Spaniards themselves who had contributed the term "guerrilla" when their irregulars stabbed and fled Napoleon Bonaparte's divisions that occupied the Iberian peninsula from 1808 to 1813. "Guerrilla" meant "little war," and this kind of combat was an endless series of bloody little wars.

Little more than five decades later, the situation was totally reversed. If such deities existed, the gods of war must have noticed the irony of a conflict in which Spanish fighting men were the regulars—operating in large units with strictly ritualized and predictable tactics—while their enemies were fast moving small groups of irregulars, as unconventional as they were unpredictable. Instead of being the occupied nation, Spain was now the occupier.

Not for too much longer, though, if several dozen *insurrecto* groups had their way. New ones appeared every month as word of the victories of such leaders as Carlos Manuel de Cespedes and José Xavier Arias spread. Encouraged by successes, the Arias Brigade found enough recruits so it could put as many as one hundred and fifty combatants into a single action.

And still the cannon remained hidden under tarpaulins covered with brush in the hills. Several of the Cubans were impatient to show off their most powerful weapons. They pressed Arias on this daily.

"Our most powerful weapons are surprise and speed," he told them patiently.

"And the longer we keep the secret of the cannon, the greater the surprise will be when we use them to smash forts," his sister agreed. "Cannon are to kill forts that rifles can't even wound."

Several of the *insurrectos* nodded.

Once again the widow's logic made sense.

She was a strange woman—independent, and cold to even the most discreet male advances, but very clever. Indeed, many believed that she thought like a man. After a successful raid in April, an admiring guerrilla had said it to her face. "Don't be a fool," she'd replied irritably.

Today she was not angry, however. This afternoon she had her temper in check.

"And we *will* kill Spanish forts—soon," she predicted.

The Arias Brigade struck again and again during the next eleven weeks. Sometimes the assault force was a dozen fighters. Other raids were made by sixty or seventy. Since earlier attacks had put as many as one hundred and fifty Cubans in the field, Spanish officers were encouraged.

"They're growing weaker each month," *Teniente* Bortelo exulted to his superior. "By August first, I'll bring you José Arias' head on my lance."

"And his sister?" the captain asked.

"I'm saving her for my bed," Bortelo boasted with a confident smirk. Spies' reports on Isabella Garcia's important role in the *insurrecto* effort had angered him for half a year. He'd teach that proud bitch to know her place. When she heard the agonized screams of her stupid guerrilla comrades dying inch by inch, she'd beg for the privilege of surviving as his devoted mistress. And when she began to bore him in a year or so, he'd sell her as a slave—perhaps to a quality brothel in Havana. She'd bring a good price with that body.

Bortelo was not the only Spanish officer in Oriente Province who believed that the rebels were losing manpower. In fact, it was exactly what José Arias and his sister wanted their foes to think. Attacking with smaller units was a tactic to deceive the Spanish commanders. If they were over-confident, they'd be more vulnerable when the Cuban artillery finally smashed their stone redoubts.

The rebels began to strike less frequently.

Sometimes eight or nine days went by without a raid or an ambush, and the number of men in each attack continued to decrease.

All of this was part of the carefully thought-out deception program and timetable. It was no longer just lieutenants and captains who believed that the guerrillas were fading in eastern Cuba. Now colonels and generals—even staff officers sipping sherry in the main headquarters in Habana—felt that the Cuban rebellion was subsiding, just as they'd long predicted it would.

It was the twenty-seventh night of July, a week

before the cannon would finally thunder. Isabella Arias Garcia sat on the ground in a temporary camp, apart from the other guerrillas who were talking some twenty yards away. There was no campfire. There were no lanterns or other light that could betray them. Though it was clear that the Spaniards were relaxing their patrolling, security precautions among the fighters of the Arias Brigade were even tighter than in the past.

As she often did when she was alone in the darkness, Isabella Garcia thought about the American ship and tried not to weep. Her burning hatred for the Spanish Army that had driven her to send her lover away helped some, but it did not ease the soreness and longing within her. Sitting on the hard ground here in the hills with her eyes closed, she could relive that first meeting on the deck of the *Sarah W. Lee*.

She could see her lover and his youthful captain clearly in her mind's memory.

In a moment it was all different.

She no longer saw.

She felt.

She was in the strong arms of Patrick Fitzgerald again. Seconds later his weight was upon her. She shuddered and struggled to choke off the groan of longing. It was not easy, but she managed to stifle the sound. The shapeless fire still glowed deep inside her.

With more than one hundred men nearby, the heartsick widow was isolated and far from anyone. It would be like this for a long time, she realized grimly. Since Bortelo was aware of the intimate connection between the *insurrecto* leader's sister and the American first mate, it could be dangerous for the entire Yankee crew if the ship touched at any port of this turbulent island.

Not *could*. It *would* be dangerous.

Bortelo must know by now of her own role in the guerrilla war. She recalled the dirty look in the *teniente's* eyes when he'd stared at her. The man was a sadist and a thug. Bortelo would make sure that Fitzgerald and the ship would be seized if they returned.

She was breathing hard, as if she'd been running. Her hatred of Bortelo was making her pant.

His atrocities alone made him unfit to live, of course. But it was the fact that he stood between her and her magical lover that turned Bortelo into her *personal* and *mortal* enemy. Aching for Fitzgerald, she took a silent oath beneath the summer stars.

She would kill Bortelo herself.

She would slay the monster, as knights had done in medieval sagas.

She would destroy this vicious dragon, and then peace—and Patrick Fitzgerald—could return to Cuba.

She was considering this prospect when the courier emerged from the darkness. He brought a message from the freedom fighters' key spy at Spanish Army headquarters in Guantanamo. The news was not good.

Word had reached *Teniente* Bortelo that the Arias Brigade had at least two cannon hidden somewhere in the hills and gullies west of Third Cavalry headquarters. The guerrilla leaders listened to the report in something close to a state of shock.

Isabella Garcia was the first to speak.

The startling report had jerked her back to military

reality. Her keen, angry mind was working at full speed.

"All right, we've lost the element of surprise," she said crisply.

"*Madre de Dios,*" another rebel leader lamented, "they'll flood the hills with patrols. They'll find the cannon."

"Not if we move quickly enough," José Arias countered.

"He's right," Isabella said. "Let's advance the big attack by two days. No, three. We can blast them before their lazy officers ride anywhere near here."

"I agree," Jose said. "Our first priority must be to speed up all our preparations and the whole schedule by seventy-two hours. Alert every unit commander."

Then he saw her shaking her head.

"Our *first* priority, dear brother," she announced in a voice as cold and hard as a sword blade, "is to identify the spy or informer in our brigade."

"And then we'll kill him!" Arias' personal aide declared.

"No," the pharmacist told them. "We'll feed the swine false informatin that will divert Spanish troops away from Guantanamo just before we attack the fort. When that's done, I'll cut his throat myself."

The *insurrecto* leaders rose to relay the new orders. Isabella Garcia was pleased by the speed-up in the schedule. After all, the sooner the Cuban freedom fighters blasted their way into Third Cavalry headquarters, the sooner she could kill *Teniente* Bortelo.

There was no question in her mind that she would.

It would be unthinkable if some other Cuban were to slay him. Perhaps she had better make that clear.

"*Compadres,*" she called out.

They stopped, and turned to listen.

"There's one more thing. When we break into the fort, Bortelo is *mine*."

The men thought that they understood fully. The *teniente* had slain her husband, so it was logical that she'd want to destroy the vicious cavalryman.

"It is a matter of family honor," José Arias said in well-meaning, but misguided explanation.

She decided that it would serve no purpose to correct him, so she ignored the pharmacist's *macho* comment.

"Tell all the men. I want this clear," she said loudly. "*Bortelo is mine!*"

She had the wild look in her eye again.

Even in the moonlight the men could see that. Not one of them had the slightest inclination to dispute her wish. When Isabella Arias Garcia was in this odd state of controlled, but intense fury, practical men did not disagree with her.

It would be a waste of time.

Or possibly worse.

So the hunt for the traitor began.

And the word went out to the key commanders that the attack on the fort was moved up to August the first.

It was finally happening.

In seventy-two hours—nine months after the *Sarah W. Lee* had sailed away to some unknown destination—the American cannon would thunder at last.

With the help of God and the Virgin, Guantanamo—

then the rest of Oriente Province—and finally all Cuba, would be free. The fighting might go on for months or years, but it had to be.

The time had come.

The long-awaited hour of the cannon was near, and nothing could stop it now.

Chapter Fifteen

On the first of August—the day of the great *insurrecto* attack at Guantanamo—the *Sarah W. Lee* was far from Cuba. The ship was en route from Jamaica to Barbados with a cargo of farming tools, shotguns, hardware and Scotch whiskey for the planters who ran the sugar plantations.

It took more than four months for Davis and Fitzgerald to learn of the dramatic events of that day. The man who told them the story in mid-November was a Dutch navigator whose vessel had been in Guantanamo Bay when the guerrillas struck.

They had run into the Dutch mariner by chance in a pleasant enough restaurant in Fort de France, capital and main port of the French-owned isle of Martinique. His name was Van Hooten, and his drink was gin—straight. The sturdy tow-haired Hollander called it *genever,* and he drank it in quantity with no visible effect.

"It was a slaughter, *Mynheeren,*" he told the Americans as he downed his fourth double, "and I don't mind admitting that I was frightened. Well, very tense."

Then he chuckled.

"Hell, I was scared half-shitless. I've seen a lot in my seventeen years out here—some of it pretty ugly—but nothing like this. Ever been to Guantanamo?"

The two Americans nodded as he sipped more *genever.*

"Then you'll understand what I'm talking about. I didn't actually see it all, but I saw plenty and I heard the rest from men who were right in the thick of it. Tough bastards they were, too."

"Spanish officers?" Davis tested.

The Dutchman shook his head.

"All but Colonel Mega and three or four other Spanish officers were cut to pieces," he reported. "No, I got it straight from the guerrillas. Call themselves *insurrectos,* or something like that. God, they took damn heavy casualties also. Even with their cannon, the Cubans paid a high price that day."

He gulped more of the colorless liquid.

"This is some of the worst gin I've ever had," he judged without malice. It was a matter-of-fact estimate from an expert. "My dog pees better stuff. Isn't that hard to make the stuff right, you know. We Dutch invented it."

"Tell us what happened in Guantanamo," Shelby Davis suggested. He could see that Fitzgerald was much too taut with concern to speak calmly or to talk in a way that wouldn't alarm the navigator.

"Who won?" Fitzgerald blurted.

"The *insurrectos,*" Davis answered before the Dutchman had a chance to.

The first mate looked puzzled.

"If they hadn't, they wouldn't have been around to describe the battle to our gin-drinking friend. Am I right, Mynheer Van Hooten?"

"You certainly are, Captain. Very logical you be. Fine mind, sir. Born to command."

"You're too kind," the Georgian said. "Why don't you have another gin, as my guest, and tell us all about the battle?"

The tactic—and the liquor—worked.

The shocking events of August the first were still starkly etched in the navigator's mind and memory. He recalled them in stunning detail. His voice rose and fell; his facial expressions changed, and he gestured dramatically as he relived the intense experience.

The attacks had begun before dawn.

A dozen guerrilla groups had struck simultaneously. They hit scattered Spanish units all along the wide arc of the Third Cavalry's outer defense perimeter at four in the morning. Crawling infiltrators with machetes and daggers took out Third Cavalry sentries without a sound. Then rebel assault teams that outnumbered the troopers at least two to one suddenly appeared.

There must have been more than one thousand *insurrectos* involved in those devastating and utterly unexpected assaults. Only a small number of Spanish soldiers managed to escape through the encircling guerrillas. But there was a second line of Cuban fighters waiting beyond—dozens of farm women with machetes. They hacked up all but three of the cavalrymen.

That trio tried to spread the alarm, but the guerrillas moved swiftly. The whole thing was well planned. Twenty-five minutes after they'd wiped out the perimeter units, rebel forces were moving by horse and foot to storm the next line of Spanish defense positions.

The officers in charge of three of those seven outposts had already sent back galloping messengers to warn Third Cavalry headquarters about what was happening. But two of the dispatch riders were themselves dispatched by Cuban sharpshooters lying in wait. One of the expert snipers was the sister of the rebel *commandante*.

The second line of defenses was under fierce attack when the breathless and bleeding rider galloped into still-sleeping Guantanamo a few minutes after five o'clock. The wound from the bullet that had passed through his upper left arm was painful, but not very serious.

It certainly didn't compare to the second wound he received when only one hundred and fifty yards from military headquarters. Three more guerrilla snipers were waiting there to make sure that no messenger got through.

One missed completely.

The second's slug struck him in the chest, just missing a lung.

The third sharpshooter's bullet tore into the courier's belly.

The trooper was half dead when his horse clattered into the cobblestone courtyard of the stone fort that was Third Cavalry headquarters. However, he lived long enough to gasp out word that "many hundreds" of guerrillas were attacking outposts. *Capitan* Colon immediately sent out patrols to every perimeter position.

Of the thirty-six men who rode out from the massive fort, eleven got back between six and seven o'clock.

The sun was up, and they had seen clearly.

There were *insurrectos* everywhere.

On the ridges and in the gullies. In the dense shrubbery and in the ditches. Even in the trees.

"More guerrillas than anyone could imagine," one sweaty scout told Colon.

"The outer perimeter?"

"There is no outer perimeter, *Capitan*. And only three of the next row of positions remain. They're coming, *Capitan!* They're coming soon!"

With Bortelo at his side, Colon hurried to report to *Coronel* Mega. Even though he wore a tight corset to improve his appearance, Mega was a competent professional. He wasn't a foppish dandy like so many of those waxed-mustache staff officers preening in Habana.

"What's your estimate, Colon?" the colonel demanded.

"They should be within sight of Guantanamo by half past one or so—three p.m. at the latest. It depends on whether they have transport or heavy weapons, of course."

"*What* heavy weapons?"

Colon glanced at Bortelo and shrugged.

"We did receive a report some days ago that they might have cannon—perhaps as many as three. It was never confirmed, sir."

"Just a rumor from some cheap informer," Bortelo

added. "As the captain said, we haven't seen a scrap of evidence to confirm it."

"Did I get this report?" Mega asked.

"No, *coronel*. We don't usually waste your time with unconfirmed rumors," Bortelo said.

"Well, we'll know soon enough," Mega predicted.

The main force of the garrison would remain in the fort to beat off the enemy attacks. After several futile assaults on the thick-walled redoubts had broken the foe's momentum and littered the area with heaps of dead Cubans, troops of fresh cavalry would gallop out in classic charge to hunt down and destroy the weakened remnants of the guerrilla legion.

And that would be the gory end of the Arias Brigade.

Standing at an observation post in the fort's tower, *Coronel* Mega looked out in vain for the Cubans at 1:30 . . . 2:00 . . . 2:30 . . . When he didn't see them by 3:00, he felt better. The second line of defenses must have stopped their advance. Mega decided to send out a cavalry troop to reinforce those positions.

But then he heard *something*.

It was from the north . . . No, the south . . . No, the west.

Within twenty seconds he realized what was developing: a triple-pronged attack. The damn rebels would come howling into the outer neighborhoods of Guantanamo by five o'clock. By six, the fools would be shooting their rifles at the fort.

But they didn't come howling, and they weren't fools. They moved slowly and methodically. It wasn't until seven p.m. that Mega saw what he had most feared.

Cannon.

Their silhouettes were unmistakable in the late sun of summer.

"*Mierda!*" the colonel swore before he went down to do his duty.

The freedom fighters advanced through the streets and alleys cautiously, pausing every ten yards or so to check for snipers or ambush. When the *insurrectos* got within a mile of the fort, they halted. Guerrillas stole from door to door and directed the occupants of each house to evacuate before the heavy firing began. When the civilians were all gone, Cuban sharpshooters began to move across the rooftops towards the fortress.

They made almost no noise.

They crouched low and moved in short sprints or crawled.

Marksmen atop the walls of the fort tried to pick them off, but they were as dim as fluttering bats or mere shadows.

Now the sounds of the wagons carrying the cannon were audible. The Spanish officers tried to spot the big guns, but couldn't.

At 8:13 p.m., as the last tiny beams of sun vanished, the rebel cannon boomed. The crews seemed to know what they were doing. After only two ranging shots, they began to hammer specific targets.

One battered at the main gate.

Another lofted shells over the walls and into the courtyard, to kill the soldiers assembled there.

The third smashed at the fort's observation tower until it was a gutted ruin. Then that sixteen-pound gun turned to help smash at the big metal-studded portal. At the same time, Cuban snipers poured a deadly fire against the soldiers on the walls. Another sixteen-pound shell ripped a chunk from the gate. Then another blew up against one of the portal's massive hinges.

Four or five more hits would blast the door ajar, the colonel realized, and then the guerrillas would come charging in—wave after wave. That report from the scout had been right. The rebel force was far stronger than anyone had guessed.

Mega could not afford to play the waiting game.

His horsemen had to counterattack now, had to sally in a surprise charge and cut their way through to those cannon. The rebels' artillery must be silenced—*now*. This was the Third Cavalry, dammit. They'd drive that rabble into the Caribbean.

Mega gave the order, and the gate swung open at five minutes to eleven. It couldn't open fully because one hinge was damaged, but the horsemen raced out. They swung smartly into lines. They charged.

Even in the moonlight, it was a glorious sight.

Three hundred and eighty crack cavalry thundering to attack!

Hundreds of *insurrecto* rifles and pistols rained death on the riders. They fell by the dozen. But they galloped on. *Teniente* Bortelo led one squadron of lancers. *Capitan* Colon rode at the head of another. Now they were across the open area. They split up into a dozen columns to charge up the narrow streets, fanning out to find those enemy cannon.

The guerrillas were waiting for them.

Marksmen raked them from almost every door and window, from rooftops and stables and even from be hind bales of cotton. More riders fell, and still more. Of the three hundred and eighty who sortied so confidently from the fort, nearly ninety were dead and some hundred and sixty wounded. A number of them fell near a beautiful, dark-haired woman who stood beside a statue of King Ferdinard, with a long-barrelled pistol in each hand and another pair stuck in the sash of her tight-fitting dress. There was a twelve-year-old boy behind her, reloading and handing her new weapons.

Still more cavalry dropped.

Dead riders, crippled horses and broken lances were everywhere. Men were screaming on all sides. Some hurled curses. Others cried out in pain or fear. As Bortelo galloped around a corner, he glanced back. More than half of his men were gone.

Another hail of bullets was followed by a crossfire as the Spaniards reached the small square. Seven more troopers toppled from their saddles. Bortelo swore savagely.

Then he saw her.

It was that widow bitch, the slut sister of the guerrilla leader.

Bortelo pointed his sword directly at her and roared his frustration and hatred into the night.

"Charge!"

The bugler behind him sounded that stirring call twice—loud and clear—before a Cuban bullet tore out his throat. The horsemen rode forward at top speed with their lances levelled to kill.

Isabella Arias Garcia stood her ground. As *insurrecto* riflemen cut down a dozen of Bortelo's troopers, she took careful aim with her pistols. She was screaming too.

"He's mine! Remember he's mine!"

Her first shot caught his black stallion squarely between the eyes. The big horse dropped. Bortelo barely managed to jump clear and avoid being crushed. He leaped to his feet, saw her behind the fountain and ran to finish her off.

Her second shot opened an inch-wide hole in his stomach. Shock, pain and numbness swept over him as he crumpled to the cobblestones. With their leader grievously wounded—perhaps mortally—and no chance of finding those damned cannon, the remaining thirteen troopers swung their mounts to try to fight their way back to the fort.

Now he had no one to help him. His blood seeped across the stones. He couldn't see her too well, could barely make out what she was doing. She was picking up a broken Spanish lance, and suddenly he sensed what she meant to do. Well, she'd die first. Drawing strength from his fury, Bortelo reached for the dragoon's pistol in his holster.

He managed to draw it.

There she was.

With a triumphant grin of hate, he swung the pistol to kill her. The sound of the gun echoed through the square, but *Teniente* Bortelo didn't hear it. He was dead—with a lance through his groin.

She had kept her promise.

The Spanish attack was broken. All the surviving cavalry were driven back into the fort, and the shelling of the gate continued. The three big guns concentrated on that single target, steadily reducing it from an impenetrable barrier to kindling and twisted metal. It finally collapsed just before one in the morning.

Then it happened.

Exactly as *Coronel* Rodolfo Mega had dreaded.

The rebels swept out of the streets and alleys. Spanish artillery in the fort took a heavy toll, but the *insurrectos* poured in anyway. There was hand to hand fighting for twenty-five minutes before the royal banner was ripped down and the last resistance collapsed.

"I guess I was fortunate to survive," Van Hooten said with a shake of his head. "My damn luck to be visiting some pretty ladies in a cat house in the middle of town when the whole thing happened. Bodies all over the streets. Riderless horses—half crazy they were—galloping everywhere. What a horror!"

He paused to swallow more gin.

"Then what happened?" Davis questioned.

"The guerrillas cleaned out every bullet and weapon in the fort and headed west. They were dragging out the Spanish cannon as I left."

Fitzgerald had to ask.

"And the woman who killed that lieutenant?"

"Beautiful, and impressive. I saw her myself. A remarkable female . . . Extraordinary. I wouldn't want to be her enemy. She's the sister of the *insurrecto* leader, they say. That's a woman and a half. You'd remember that one if you ever met her."

He saw the flicker in the mate's eyes.

"You know her?"

Fitzgerald nodded.

"Quite something, isn't she?" the Dutchman continued.

"Where is she now?"

The navigator drained his gin and shrugged.

"No idea. The guerrillas were heading into the mountains. Half the Spanish Army probably went after them. She could be anywhere—if she's lucky . . . Or dead."

Van Hooten turned to Shelby Davis.

"We dropped some cargo in Habana five weeks ago. Fresh Spanish units were arriving as we left, and the guerrillas were rising all over the eastern part of the island, with her brother's outfit one of the most active. The Spaniards have put a price on his head—and hers."

"So she was alive five weeks ago?" Fitzgerald tested.

"Guess so. Havana's a mess, my friends. Troops everywhere, and they're nasty. Sore as hell, mean to everyone—even foreign seamen."

"They're scared," the Georgian judged.

"Can't blame them after seeing those guerrillas in action. Tell you one thing, *Mynheeren*. My skipper won't go back to Cuba for a while. No, sir."

Davis and Fitzgerald started for their ship a few minutes later.

"Cheer up, Paddy. She's *alive*."

They walked on in silence.

"They won't get her, Paddy," Davis assured with more confidence than he felt. "She's smart and she's strong, and she knows a thousand places to hide on that island. Besides, the *insurrecto* movement seems to be growing. They may win."

"What if they don't?"

"Then you'll go in to bring her out. It's more than a year and a half since Lee surrendered. Life and feelings back home must be returning to normal. The Yankees can't stay that bitter much longer."

"What are you saying, Captain?"

"I'm telling you that they'll stop this pirate lunacy in a few months, and we should be able to go home. Maybe not as the *Georgia*. Maybe we'll have to slip into some port in Louisiana or Texas as the *Warren*. We'll unload, sell the ship, divide the money and scatter. You can use your share to get her out of Cuba."

They were almost at the dock.

"Really think so?" Fitzgerald asked uncertainly.

"Of course. Money talks in Cuba the same way it does anywhere else. Nobody in Havana's ever heard of you, and Bortelo's dead, so he can't cause trouble."

"How will I find her?"

"Come on, Paddy. You're an Irishman. The Irish can do anything, remember? You'll find her. Why, by summer you'll be married to that lady!"

The *Warren* left Martinique the next afternoon with a mixed cargo bound for Santo Domingo. Just before she steamed out, a French naval officer came aboard with another warning about the pirates. More bodies had been found floating forty-six miles west of Guadeloupe—on the very sea lanes that the *Warren* would use.

"*Prenez garde*. Be careful, *Monsieur*," the French officer advised.

"We always are," Shelby Davis replied truthfully.

Every gun was manned around the clock as the former Confederate raider steamed north. Extra lookouts were posted. They saw very few vessels, mostly small fishing boats. The only large craft they noticed was a twin-stack freighter flying the Danish ensign. It passed by some two miles away as they neared the south shore of Puerto Rico.

Shelby Davis studied it warily through his telescope.

"For a minute I thought I recognized that silhouette," he told Dr. Preston, who stood on the bridge beside him, "but I guess I was wrong."

He wasn't.

Of course, he couldn't really be blamed for the mistake.

The pirate ship's disguise was excellent.

Chapter Sixteen

The Yankee's hatred did not subside.

The news was bad—everywhere.

At every port where the *Sarah W. Warren* dropped anchor during the next three months, the reports from American sailors whom Davis and his crewmen met were the same.

The South was being punished in a hundred ways, and looted in a thousand. Stern Northern officials were seeking vengeance as the new rulers of the states that had been their enemies. "Carpetbaggers"—a colorful term for crooked politicians and shady businessmen—were stealing vast sums as they moved through the ruins of the Confederacy. Whipped up by sensationalist newspapers and embittered members of Congress, many decent Northern citizens were being propagandized into abandoning Lincoln's compassion for limitless hostility.

The official term for this efficient rape of The South was "Reconstruction."

Dismemberment and self-serving theft were more accurate descriptions, but those who dared to say so were usually shouted down. The uncles and mothers of Union soldiers who'd been maimed or killed were in no mood to think rationally. They wanted to hurt those who had hurt them. The anger was still fierce, the wounds still painful.

The rage over Lincoln's murder had not subsided.

Shelby Davis learned that as recently as February, the U.S. Navy had increased the reward for the *Georgia* and her crew to $75,000. Soon it would be two years since the War Between the States had ended, and there was still no hopeful sign that the *Georgia* could return in peace.

And the word from Cuba was no better.

Most of the *insurrectos* had been killed or captured. Nearly all the prisoners had been tortured before entering dismal dungeons or penal colonies in regions where malaria and short rations quickly reduced them to walking skeletons. Several of the rebel leaders had been dismembered—drawn and quartered in grisly public spectacles. Vengeance ruled Cuba too.

The only "good" news was that the Spaniards were still pursuing the remnants of the elusive Arias Brigade somewhere in the Sierra Maestre range of mountains in Oriente Province. Even this report did little to cheer Fitzgerald. The reports from the U.S.A. left him as joyless as the other crewmen.

So it was hardly surprising that many of the ex-Confederates turned to the traditional distractions of sailors—the diversions and pleasures that centuries of mariners had used for surcease. The men on Greek and Roman vessels, on Phoenician triremes carrying merchants and cargo long before Christ and on ships of every kind since then had faced the same boredom and discontent.

The sailors of every era and civilization had found quick and shallow satisfaction in liquor and women—the cheapest kinds of both. Davis could not stop them, nor could he blame them. He could warn them. He did. At each port, he reminded them of the damage loose tongues could do. He left it to the first mate to describe anew the horrors of venereal disease and the hazards of waterfront thieves. Fitzgerald's Hibernian tongue-lashings seemed to have more effect than the clinical lectures of the ship's portly physician.

"And stay in groups of three or four," the first mate reminded regularly—staring at Hinkley as he spoke. Fitzgerald was still concerned that the disgruntled cook might leak their secret, and he was ready to beat Hinkley to a pulp at the slightest sign that he might. Every other man on the ship felt the same way about the whiner.

"They're getting restless," Shelby Davis told Dr. Preston as they watched the crew hurry ashore that April afternoon in Port au Prince.

"And you?"

The Georgian shrugged agreement.

"You're quite perceptive, Doctor."

The chubby physician snorted in derision.

"Don't intend to be modest," Preston announced, "but a blind veterinary could see that you're itching—and it isn't fleas."

"No, it isn't fleas."

"Then I prescribe a dose of relaxation, some of that irresistible Haitian music, a large glass of fine old Barbancourt rum and perhaps some *exercise*."

Amused by the physician's discretion, the handsome Georgian pretended that he didn't understand.

"What sort of exercise, Doctor?"

"Do you play whist?" Preston inquired solemnly.

"I'm not much for cards."

"Then you'd better try something more active. How about dancing? It's dignified enough for a captain. I hear that the locals do a very elegant dance called the *merengue*."

The physician smiled slyly.

"Find a pretty teacher. I'm told that some of these coffee-and-cream colored ladies don't mind giving lessons to visitors. And they'll tell you about the local flora and fauna, too. Should be highly educational."

The charm and beauty of Haiti's tall, slim women was as famous as their elegant grace. Indeed, their attractiveness was legendary across the Caribbean and far beyond. Many were eye-catching mixtures of French or Spanish and former black slaves from Dahomey and other parts of West Africa. Intelligent, chic and worldly, they were widely admired for their cosmopolitan femininity.

And their wondrous passion.

The fidelity of the married women was almost total, but wars and insurrections had slain many males and left a surplus of unwed females. It was these high-spirited women whose uninhibited ways with lovers were internationally esteemed. It would be naive and simplistic to call them promiscuous.

They merely had their own rules.

If they wanted a man, they let him know it. If they didn't care for him, they made that clear too.

These were bold blossoms, not shy flowers.

It was such a bouquet that the canny doctor had in mind for the long-celibate Georgian. They were simultaneously ladylike and lustful, the ideal combination for a Southern gentleman such as Shelby Davis.

"Are the lessons expensive?" Davis fenced.

"I'd say you can't afford not to take them. That's my *professional* opinion, Captain. And don't worry about any language problem."

"They speak French and a French-based *patois*, don't they?"

"Many of these ladies speak an international tongue. It's called *friendly*," the physician explained dead-pan.

"I know that one."

"Thought you might. Good-by, Captain," Preston said and turned away.

"Why don't you come with me, Doctor?" Davis called out cheerfully.

The chubby physician stopped and spun in astonishment.

"Me?"

"Why not? I've heard you were quite a fine *dancer* back in Carolina. According to those plantation owner's daughters, you were—"

"Now watch that, Captain. I was always proper with those young ladies. Well, *almost* always," Preston modified as a glow of remembrance lit up his eyes.

"Whatever you did was purely for the ladies' health, I'm sure," the Georgian jested. "And I'm ordering you to come with me for my health. How safe would any of us be alone in that lively port?"

Preston thought about the elegant Creole belles ashore.

"Did you say it was an *order*?" he asked.

"Absolutely. You'll be court-martialed if you don't obey," Davis threatened with a grin.

"Then I've no choice?"

"None. You can tell that to your wife," Shelby Davis suggested.

"I don't intend to tell her *anything*—not about this," the physician confided and followed his captain down to the dock.

The city they strolled into was a bustling and polyglot community. The hues of the clothing worn by the residents were bright and varied, with many bandanas of lively red or green and bold shirts reflecting every shade of the rainbow. The color of ninety percent of the people themselves was basically black. Although this was the first place where Columbus had landed on his historic journey in 1492, the vast majority of the Arawak Indians whom the Spaniards found were killed by the Europeans or died from disease within sixty or seventy years.

So the Spanish conquistadors and the French who later took the island by force had imported vast legions of black slaves for the sugar, coffee, indigo and cotton fields. The French changed the island's name from Santo Domingo to Saint Domingue, just as the British had earlier changed the Dutch name of Nieuw Amsterdam to New York. Much more important and practical than the name change was the army of enslaved Bambaras, kidnapped Quimas, strong Mandingues and grim Ibos brought from Africa. Only a few hundred of the original Indians survived by the time that Robert E. Lee's father joined George Washington's forces.

Some thousands of French had come to rule this island. They became the rich and the powerful, backed by tough and well-armed French troops who never hesitated to smash any sign of slave revolt with ruthless and bloody efficiency. The colonial lords did what rich and powerful men of many other nations did in such tropical outposts, especially places where slavery flourished. They took pretty native women to their beds. The results here—as in so many places, including the home states of Shelby Davis and his crew—were thousands of half-white children.

Though outnumbered some ten to one by the pure black slaves, these mulatto offspring developed into a special and useful class. Well, useful to the French, who gave them access to education and sent quite a few to Paris to learn medicine, law, engineering and other important skills. In France, these students also absorbed the graces of French lifestyle, food, art, history, attire and music. They came back with the French style, and many of them came back snobs who looked down on the poorer blacks still toiling on the plantations.

This did not trouble the French, who—few in numbers here—used these coffee-colored aristocrats to help govern the less educated masses and rule the island. These thirty thousand cultured *gens de couleur*—people of color—were as haughty as the French, who let them own land and slaves. The embittered black slaves—more than six hundred thousand of them—hated them fiercely as traitors and oppressors.

There had to be an explosion.

It came in 1791 when the first slave uprising swept across Saint Domingue. Fighting against the French and their half-white and quarter-white allies erupted in every village and town with a heavy loss of life and immense property damage. Ironically, it was inspired not only by the successful American revolt against Britain but also by the democratic slogans of Robespierre and other fiery orators who spearheaded the French Revolution. The Paris monarchy and its aristocratic elite were destroyed on the guillotine, but their republican executioners nevertheless sent more troops to crush black Haiti's desperate bid for freedom.

Many died in the fighting.

But the Haitians' proud spirit would not yield. The wars to drive out the French lasted for years. Then there followed a series of power-crazy local generals and despots who ruled the tragic isle as cruelly as had any foreign monarch. One madman proclaimed himself emperor. Though Haitian courage and malaria had ended the French military occupation, this land was far from free for decades. Haiti—which in 1791 became the second nation in the Americas to proclaim its independence—was still struggling towards working democracy. Slavery had long been dead here, and President Abraham Lincoln himself had officially recognized Haiti's independence in 1862. But the distrust between the hard-working black majority and the pro-French mulatto elite continued.

"Ending slavery hasn't solved their problems," Preston pointed out as he and Davis walked the rutted dirt streets of Port au Prince. Only three or four main avenues were paved in the bustling Haitian capital.

"It was a beginning, Doctor," Davis replied. "I never thought I'd agree with Abe Lincoln—no, with *those Yankees*—but slavery's time is done. It's finished, and I don't mind."

"Shelby Davis an *Abolitionist*?"

"Put any label on it you want, Doctor. Slavery's finished here in the Americas, and it'll be gone everywhere before long. Cruel bastards such as Bart Beecher aren't that rare, I'm afraid. There are plenty of those brutes in every country."

It was odd to hear the young Georgian speaking so bitterly about a man he hadn't seen in over two years—a person whom he'd met only once for five minutes.

"Didn't realize that blockade runner made such an impression on you, Captain."

"It's mutual. He swore to kill me, you know," Davis reminded. "That's the kind of thing you remember. But even forgetting Beecher, there's a moral question about one person owning another. I did a lot of thinking about things like that during those months when I could hardly sleep. . . . The sermon's over."

"What?"

"You can relax, Doctor," the Georgian assured in a less earnest tone. "I'm not trying to cram my ideas down anyone's throat. Hell, this isn't the time for such serious talk anyway. We're here to unwind, not debate."

"That's what shore leave's for," Preston agreed as they stepped aside to let a wagon laden with rich smelling sacks of coffee pass.

"And *that's* what we need now—some fine Haitian coffee. How about it, Doctor?"

Then Davis pointed at the two-story Hotel de Paris across the street.

"You're the captain."

It was not easy to enter the wooden hotel. At every step they took, they were challenged by good-humored, but persistent street vendors. Men and women of every age from fourteen to seventy-four—most of them barefoot and all of them amiable—offered a wide variety of local products.

Fruit. Five different kinds: mangos, guavas, pineapples, two varieties of oranges and three of bananas.

Candies made from sugar cane and chunks of unrefined brown cane itself.

Bottles, large and small, of six brands of rum and rum liquers.

Also, beer and wine and assorted soft drinks.

Wooden carvings by the hundreds. A single vendor somehow carried forty or fifty statues of birds, fish, women with baskets on their heads, farmers, men playing drums and other figures.

Exotic wrought-iron metal sculptures, black and complex and eye-catching.

Every vendor—including women who bore their fruit wares in straw baskets atop their heads—was appealing, cajoling and bargaining. Even a shy faced artist offering dramatically colored paintings of the market place and others of fishing boats was ready to "negotiate."

The vitality of the teeming town was extraordinary.

Mere ninety-degree heat and intense humidity could not depress the people of this city. Even as Davis and the bright-eyed physician made their way through the crowds to the whitewashed wood and plaster hotel that looked like a wedding cake, they felt the vigor of Port au Prince.

One young boy selling large orange-red blossoms pursued them to the door of the hotel itself. His clothes were frayed cotton, but his determination was cast iron. He smiled warmly as he thrust the flowers at them.

"*Pour votre jolie femmes*?" he pressed.

"For our pretty women?" the Georgian translated. "We don't have any, son."

"But we will," Preston predicted merrily, and paid the youth the equivalent of twenty-five U. S. cents. The two Americans entered the cool, high-ceilinged lobby, where they paused to look around. They saw bamboo furniture adorned with big cushions sheathed in floral prints, the famous Haitian cotton fabric. On one wall hung a large oil portrait of a big man, apparently mulatto, who radiated authority.

"That is *Monsieur le President,*" an attractive woman in pale blue announced. Her skin was white and her accent pure Paris.

"You speak English?" Preston noted.

"It's almost the same as *Americain, n'est ce pas?* You are *Americains*, I think."

"*Oui*, Madame," Davis replied, "and you are very pretty."

With those words he gave her the big bunch of flowers.

"The boy who sold us these said they were for pretty women," the handsome Georgian told her, "and you're the prettiest woman we've met here."

"And how long have you been in Port au Prince?"

Davis and Preston looked at each other slyly.

"At least fifteen minutes," Davis replied.

"It might be eighteen," the physician suggested.

"I think you're right, Doctor," the Georgian ratified with a grin.

The woman—trim and blonde in her mid-thirties—studied Preston now.

"*Un medecin?* I too am a *docteur!*"

Genevieve Carpentier was a specialist in tropical diseases, a six-year veteran of Haiti and enthusiastic about meeting another physician.

"There are twenty-three of us for the entire nation," she explained as she led them to a table in the adjacent dining room. She showed a good deal of her excellent legs as she sat down. It was probably no accident, Davis guessed. The local women were much too attractive and forthright for a foreign female to be shy.

He was right.

And exceedingly handsome, Dr. Carpentier decided. He was eight or nine years younger than she was, but that was no problem. It was actually a great advantage, the realistic Parisienne calculated. Since the ship would only be here for three or four days, a strong young bull of a lover was far preferable to some middle-aged man with less stamina and desire.

She would have to separate the *Americains*.

Dr. Carpentier had spent several interesting nights—and one memorable weekend—with two men in her bed, but that didn't appeal to her any more.

No, she'd find another woman who could keep this sweet, chubby ship's physician busy. As she sipped the very strong rum-laced coffee and thought out her plan, her silent wishes were answered. The reply came in the form—the tall, lush form—of a light-skinned black woman in a tight pink dress.

She was twenty-two and quite lovely.

And had been without a lover for weeks, the French blonde knew.

It was almost too easy. Dr. Preston was one of those respectable middle-aged Southerners who hungered for young women in general—and the long-forbidden black beauties in particular. Therese Geffard, a distant cousin of Haiti's honest and able President Fabre Geffard, was equally aroused by the idea of bedding a cultured white physician of mature years.

It would be a feather in her cap, and *amusant* to tell.

She would enslave him with her beauty, she told herself confidently. He would weep and suffer terribly when he had to return to the sea. He'd dream of her forever, of course. Once she locked those long legs around him, the plump *Americain* would be another fine conquest for her collection.

At five o'clock they all switched from coffee and rum to a rum-based brandy. Therese Geffard licked her painted lips, thrust her ample breasts at the ship's doctor and smiled at him in open invitation. These tried-and-true methods worked as usual. Preston was more than ready to go with her at five minutes after six when Therese Geffard invited him to "a small party."

"See you in the morning," Davis told him, and watched them leave.

"And what are your plans for the evening, *mon*

capitain?'' the French woman asked a few minutes later.

''I was thinking of going dancing.''

''How fortunate you are. I'm a splendid dancer—and I know of a charming restaurant with a delightful *orchestre*.''

Davis smiled and nodded.

''Do you think I'm too forward, *Monsieur?*'' she flirted.

He shook his head as he signalled to the barefoot waiter for the bill.

''I think you're a very pretty doctor who's being kind to a visitor,'' he assured her smoothly. And that pleased Genevieve Carpentier. It was appealing to deal with a man who was as gallant as he was handsome.

This *capitain* had style.

If he loved as well as he spoke, the night would be *formidable*.

They rose to leave, and she took his arm. It was lean and muscular. She liked a man with a firm body, a man as sleek and strong as was she. They walked through the lobby out into the street. It was still hot and humid, but there were many fewer people now. There was much less bustle and noise.

But there was another sound.

It was not loud, but Davis' alert young ears heard it clearly.

''Drums?''

''*Vodun* drums. Some foreigners would say *voodoo*, but the people here call it *vodun*. There are many believers.''

Shelby Davis frowned in mild surprise.

"I thought this country was mainly Catholic, Doctor."

She gestured for a horse-drawn taxi.

"*Mais, oui*. The people are ninety-percent Catholic and one hundred-percent *vodun*. Their faith is a powerful mixture of both. They respect Christ and they take their *loa* seriously, too."

"*Loa?*" Davis wondered as the cab pulled up beside them. It was decorated with flowers and feathers and bits of bright-colored cloth.

"The gods of *vodun*," she explained and pointed at the various strips of cotton and clumps of feathers. "Those are not mere adornments, *mon capitain*. Each has a meaning and worth to the believers."

Now the drums were louder.

They were coming from somewhere up the big mountain.

For some reason Shelby Davis felt uneasy.

"Those stories I've heard about voodoo—excuse me, *vodun*—aren't true, are they? The talk about the zombies, the living dead? And tales of human sacrifices? You believe any of that?"

She hesitated for several seconds before she replied.

"I have seen some strange things here," she said carefully.

Davis listened to the drums again.

"I don't know why, but those drums sound dangerous," he confessed as he helped her into the taxi.

"If that's the *Sect Rouge*—the Red Sect—they are," she told him.

They both saw the driver's head jerk.

"*He* knows what they do. The very name frightens him," she declared.

"Just what do they do, Doctor?"

"They kill, *mon capitain*. They kill in strange and terrible ways. Ask me no more."

Then she told the driver where they were going, and immediately changed the subject to the various dances that she and Davis would enjoy after dinner. The Georgian tried hard to listen, to concentrate.

It was not easy.

All the way out of the city and up the twisting road to Petionville, the drums kept getting in the way.

It was probably all the rum they'd drunk, he told himself.

But the drums gave him no peace, no respite.

They were sending some secret message booming across the hills.

What could it be?

Chapter Seventeen

Dr. William Preston's good manners were well-known across the Carolinas.

He was a courtly physician and gentleman who never did anything immature or vulgar.

Right now he was sweating and staring and bug-eyed as a lustful schoolboy.

He had never seen Therese Geffard naked before.

The beads of perspiration on his chubby face pleased her, for she enjoyed the way her shapely body aroused men. It had all gone well. They had ridden halfway up the mountain to her elegant bungalow, far above the dust and humidity that choked the city below. Port au Prince was where the poor lived. ''Better'' people, such as voluptuous young Therese, resided up on the green slopes where it was always much cleaner and fifteen degrees cooler.

But it wasn't the temperature that was making William Cicero Preston sweat. And before I'm done with him he'll sweat a lot more, the mischievous twenty-two-year-old thought smugly.

Of course, I'm the most beautiful woman he's ever seen, she concluded as she gauged the raw animal hunger in Preston's eyes.

He'd been staring like that from the instant she'd returned to the comfortably furnished living room in her favorite crêpe-de-Chine robe. It was almost transparent. Then his mouth had opened when she'd let the delicate garment flutter to the floor.

Let him see all of her splendors.

Let him be dazzled like the others.

Therese Geffard was hardly typical of her family. Her three sisters were models of virtue and propriety. Yet there was something in this youngest of Rene Cesar Geffard's daughters that drove her to conquer men. Was it merely to show her superiority over her well-married sisters, or was she trying to humiliate them? Some members of the mulatto elite had speculated that it could be a lack of self-esteem or some nameless force that drove her to prove her attractiveness again and again.

Other members of the Creole aristocracy sometimes argued that she was merely looking for "the perfect man." This view of her as a "romantic dreamer" certainly was kinder than the more widely held opinion that Therese Geffard was cheerfully sex-crazy—an addict who needed more and more.

Whichever was true, she was out of control.

Both her mind and her body now required these

carnal adventures. The many costly presents that her fascinated admirers gave were only icing on the cake. She was much too lustful to be a courtesan for profit. It didn't matter whether a man was wealthy as long as he was obsessed and passionate.

The look on Preston's face as she swayed towards him indicated that the middle-aged physician was both.

She reached the chair where he was sitting.

Radiating body heat and a musky perfume, she stopped six inches from the yearning man.

His eyes grew even wider as his desire swelled.

Yes, he was ready, she judged.

Slowly and regally, she reached down to take his hands. He was breathing hard, so choked with wanting that he could not speak. She drew him to his feet and placed his sweating hands on her freshly powdered breasts.

He made a noise, a deep groan of surrender.

Now he was kissing her firm young breasts and making other sounds. His hands moved across her body to caress her back and flanks, traveling first slowly, then urgently. He was clutching the backs of her thighs, pressing her against his loins.

He was startled when she pulled back.

He didn't understand that she always did this—paused to assert her control.

They would proceed when *she* decided.

"What . . . what is it?" he whispered hoarsely.

She let him want and wonder for several seconds.

"It is time, *cherie,*" she announced triumphantly.

She turned and walked slowly to the big brass bed in

the next room, letting him appreciate her shapely flanks as he followed her helplessly.

Now he'd do what she wanted, just like the others had.

She undressed him as if he were a child, and then she lay down and parted her legs wide. He was on the bed in an instant, feverish and impatient.

No, it was her turn first.

She cupped his head in her hands and guided it to the deep, scented cleft between her breasts. He responded like a well-trained puppy. He began kissing and touching eagerly, and when he was panting wildly, she gently moved his head so he'd make love to her belly and thighs. She felt the heat and the wetness within her as his frantic touches and kisses ignited her loins.

And her hips began to move.

She was wide open now, and smiling. This man had probably never made such love before, she thought dreamily as the sensations spun through her womb, but he was doing well. The fact was he didn't know what he was doing. Dizzy with the sensual experience, the physician continued blindly until her body shook with the shudders of completion.

She cradled his head against her silken stomach for a minute, enjoying her satisfaction and listening to his gasps. He gasped even more when she firmly drew him up and guided his hard maleness inside of her. The first time he was finished within moments. The second time took much longer.

He was quite good for a man of his age, she judged with a sigh.

She would train him to be even better.

Three miles further up the mountain, Shelby Davis and Genevieve Carpentier sat on the breeze-swept veranda of Petionville's renowned *Chez La Reine* restaurant picking at ample portions of spicy *crab farci*. As they looked down at the oil lamps of the port city below, the Georgian returned to the question of voodoo.

"You know, people are afraid of it back home too," he said between bites of the delicious hors d' oeuvre. "When the Spaniards still ruled Louisiana in 1782, Governor Galvez banned the importation of slaves from Martinique because he suspected they'd bring in voodoo."

"Did they?" she asked.

"People say they did. They're still worried about voodoo in New Orleans. I heard that some years ago the blacks were forbidden to do any dances at all in Congo Square for just that reason."

"Congo is the name of one of the three main *vodun* rites."

He couldn't help asking.

"Is that what the Red Sect does?"

She sipped at the chilled beer before answering.

"They do the Petro, some say. I'd rather not speak about them."

The practices of the Red Sect must be utterly horrible, Davis calculated, if they could dismay a trained physician.

"And what do they call the witch doctors?" he wondered.

"If you mean the *priests*," she corrected, "it's *Houngan*. The origin is African, of course. In the tongue of the Fon people of Dahomey, *Houn* means *spirit* and *gan* is *chief*. Some say the slaves brought what you call voodoo with them from Dahomey about one hundred years ago."

"Is there more?" the handsome Georgian asked curiously.

"A lot more. Nobody knows it all except the *Houngans* and the *Mambos*. They're the priestesses, and just as powerful and important as the priests."

At that moment the owner of the restaurant approached their table. She was probably the most striking and dramatic female whom Shelby Davis had ever seen.

Six feet tall.

Jet black with long coils of glistening hair.

Big shoulders. Very wide hips. Large breasts that jutted out almost five inches.

And yet far from fat. No more than one hundred forty pounds distributed perfectly over a splendid frame.

Enormous eyes and oddly slim hands with delicate long fingers—several of them adorned with rings of gold.

A great eye-catching head with large, but refined features.

An ebony queen.

Of course, that explained the name of the restaurant. *Reine* was queen in French. This woman moved like a queen, and spoke with the assurance of one.

"Are you content?" she asked simply in a richly timbred voice. Deep and resonant and still utterly feminine, it suited this striking woman well. It added further to her grandeur. There was something majestic—and highly attractive—about this larger-than-life beauty.

No man could ignore her.

There were few women whom she would not distress

or intimidate. The sight of their men eyeing her warmly would assure that. The ordinary always feared or resented the extraordinary, Davis reflected. He wondered just how different she might be.

As a person.

And as a lover.

Aware that he'd never get to bed with this stately black goddess, Davis let himself wonder—for just a few seconds—what it might be like.

"Everything is splendid, Madame," he assured her. "The food and drink, the service and the view—all excellent."

Her smile of acknowledgment was vast and bottomless.

"My name is Celeste. You are welcome to my house," she told him. She was looking at both of them, but the Georgian sensed that she was speaking only to him.

He had no idea that, behind that perfect face and deep smile, she was considering whether he would be *suitable*. He was extremely handsome, seemed alert and intelligent, and showed no signs of arrogance or immaturity. She liked his quiet air of competence as well as the fact that he was American rather than French or British. The Americans were usually less rigid or pompous.

She would have to speak to him further.

It would be good if he were *suitable*.

She could not perform the rites of love with *the others*, and her queenly body told her in a dozen ways that it should be done now. If this foreign sea captain was the chosen one, there was little time to waste.

"It is good to see you again, *Docteur*," she said to

the French woman, "and to welcome your companion for the first time."

"Where else would I bring a handsome young *capitain*, fresh and hungry from the sea, Celeste?" Genevieve Carpentier replied gaily. "This is the best restaurant in Haiti, isn't it?"

The big woman beamed and bowed her head graciously. It was not modesty. She had none, nor did she make any pretense of it. It was aristocratic acceptance of a deserved compliment.

"And what are you hungry for, *Capitain*?" the restaurant owner asked. She looked into his wide blue eyes for just a moment—and she knew the answer. It was more than food. For now, she would pretend that she did not see. She would discuss the menu with him to draw him out and to learn more about this stranger. She explained each dish carefully, deliberately drawing him into questions and conversation.

After six minutes she blinked her large eyes in silent pleasure like some immense cat. This man would indeed be *suitable*.

So she took their order, made her plan and glided away to do what was necessary. Clad in a red velvet jacket and white cotton pants, the waiter brought Shelby Davis and Genevieve Carpentier a cold bottle of *blanc de blanc* champagne "with the compliments of Madame Celeste." Then the courses began to arrive, each tastier than the last. The yellow-haired French woman told amusing anecdotes—including two bawdy ones—encouraged Davis to speak about his life and nautical career, and deftly persuaded him to order another bottle of the bubbly white nectar.

Soon they would dance.

The *orchestre* here was first class, and the *Americain* would hold her close. In a while, the wine and the music and her charms—as well as her body against his—would prevail. Celeste kept three rooms for patrons who were too tipsy or too lustful to go down the mountain. They'd rent one of these, and it would be a glorious evening.

Everything went as the doctor anticipated.

The champagne enlivened them and the music moved them, and they danced very well together. Now and then, Genevieve Carpentier pressed her loins against his. It would be excessive to rub all over him like some peasant in heat. A hint and a promise should be enough for a healthy young gentleman such as this Yankee.

It was. He was clearly becoming more physical though, in a discreet way. Then it happened. Celeste signalled to them as the band paused for a ten minute break. A messenger had arrived to see the *docteur* on an urgent matter.

He was a short, thin man. He was panting as he described his forty-mile gallop over the hills. He'd been sent to tell her that there'd been a fire at *le clinique* in Ville Bonheur. She was needed at once.

"I have a fresh horse," the big woman offered.

"*Merveilleux*, I'll leave immediately."

Then the blonde looked at Shelby Davis. It would not be wise to expose him to the other needing females down in the capital. One of those smoldering bitches would drag him off in an hour.

"Why don't you wait here?" she suggested to the Georgian. "Celeste has a spare room or two, and it's much cooler than down in the city. Relax, and I'll be back for you tomorrow afternoon. We can finish our dance then,'' she promised with a sly grin.

The mariner nodded in agreement.

''Take care of this delightful man for me, Celeste,'' Genevieve Carpentier appealed.

''You have my word, Madame.''

So the lithe French doctor hurried off into the night to her clinic, putting duty before desire. Her horse was hardly out of sight when the orchestra began to throb again.

The big woman reached out her arms in invitation.

''I am to take care,'' she reminded.

She was the finest and most sensuous dancer Davis had ever known—or even seen. She floated across the floor like a feather, and her body moved with his as if they'd known each other for years. She radiated grace and serenity and confidence that all would be well and right. Davis caught the scent of jasmine, and when she brushed against him ever so lightly, he realized that she wore nothing beneath the purple silk gown.

She did not talk very much.

She didn't have to.

Her body, her eyes, her movements spoke eloquently.

By midnight, only three other couples remained on the dance floor. The last of those left at ten after one. Celeste blinked again in that feline way, dismissed the musicians with a regal glance and led Shelby Davis to a large bedroom, with a bathroom and veranda, at the rear of the building.

''It is quiet here,'' she said.

''Good. I think I'll sleep late,'' he replied drowsily.

They exchanged good-nights. He washed his hands and face, noted with approval the shaving kit and soap for morning use, and disrobed to go to bed. Though it was cooler here up on the mountain, it was still very warm, so he lay down atop the sheet to air out his body.

And think about the two women. His mind was on the extraordinary Celeste as he began to fall asleep. Then the door opened, and he saw her framed against the light in the next room.

It was her.

She was humming an odd melody as she glided across the floor—a song of strange rhythms.

And she was gleaming.

She was nude. Without her clothes she seemed even larger. She had anointed her body with oil, and she was an astonishing sight—an incendiary one. Davis felt the fires within him leap higher in instant response.

"I come to take care of you," she announced.

But it was Davis who took care of her. From the moment that she lowered that magnificent body onto the bed beside him, it was Shelby Davis who led the way—gently, but firmly. As his hands explored and caressed, she began to purr and sigh. He kissed her ears, neck and shoulders. His fingers were everywhere, tender and teasing and tantalizing.

He was so different from most men.

He was bringing her up . . . up . . . up . . .

Unlike the others, he did not leap upon her for hasty and mindless satisfaction of his own appetites.

He was celebrating every square inch of her oiled skin.

The small of her back, the pulsing vein in her throat, her flat belly and the mound beneath it—all tingled beneath his attentions.

This man knew women.

He was in no hurry, and the soft sounds he made said that he was enjoying her pleasure. No man had ever lingered so long and skillfully at her swollen breasts—or so appreciatively. With her nipples stiff with need and her head twisting from side to side, she suddenly felt her hips twitching.

It was as if they had a life of their own.

Her legs parted.

Why didn't he take her?

How long would he continue this unbearable and wonderful arousal?

Didn't he realize that she was wet and wild with wanting?

Now her hands reached out for his strong lean body, stroking and touching to tell him that it was time. She was so ready. Her throat was parched, and her remarkable body was arching and pleading in raw need. Her fingers circled his most sensitive parts to urge him on.

She could not endure any more.

"Now . . . now . . . NOW!" she insisted.

This was no mere appeal. It was a deep-throated demand, the order of a queen.

And he entered her like a king.

No, an *emperor*.

It felt as if every space within her was filled and glowing. She closed her powerful legs around him with a gasp of joy and victory, and her hips rose up to meet his deliberate thrusts.

This devilish man was still leading, and she could do nothing but follow in helpless happiness.

They were almost there.

Why didn't he accelerate? He had to. He must. She was heaving and moaning. What sort of man was this? The whole bed was shaking under their exertions. *Aaah*, he was moving faster at last.

At last. At last.

Faster.

Her arms tightened about him. Her frantic fingers grasped at his back, raked his flanks as she saw the peak just ahead.

Then they reached it, together.

She shook and cried out and shook again, struggled to draw him even deeper, though that was impossible. He grunted in completion, but did not stop. He was still moving within her. She shuddered again and shrieked in primeval pleasure.

For a moment she was almost frightened.

She had always set the pace for other lovers. She had no way of knowing that Davis had months of abstinence to dissolve, that his appetites were far from slaked. She sighed and murmured soft approval, then appeals. His desire had not softened. The *Americain* was starting all over again.

And she was swept away.

Her body was slippery with oil and perspiration. The twisted sheets were drenched with Celeste's scented sweat, but he would not stop. He didn't even pause until she had twisted and screamed twice more.

Again they reached the heights together. Now he

finally slowed, still sliding back and forth to savor her—like some connoisseur sipping a fine wine. Every millimeter of movement sent tiny electric currents spinning through her body. All she could do was sigh and sigh in animal pleasure.

He was done.

Or was he?

As they rested in sweaty exhaustion, she reached out—and he responded at once. This time she was the guide. He did not resist. Soon she was crouching above his loins with his rigid member within her. This time she was the one who moved slowly and deliberately, and he was the one who groaned. She made up her mind to stretch the experience as long as possible, and she did.

Seconds flew by. Minutes passed. She slowed. She paused altogether. The muscles of her inner walls pulsed with calculated promise. She began again, and soon they were moving to the same profound rhythms. He grasped her heavy breasts, but she would not let him pull her down. He must know that a queen was his lover.

Something was flickering inside her.

It was growing, surging.

Her control was wavering. In seconds she was wild again. This explosion was even deeper. Now they were both exhausted.

"*Cherie, cherie,*" she crooned contentedly. They held each other for several minutes, and he felt the rumbles and purrs within her.

It was half-past two when they fell asleep.

When he awoke at ten the next morning, Celeste was gone.

Dehydrated from his exertions the night before, Shelby Davis licked his dry lips.

He could still taste her oil.

Chapter Eighteen

The drums began to sound again an hour later.

Dr. Preston did not notice them, for he was fully occupied taking a bath in a huge marble tub with a soapy and playful Therese Geffard.

But Davis did hear them. Since Celeste was nowhere in sight, he asked the waiter who was serving him breakfast what they meant. The man shrugged noncommittally. Either he didn't know or would not say.

"*Maman,*" the waiter muttered and strode away.

Finishing his excellent coffee, the Georgian wondered why the man had spoken of the drum in *patois* as "Mother." That could hardly be the name of the instrument. Perhaps the French woman would explain later in the day when she returned.

It was peaceful up here, the Georgian thought as he

speared a final piece of fresh pineapple that was too good to waste. Then he looked down towards the port. It was too far away for him to make out his vessel, but he found himself thinking about the ship. He was responsible for that craft, and for finding another cargo.

He couldn't afford to spend four or six hours up here waiting for the French physician. He had work to do, and besides, she might well be late. It could be seven or eight at night before she rode back. Davis found the waiter, asked him to leave word for Dr. Carpentier that he'd be waiting to meet her at nine p.m. at the Hotel de Paris.

His reasoning was simple, logical and male. It could be a bit awkward to have a rendezvous with the attractive Parisienne after his night of intense and passionate intimacy with the black woman. Celeste might not be quite that liberal. She was grand and extraordinary, but her temper probably was too.

He realized that he knew little and understood less about the remarkable lady-animal-gourmet who ran this establishment. Perhaps he'd find out more when he saw her again. When the waiter indicated that she too was away, Davis reluctantly told him to give her his "profound thanks" and caught a ride on a carriage going down to town to buy fresh fish at the waterfront for tonight's menu.

When he reached the ship, Fitzgerald had good news. An exporter had been there forty minutes earlier to arrange for movement of a cargo to the Jamaican capital of Kingston.

"The price was right, Captain," the mate reported, "so I took the liberty of saying yes."

"Fine," Davis approved.

"He's in a hurry. Wants to load today—tomorrow morning at the latest."

"We don't argue with customers, Paddy. Do you know where to reach him?"

"Aye, aye, sir. He's just three blocks from here."

They found the shipper together. Wagons began to draw up on the dock by a quarter to four, and by seven most of the crates were aboard. Then the longshoremen stopped, promising to return at seven the next morning when the remaining three wagons were due.

"You can give the men another night of shore leave, Paddy," the Georgian announced, "but they must be back by midnight."

Fitzgerald spread the good word. All but six men—the minimum security detachment needed to protect the ship and cargo—hurried down onto the dock. The half dozen who had to stay aboard grumbled a bit, and one cursed his fate. That was Hinkley.

Still bitter and indifferent to the safety of his comrades, the surly one-eyed cook prowled the aft deck as the orange-red Caribbean sun vanished over the horizon. He didn't care that it was his turn to take the watch. No, they were giving him another piece of dirty duty. It was more of the malicious harassment, another proof that they all despised him.

He'd teach those damn officers a lesson.

They couldn't treat Cyrus F. Hinkley this way.

Maybe those other fools didn't mind being treated like dumb white trash, but he wouldn't stand for it.

There were laughing young girls waiting on shore, and he meant to have his share. He was entitled to some of that juicy flesh. He wouldn't want to be seen with black women at home, but out here two thousand miles away where nobody knew him, it didn't matter. Besides, he could sneak ashore alone and none of the other crewmen would know.

This damn ship didn't need six men on guard anyway.

Hell, there was nothing in those crates worth stealing.

He didn't owe that high and mighty captain and the dumb Mick mate a thing. Nobody on this tub had ever done anything but abuse him, Hinkley thought angrily. There were all snotty bastards. He hated them as much as the lousy blacks. They were liars and cowards, every mother's son of them. It was their rotten fault that he was suffering in exile, wandering from port to port like a dog without a home.

Home.

Why wouldn't the bastards let him go *home*?

At half past eight, the mustachioed ensign from Texas, who was the officer in charge, went below for some food—and Hinkley made his move. He slithered down one of the hawsers to the dock, crouched low as he caught his breath behind a large iron stanchion, and escaped into the blackness.

He had $3.90 in his pocket.

That ought to buy a woman and a jug.

As Hinkley prowled the streets behind the waterfront, Shelby Davis sipped a tall fruit-and-rum punch in the bar of the Hotel de Paris. He'd passed an hour chatting with a highly cultured Haitian lawyer and his schoolteacher wife, both of whom spoke good English and enjoyed talking to foreign visitors. It was the attorney who explained to him that the voodoo term for gods—*loa*—came from the French word, *lois*.

"*Lois* means laws," Monsieur Henri Pichon said as Davis wondered when the blonde physician would arrive. "So the *loa* may be seen as the power of certain magical laws that can be used, for good or evil, by those who know how to please them. That's what the symbolic blood sacrifices of chickens and goats and other creatures are all about."

"What other creatures?"

The lawyer shrugged. "Various sorts," he replied vaguely, and went on to describe the strengths and powers "popularly attributed" to such *loa* as Damballah "the Serpent God," Legba "who opens the gate to the spirit world," sensuous Erzulie, Agwe—*loa* of the sea—and the dreaded Baron Samedi, *loa* of death.

"This is all common talk, *Capitain*," Madame Pichon added immediately. "We hear this as everyone does, but we are not personally familiar with such *affaires*."

Then Davis recalled what the waiter had said over breakfast at *Chez La Reine*.

"Maybe you could answer a question?"

"It would be my pleasure," the attorney assured.

"I heard a drum this morning, and when I asked what it meant a Haitian said *Maman*. What did he mean?"

The Pichons looked at each other.

"The large drums used in the Rada rites—of which I know *nothing*—are played in groups of three. The biggest is called the *Maman*."

"Mother?"

"*Oui, Monsieur*."

"We really must go, Henri," the wife said sharply.

"Of course," he replied as he rose. "May I add that there is a great deal more to our country than this colorful thing called voodoo? *Eh bien*, enjoy your stay."

"I already have—thanks to nice people like you. I do hope that I haven't offended you with my tourist questions."

"*Non—pas du tout*," the lawyer assured.

They left, and Shelby Davis glanced at the pendulum clock on the nearby wall. It was nearly nine. Genevieve should be here soon. He thought about the French physician and the pleasures that this evening promised. Then his mind swung to Celeste, the erotic queen. It was too bad that he could not see her again.

He would not forget the big woman.

He would surely return to her on the ship's next visit to Haiti.

He had to.

She was human female, and animal. And something more. He wasn't sure what that something might be. It would be interesting to find out.

Now he shook his head in annoyance as he realized that he'd missed an opportunity to question the Pichons about the *Sect Rouge*. Draining his glass, he told himself that they probably wouldn't have wanted to discuss it anyway. Well, there were many religious groups and sects, and each was entitled to preserve its secrets.

The clock struck nine, and he ordered another drink.

She'd be along any minute now.

He sipped his drink slowly, but she did not appear. Was something wrong? Could she have misunderstood his message? Was it possible that Genevieve Carpentier was waiting impatiently for him up the mountain at *Chez La Reine*?

Ten o'clock.

She must be up there—probably furious.

With the help of the hotel's porter, Shelby Davis hired a horse-drawn cab for the forty-minute ride up to the restaurant in Petionville.

She'd be hungry by the time he got there, and that would make her even more angry. Shelby Davis faced that prospect without worry. He had soothed irate females before.

Even though the mix-up wasn't his fault, he'd apologize.

Women always expected you to. It showed that you cared.

The second step would be to feed and wine her exceedingly well, at obvious expense. That always helped too.

Then they'd come down the mountain to a bedroom at some good hotel for the third step. She'd be pleased that he was spending his last night in Haiti in her arms. And so would he.

Everything would be all right. There was nothing to worry about.

Then he heard those drums again.

Chapter Nineteen

Sisters.

It was an attractive idea, Hinkley thought as the carriage creaked up the mountain.

The man had promised in his broken English *twin* sisters, and both *virgins*.

It was almost surely just another pimp's lie. The one-eyed cook had heard many similar promises from shabby men in Caribbean bars and alleys, and he was too smart to take this sales talk seriously. Cyrus F. Hinkley was no fool. No sir, he was no gullible kid. He was thirty-six years old, and he knew his way around.

Tipsy as he was after half a bottle of the heavy local rum, he understood what to expect. There'd probably be two women and neither of them a virgin. One would be a fat old sow with half her teeth gone and the other a skinny adolescent as flat as a board. They might be cousins, or maybe mother and daughter.

That would be something. A scar-faced pimp in Puerto Rico—no, it was some other island—had provided such a pair. They hadn't looked the least bit alike. The older one had had an awful body odor, and the younger was too scared or dumb to speak. That had been a fake, Hinkley thought, but it could happen this time.

Between the rum and the jouncing carriage and the twisting road and those stupid drums, it was hard to think. Why did these savages have to beat on those drums all night? Didn't the simple idiots understand they weren't in some African jungle anymore? Too bad that fool Lincoln wasn't around to hear *this,* the cook thought contemptuously.

"Abe Lincoln was a moron," Hinkley said loudly.

The Haitian holding the reins said nothing. Speaking almost no English, he was shielded from the hate that made Cyrus F. Hinkley the most disliked man on the *Sarah W. Warren*. The driver wasn't really interested in Hinkley's hating mind anyway.

It was the body that *they* needed.

The orders of the Mambo had been specific and stern.

A living stranger was to be lured to the crossroads tonight between ten p.m. and midnight, the earlier the better. Eight of the true believers would be waiting to bring the stranger to the *oumphor*. That temple would witness the holy slaughter of the "goat without horns" —the captive.

It must be done.

The *loa* Baron Samedi demanded flesh and blood tonight.

This was the way of the *Sect Rouge,* and nothing could change it. Anyone who tried would be dismembered. And the believer who brought the "goat without horns" would earn the special favor of Baron Samedi for a long time.

His crops would not wither in the drought.

His chickens would not fall sick and perish.

His loved ones would thrive, and no one could cast a spell strong enough to steal away his woman's soul. It must have been some friendly *loa* who directed this tipsy stranger to me, the driver thought reverently, and he made a silent vow to show his appreciation in whatever way the priestess commanded.

She was the greatest of all the Mambos.

Everyone in the *Sect Rouge* knew that. She knew how to steal the soul of a dying man as he expired and turn his body into the living dead. She was skilled in the secret ways of making the healthy sick and the sick healthy. She could—with the help of the *loa,* of course—"possess" the strongest with her rites and spells.

It was not far now to the crossroads.

The believers would be lurking very near in the brush, waiting with the rags and the dried intestines of last month's sacrifice to loop around this new victim's throat. That was part of the magic. Part of the body of one sacrifice must be used to kill the next one.

The chain must be unbroken.

Such was the will of Baron Samedi. It had to be kept secret, of course. Only a tiny fraction of the Haitian people could belong to the *Sect Rouge*. The great Mambo had explained it many times. The others offered their *loa* puny sacrifices such as roosters and goats. The others were weaklings and nonentities. They were to be pitied for their cowardice.

Now the driver saw the broken tree that had been struck by Baron Samedi. Ignorant farmers had said it was lightning, but those of the *Sect Rouge* knew the *truth*. The crossroads were just around the curve. Soon they would drink the stranger's blood. They would stamp their feet and sway.

They would spin as the drums boomed.

The Mambo would shake and swing the *asson*, the special rattle made of a calabash gourd encased in strands of the backbones of snakes.

They would chew on the dead man's flesh.

They they would crack their whips as the drums grew faster, and they would dance. Men would shout and croak in voices not their own. Women would reel and stumble and faint. Shortly before dawn, they would strip off their special robes of ritual and change back to ordinary garb. Looking just like everyone else in this area, they would quietly make their way home.

And Baron Samedi would be pleased.

There was the crossroads. All the preliminaries had been completed an hour ago. They had danced around the nearby graves, marked them with poured crosses of home-brewed *clairin* rum and placed small bowls of animal blood on each. The place had been purified properly. They could catch the "goat without horns" whenever he came.

When the horse reached the crossroads, the driver reined the animal to a halt and climbed down. He gestured to Hinkley to do the same, and then pointed to a clump of trees.

"We here? 'Bout time, dammit. Where are the girls?" the surly one-eyed cook demanded.

"*Jolie . . . jolie*. . . Pree-tee," the driver lied and shaped a lush female figure in the air with his calloused hands.

"Damn well better be, or you'll feel *this,*" Hinkley threatened as he showed the handle of the carving knife he carried whenever he went ashore anywhere in the Caribbean.

Behind his bravado, Cyrus Hinkley was afraid of almost everyone. He'd been the lowest of the "white trash" back in Mobile, with only the slaves below him on the ladder of life in Alabama. That was why the freed blacks threatened him most of all.

Hinkley followed the driver for some twenty yards.

Then *they* grabbed him.

They came out of nowhere—like ghosts. Silent and many, they were dressed in white robes that hung loosely like shrouds. They materialized on all sides in three or four seconds.

Thieves!

They'd rob him—or maybe worse.

Hinkley reached for his knife and opened his mouth to scream.

Two of the *Sect Rouge* men wrested the knife from his right hand. Another pulled at his hair to jerk his head back as another pair looped the dried intestines around his neck. Two others twisted his left arm behind his back, while another rammed a large rag into the cook's open mouth and choked off the cry of terror.

Hinkley made one more frantic effort to break free. That ended when another believer—by day, a respected banker in Port au Prince—kicked him between the legs. The impact of that leather-shod foot jack-knifed Hinkley with blinding pain and ended all resistance. The hurt twisted in his groin like a hot poker. Tears poured down his cheeks. He felt his stomach knot in automatic reflex, and he wondered whether he could fight down his body's impulse to vomit. If he couldn't, the rag in his mouth might leave him choking on the contents of his own belly.

Hinkley's feet barely touched the dark earth as the *Sect Rouge* believers pushed, led and carried him deep into the thick tropical forest. It seemed like a long way. It was actually only a bit more than half a mile. A runner sprinted ahead with the good news.

"He comes! The 'goat without horns' comes to join us!"

The pain had subsided by the time the cook was hustled into the temple. The sound of the three Rada drums filled the large straw-thatched hut, with the biggest— Maman—loudest of all.

The crying had stopped, so Hinkley could see clearly by the flickering light of the candles. Most of the men and women who surrounded him wore red robes, a few others white. They were dancing all around him—twisting and whirling and thrusting their arms at him in some bizarre spastic ritual.

There was a huge woman leading the ceremony.

Very tall, at least six feet. Extremely beautiful and coal black, with extraordinarily large eyes that glowed like a cat's.

It was the high priestess.

It was the woman with whom Shelby Davis had shared his passion less than twenty hours earlier.

It was the queenly Celeste, Great Mambo of the *Sect Rouge*.

She raised her right hand, and the drumming stopped.

She spoke several words in the *patois*. Then one of Hinkley's captors stepped forward to give her the cook's knife, and she smiled. It was a terrifying look that combined joy and evil. Horrified and weak with panic, Hinkley hoped that he would faint. He had endured enough agony.

But he did not faint. He sagged forward in fear, but was jerked back by a strangling tug of the bizarre cord of intestines pulled tight around his gagging throat. How did he get into this nightmare? This whole thing was grotesque—like the Hell that brimstone Baptist preacher back home had warned about so loudly.

Who were these maniacs?

What would they do to him?

She spoke again, and he was dragged out—by that thing around his throat—like an untrained dog into a large clearing. She shook the rattle. There was no drum beating now, but the *Sect Rouge* believers danced anyway. They shuffled and swayed to the rhythms within their heads, while softly humming some ancient African tune and grinning.

They had reason to be happy.

The best was soon to come.

Now the others hurled themselves to the ground and *she* began to dance. It was frightening and oddly erotic at the same time. Hinkley stared at her splendid body and blinked at her sensual movements, but he was unable to make more than a low grunt. She began to clap her hands. Hinkley wondered why.

Moments later, six young women in white stepped forward.

Each was carrying a large shallow bowl of glazed pottery.

What the hell could it mean?

Hinkley found himself dragged and pushed forward towards the big woman who towered five inches above him. The other females ringed him with their bowls, as if offering him something to eat. Now all the men in the circle were stamping their feet softly and chanting almost inaudibly.

The priestess leaned close and patted his head.

Then she smiled, but this time her teeth showed.

She was still smiling when she cut Hinkley's throat.

The blood spurted. But the white-clad women with the bowls were ready. They knew what to do; they had much experience. They held their bowls so as to catch every drop. It would be a sin to waste even one. It would offend the Mambo and draw down the wrath of Baron Samedi.

This was the *Sect Rouge*.

The *rouge*—the red—was blood.

Human blood.

As Hinkley's carmine life fluid gushed and weakness swept over him, the Mambo deftly plucked the rag from his mouth. The dying cook could only gasp weakly. The believers nodded contentedly.

That was the sound of his soul departing.

A final whimper, and then Hinkley's head dropped to

his shoulder. It was done. The "goat without horns" was dead. Once again the "grey pigs"—as the believers called themselves—had served Baron Samedi well.

The Mambo raised Hinkley's knife again, and began to cut away slices of his warm flesh for everyone to eat. There were fifty-six of the faithful at the ceremony. Each must drink of the sacrifice's blood and eat some of his body. There was a great deal of carving to be done if everyone was to be fed properly.

The Mambo did her job well, as always.

Crooning the ritual melody of death in a deep fine voice, she literally cut the remains of Cyrus F. Hinkley to pieces. She butchered him as if he were a dead steer, taking special care not to waste any meat. When all the flesh was hacked away, she finished by removing his heart, lungs, genitals, ears and intestines. She took care to keep the latter intact, for they had to be dried out for use on the next human sacrifice.

It was as she finished this dissection that one of the believers called out and pointed.

An unbeliever was watching from the darkness.

The high priestess pointed her left hand and waved the bloody knife. They all ran in obedience to the great Mambo's command.

The intruder must be caught and silenced forever.

The spy must be destroyed.

Chapter Twenty

As his carriage turned the curve, Shelby Davis saw the lights of the *Chez La Reine* restaurant a mile further up the mountain.

Then he saw something else.

It was a slim figure running. It was a woman. Racing, stumbling and staggering, she charged down the twisting road as if Death itself was chasing her.

It was.

Now he recognized the figure with the yellow hair. It was Genevieve Carpentier. Her clothes were in disarray, and tiny red cuts showed where jungle thorns had gashed her face and arms. There was sheer terror in her face. She was sprinting so fast that she didn't even notice the horse-drawn taxi for a few seconds.

Then she saw it and began screaming.

"Help! Help! Save me!" she shrieked.

The startled driver stopped the horse, and before the cab came to a full halt, the Georgian vaulted to the ground. She came reeling forward hysterically, crashing into his arms.

"They're coming! They mean to kill me! They'll kill you too!" she blurted in a voice edged with raw panic.

"What is it, Doctor? Who's coming?"

"The *Sect Rouge*!"

She sounded half mad. Davis wondered whether she'd lost her mind, and reached to comfort her. She tore free from his grasp, turned and pointed.

"There they are! I saw them butcher the one-eyed man. They ate him! They drank his blood!"

Dozens of figures emerged into the moonlight. They wore red robes, and they carried knives and whips. They were running straight at Davis. Behind them loomed a tall figure.

It was Celeste.

She too held a glittering blade, and her face was pure rage.

Davis swept the French woman up into the cab, and not a moment too soon. The terrified driver was already turning his horse to flee down the mountain. He'd heard of those who wore red robes and did unspeakable things in the night.

They were only twenty yards away. Leading the homicidal pack was the waiter who'd served Shelby Davis breakfast this very morning. He looked completely different now.

"Samedi! Blood for Baron Samedi!" he roared.

As the carriage turned, the wild-eyed waiter made a frantic leap to catch it. He caught hold of the rear with one hand, and grinned in triumph as he began to pull himself up. His expression changed drastically when Shelby Davis broke his jaw with as hard a punch as he could throw.

The man dropped to the road, and the taxi clattered on with the cult members shouting curses as it pulled away. Genevieve Carpentier was sobbing uncontrollably. The driver whipped his steed again and again. It was extremely dangerous to race down this winding road at such speeds in the darkness. Only a lunatic would do it.

Only a fool wouldn't. One had some chance if he drove well and had good fortune. There was no hope at all if the *Sect Rouge* caught them. Those pious murderers would reduce them to bones by morning.

"You must go. You must leave Haiti *at once*. Tonight!" the French physician pleaded. "You have seen them. Now you know who some of them are—and they know you."

"And you, too," Davis pointed out grimly.

"They are cannibals, *Capitain*. It is *fantastique*," she said with a shudder. "Cannibals in this peaceful island—*today!*"

The Georgian heard her words, but his attention was focused on his crew. Would they all get back in time? Suddenly he thought about the ship's physician and the sultry young mulatto. On this last night in port, Preston was surely in her bed.

"Therese Geffard? Where does she live?" Davis asked urgently.

"Perhaps half a mile down this road—and off to the right some one hundred yards. Why?"

"We have to stop there for Preston."

"We *can't* stop! It would be suicide!"

The handsome Georgian shook his head.

"What we can't do is leave him behind to be eaten," he corrected. The driver was an unenthusiastic as she was about stopping for anything—even for a second. Davis persuaded him to cooperate by threatening to throw him off the carriage for the *Sect Rouge* to devour.

They found the house, and Davis banged on the door. When no one answered, he simply kicked it in. Seconds later, Preston and Therese Geffard hurried from the bedroom. She had an angry look and a shotgun. Aside from that, she was naked, as was the ship's physician.

"I assume that's for some jealous lover," Davis said.

"Are you mad?" she demanded indignantly.

"Just in a hurry. Get your clothes, Doctor. *Fast.* That's a real order."

Preston could tell that he was serious.

"Captain—"

"*Later*. You've got thirty seconds, or you're dead. I mean it."

Preston raced into the bedroom, and the young beauty began to tell Davis what she thought of this *outrageous* behavior. She was still denouncing him when the physician emerged. He was wearing his pants and holding his shoes and shirt.

"You can finish in the taxi," Davis announced. "*Au revoir, Madamoiselle.*"

Then he seized the shotgun and pushed Preston out the door.

"Run, Doctor. Run!" he commanded.

They jumped into the cab. Preston was startled and confused. The sight of a scratched and disheveled Genevieve Carpentier added to his disturbance.

"*Vite! Vite!*" she begged the driver. He complied with her urgent appeal for speed immediately. He whipped the horse and the taxi lurched forward at once. The ship's physician tried to button his shirt in the careening cab, wondering what the awful crisis might be. He got his answer as they reached the main road.

Shelby Davis' finger stabbed forward like a spear.

"Those are the people who want to kill us," he said coolly.

Preston saw a cluster of men in strange robes. They had knives and whips and clubs, and they were looking around intently.

"They've seen us!" Davis announced and grabbed the reins from a driver abruptly petrified with fear. The Georgian held the leather lines in his left hand and the shotgun in his right. He snapped the reins to spur the horse on. It was a matter of seconds now.

"We're going through," the Georgian announced.

It was like a cavalry charge. The horse and wagon hurtled towards the cultists. Three or four jumped aside, but the other fanatics held their ground. A blast from the shotgun smashed two of them aside, and then Davis simply ran through the others like an express train.

"Oh my God!" Preston gasped.

Davis jerked the reins for the sharp turn, and they hurtled down the mountain road at a bone-rattling speed.

Faster. Still faster.

People were shouting behind them. Preston turned to

see dozens of runners in hot pursuit. They appeared to be dressed in red. What the hell did it mean?

Down . . . down . . . down . . .

Shelby Davis struggled to control the carriage. He'd had years of experience with horses, but nothing like this. The driver beside him was praying loudly in the Haitian *patois*, pleading with all the saints for help and forgiveness. For some reason, the French woman seemed to be growing calmer. Maybe it was Davis' tough skill that caused it, Preston thought. The sight of a cool, competent leader often inspired others in battle, he knew.

"I'm a good shot," she shouted. "I'll take the gun."

"Don't fire unless you have to," the Georgian answered. "We've only got one round left."

Faster and faster.

Now the night was filled with the sounds of voodoo drums. Neither Davis nor the French woman had any question about what they were saying. It was the *Sect Rouge*, spreading the alarm.

Stop the unbelievers who are coming down the mountain.

Kill them . . . Kill them . . . Kill the unbelievers.

Preston managed to finish dressing in the wildly swaying taxi, cursing softly as he completed the awkward task of tying his shoes. There were more lights ahead. They were almost in Port au Prince.

"We're not safe yet," the Georgian announced, and he didn't slow down at all. They swept into the city at full speed. This was a terrible thing to do to a horse, Davis thought as they bounced through the almost deserted streets. His elegant grandpa—who'd taught him to ride and much more—would never have approved. He was right, too. This kind of abuse was the sort of things only fools or brutes such as that bastard Bart Beecher would inflict on animals.

It was four minutes before midnight when they reached the dock. It was crowded with dozens of his crew, returning in groups from their night on the town. It had obviously been a merry one. Several were singing, and the gait of three or four others signalled that they'd drunk plenty of rum. One gulped the last swig in a bottle and tossed it into the harbor as the carriage clattered noisily onto the pier. Davis reined the exhausted horse to a halt just yards from his sailors.

"Hey, it's the captain!" a stoker called out cheerily.

Davis stood up before he shouted his orders.

"This is an emergency. We're leaving in fifteen minutes. I want steam up, every cannon manned and loaded, and all riflemen with their weapons on deck. Battle stations! *ON THE DOUBLE!*"

Getting steam up in fifteen minutes was impossible, but the steely edge in the captain's voice cut through every hesitation. Officers and enlisted crew reacted alike. They ran. They poured up the gangway on the double.

Now Preston, still groggy from the journey, rose to his feet and looked back. There were scores of flickering lights moving down the mountain. It had to be *them*—coming with torches to burn the ship. Genevieve Carpentier saw them, and so did the driver who crossed himself.

Davis reached into his pocket, took out a wad of Haitian currency that added up to four times the normal round-trip taxi fare to *Chez La Reine* and gave it to the scared driver. The horse was still panting, and flecks of foam at its lips showed the awful effects of the breakneck ride down the mountain. With no choice but to leave at once, the driver patted his steed hopefully.

"You'd better come with us, Doctor," Davis told the French woman.

"I fear that I must. Celeste would not let me live to see the dawn," she replied soberly.

"Tell the driver he can come, too."

She spoke to the taxi man in the rippling *patois* of the island. After a few moments, he shook his head and answered softly.

"He can't abandon his family," she translated and silently gave him the shotgun. The driver climbed back up onto the cab and the weary horse cantered away slowly. As it trotted from the ship, Fitzgerald ran down the gangway to find out what was happening. Preston listened as Shelby Davis briefly described the gruesome events up near Petionville, and the grave and immediate threat that the homicidal *Sect Rouge* posed to all of them.

"Jesus, Mary and Joseph," the devout mate erupted. "*Cannibals?*"

He didn't wait for an answer. He sprinted back onto the bridge to speed the crew's efforts. Davis, the French woman and William Cicero Preston followed. The riflemen were already hurrying to their posts with their weapons at the ready. Every eye was focused on the street at the end of the pier.

The cathedral clock on the square sounded midnight, and Davis assigned an ensign to start an immediate count to find out whether anyone was still ashore. Half a minute later, Fitzgerald approached with an armful of weapons.

"Ladies first," Davis invited.

She took a rifle and a fistful of extra bullets. Davis selected a rifle *and* a pair of long-barrelled pistols, plus enough ammunition to fill one big pocket.

"I think I'll have a rifle, too," Preston declared stiffly. "Used to bag a lot of rabbits and birds when I—was—uh younger."

"But doctors aren't allowed to bear arms, are they?" the mate teased.

"You didn't see *them*," Preston snapped defensively. "If you had even a glimpse of those devils, you wouldn't say such stupid things."

"He's right, Paddy," the captain said.

"*And* I'll take a pistol, too," Preston announced.

Some fourteen minutes after Davis had sounded the emergency, the ensign reported that everyone seemed to be on board except "that fool Hinkley."

Shelby Davis thought of the description that Dr. Carpentier had given of the one-eyed Caucasian victim eaten on the mountain.

"Hinkley isn't coming," Davis said simply.

"And we're not going—not in the next fifteen minutes," the ship's engineer reported from behind them. There was trouble with a piston and a jammed valve, and steam was building up very slowly as well. It might be forty minutes to an hour before the *Sarah W. Lee* could cruise from this harbor.

Davis listened to the drums.

They seemed nearer, and so did the lights that marked the moving column of *Sect Rouge* followers. They were picking up more men as they neared town. They might be hundreds by the time they reached the waterfront.

"We don't *have* forty minutes, Mortimer," Davis told the chief engineer. "If we can't steam out now, we'll float."

They did.

Within a minute or two after the last hawser was loosed from the dock, the tide began to move the *Sarah W. Lee*. It was very slow, but quite steady. In ten minutes, the vessel was half a mile from shore—out of effective rifle range and far beyond any threat from daggers, whips, clubs or torches. Then the former Confederate raider turned—very gradually.

It stopped moving.

It seemed to be stuck for a few minutes.

"What's going on with that steam?" Davis fretted.

"Think we've almost got it, sir," the assistant engineer replied.

Now the lights were on the waterfront. The whole pier they'd just left was covered with them. The believers were chanting something, and the big woman was leading them.

"Prayer or curse?" Preston wondered.

Suddenly they felt the thrumming beneath their feet, and they almost cheered. It was the familiar vibration of the ship's twin propellers turning. The steam engines were finally working, getting stronger by the second.

The *Sarah W. Lee* slid smoothly across the waters of the harbor as it picked up speed steadily. When the vessel reached the open Caribbean, Davis finally relaxed and turned to the French woman with a sigh.

"You're a very pretty mess, Doctor. Tell me, how *did* you get into this thing tonight?"

She patted her disheveled hair, quite automatically, before replying.

"To start from the beginning, it was a lie. There was no fire at my *clinique*," she told them.

It was probably a trick, Shelby thought. Yes, Celeste might do something like that to have a night alone with a man if she wanted him. She was the Mambo. She took and did whatever she desired—and she had clearly desired him immensely. She was a woman of gigantic pride and passion to match her startling stature.

Would she also have slain him if he'd stayed?

Almost surely.

Her loyalty to blood and Baron Samedi was far stronger than her need for any man. Maybe she'd have invited him to join the cult. Voodoo was not limited to blacks any more than lust or murder were. He'd have refused in any case, and she'd have smiled and cut his throat.

"So I slept for some hours at my house there, and set off that afternoon to meet you at the restaurant as we agreed," Genevieve Carpentier continued. A bridge had been washed out. She'd had to take a more circuitous route. It was after ten when her horse threw a shoe on that dark road. Unsure where she was, she spotted the lights and headed towards them for help—unaware she was approaching a *Sect Rouge* temple. Frightened and fascinated when she saw the ceremony begin in the clearing, she'd watched "like a bird hypnotized by a snake" until they'd spotted her.

"So I ran through the woods for my life. You know the rest," she concluded.

Without warning, she embraced Davis and kissed him hard.

"That's for saving my life, *Capitain*. I am in your debt—profoundly. Is that good English?"

"Absolutely."

"I will pay my debt," she assured, "and soon."

She had that warm-woman look in her eyes. It was filled with anticipation.

"Now I'd like some clean clothes and a comb," she announced. "I can wear a young sailor's pants and shirt if I have to."

"And look splendid," Preston complimented.

"How would you know of *splendide?*" she laughed. "You're not even wearing socks."

Preston looked down to discover that he'd left his socks on the straw mat that covered the floor of Therese Geffard's bedroom. He blinked in embarrassment, and then decided that it hardly mattered. Lovely Therese Geffard had made him feel young and strong and passionate again. That was worth more than . . . than almost anything.

"I know a lot about *splendide*, Mademoiselle," he declared proudly. The French woman was surprised to discover this fire in the chubby middle-aged American. He might not be so uninteresting after all.

"Would you show me to my cabin, *Docteur*?" she invited.

As they headed below, Davis ordered the navigator to plot a new course.

"Kingston, Jamaica," he ordered. They could not

deliver the entire cargo because some of it was to have been loaded in the morning ahead, but they'd bring the many crates already aboard.

He could barely hear the drums. Staring back, he watched the coast of Haiti drift from sight. Haiti meant "land of the mountains" in the ancient tongue of the Arawak Indians, he recalled. Well, he had seen those mountains—and faced death on one of them. It would be long time before he returned to that island. Celeste would not forgive or forget.

It had been an extraordinary two days. He had followed Preston's advice to end his long period of celibacy, and he wasn't sorry. He had broken free of the emotional mourning months ago. There was no point in continuing the physical mourning either.

But he couldn't help thinking of the redheaded Yankee woman whom the war and the sea had stolen from him. Well, he had to go on. He was thirty, and he would find another fine woman. Perhaps two days from now in Jamaica. Or maybe in two years somewhere else.

He'd be home by then, he reflected. He found himself wondering about his family, about whether his mother had received the letter he'd given to the friendly Canadian captain last month to mail from Halifax. Maybe it hadn't reached her. Perhaps their home had been burned by Yankee troops in the closing months of the war, or she might have died.

Somebody ought to let Hinkley's family know too, he brooded. They were entitled to be freed of their waiting. Yes, he'd work it out next week somehow. The letter would have to be carefully worded—with no gruesome details. "Your son was a fine and respected member of our crew, and his death in the storm has saddened all of us." He'd written such messages of condolence before. It was part of a captain's job.

Suddenly he felt weary. His back hurt where the big woman had raked it with her nails in passion, and he realized that he hadn't eaten any dinner. He was hungry, and he was tired of death and danger. He wasn't even sure that this endless crisscrossing of the Caribbean was right anymore.

But a captain couldn't reveal any uncertainty or weakness. He was responsible for all these men. He must show confidence and strength. Their morale and faith in his leadership were almost all they had left. He had to maintain both. That too was part of a captain's job.

He couldn't let them down.

He wouldn't.

Too hungry to eat and too tired to sleep, he paced the deck for a long time. The moon was full and the sea calm, and the steady vibrations beneath his feet were reassuring.

A mariner's lullaby in this age of steam, he thought. It was half past two before he went below to lie down. It was after three before he escaped into a long complicated dream. There were many people in it. One was the redheaded woman he'd never hold again.

Chapter Twenty-One

Eight hours later and 632 miles southeast, an old two-masted merchantman sailed slowly north in a middling breeze. The winds were not strong in the central Caribbean in May, but the British captain of the 105-footer was in no great hurry. The *Yorkshire Lady* had been cruising these historic trade routes at such speeds for seventeen years, and probably would for another seventeen if properly handled.

That it would be was beyond question.

Captain Humphrey Harwood was one of the most proper ship's masters afloat, and his crew of twenty-six was well-trained. If they seemed relaxed, it was because they knew their jobs—and their skipper. He wasn't a boozy cast-off from the Royal Navy like some of the other masters in these waters. He was a rigorous and efficient professional who had chosen the Caribbean because its weather far surpassed that of England—where his impossible-to-please wife still resided.

Captain Harwood had solved the problem of that vituperative lady by moving half the world away—and by setting up a discreet arrangement with a Spanish woman in Barbados. She was, officially, his "housekeeper." Everything "proper and tidy," as Harwood often said.

Appearances and schedules were important to him. His crew might go barefoot at sea, but every man-jack of them wore shoes in port. There was proper tea each morning at eleven and again at five, with decent biscuits. And there was always an alert lookout on duty at the bow. Since the recent dust-up about those filthy pirates, Harwood insisted on a second watcher atop the mainmast. After all, he also carried passengers from time to time. At the moment, a Chinese shoemaker, his wife and teenage daughters were on board en route from Trinidad to Montserrat.

Captain Harwood checked his pocket watch, a fine example of British workmanship. He was very proud of the reliability of things made in his distant native land. It was three minutes to one on a cloudless Caribbean afternoon. In precisely one hundred and eighty seconds, a proper lunch would be served to the ship's master and the passengers on the aft deck, under a canopy. Shade was necessary for the midday meal in this part of the world, as Harwood pointed out fairly regularly.

But the proper master of the *Yorkshire Lady* did not get to enjoy his proper lunch that day. He started it, but he never got to finish. At two minutes before one, the lookout up top sang out that another vessel was approaching. Harwood raised his telescope calmly.

It was a steam-powered craft with twin stacks spewing smoke.

The ship was moving only a bit faster than Harwood's. It was flying the good old Union Jack, the flag that always delighted Humphrey Harwood whenever he saw it. The presence of another British vessel was a pleasant reminder of which nation—which empire—really dominated the seas.

As the lunch began, exactly at one, Harwood noticed that the other ship was drawing nearer. He went through the motions of trying to maintain a conversation with his passengers, but it was a polite formality. Mr. Wu Feng spoke basic survival English, and his wife and daughters none at all. They'd left Shanghai only fifteen months earlier to join the growing Asian community of Trinidad.

It would be rude to ignore his countrymen, Harwood decided. Excusing himself, he turned to order that a message be sent by signal flags asking where the other craft was headed. He was puzzled when there was no reply. The other ship was less than a mile away. Its crew must have seen the flags.

Now the other ship was picking up speed. It was moving directly towards the *Yorkshire Lady* at an impressive twelve or thirteen knots. Ah, there were the flags with the reply.

''Prepare to receive boarding party.''

As Harwood read it letter by letter, gunports appeared on the other ship. They had been skillfully camouflaged. These were pirates—perhaps the very ones who'd looted and sunk thirty other ships during the past nineteen months. Harwood could see eight cannon on the other ship, and his vessel's entire armament was a dozen hunting rifles and two shotguns.

Maybe these were not the pirates who killed so freely.

Perhaps this was a different band of corsairs.

Or was it a disguised British warship out to catch the vicious thugs?

"What ship are you?" Harwood signalled hopefully.

Four cannons answered the question. The shells blasted holes in the wooden hull of the large sailing ship, killing three crewmen and wounding several others. Livid, but aware that no effective resistance was possible, Harwood grimly ordered that the *Yorkshire Lady's* flag be struck to communicate surrender.

But another salvo of shells smashed into the schooner.

The pirate captain was teaching him a lesson, Harwood realized. The bastard was a sadist. Looking across to the armed raider only two hundred yards away now, Harwood caught a glimpse of a large fat man who appeared to be giving orders. He seemed gross, perhaps three hundred pounds.

He was at least that, Harwood judged when the pirate chieftain came aboard six minutes later. He wore a big straw hat, an embroidered shirt and bulging pants that barely contained his jiggling belly, and high black boots. The forty pirates who preceded him aboard were a ragtag lot who jeered in a variety of accents. Some were Hispanic, others French and several sounded American. Two talked as if they were Scots.

When the crew and passengers had all been lined up, the fat man stepped forward belligerently and spat on the *Yorkshire Lady's* recently sanded and immaculate deck. Humphrey Harwood winced.

"You the captain?" the pirate leader demanded nastily.

"I am, sir. My name is—"

Harwood did not finish the sentence. The fat man prevented that by shooting him twice in the stomach at point blank rage. Humphrey Harwood gaped in astonishment, then fell forward on his face. He was four-fifths dead already. As the crimson fluid spouted from the holes in his abdomen, the young Chinese girls began to scream.

The fat man did not shoot them. He had other plans for those adolescent bodies. He simply sent each of them reeling with a tooth-rattling slap. Mr. Wu Feng stepped forward to defend his daughters. Another pirate shot him in the face.

"Good work, Lopez," the massive pirate boss congratulated. Then he saw Harwood's watch. Reluctant to risk bending over to steal it, he ordered Lopez to hand it to him. Then he kicked Captain Harwood's almost dead body over the side.

"Shark bait," he guffawed. "All right, stop dawdling, you idiots. No time to waste. Get that cargo moving, and search these prisoners carefully. Be sure you check that Chink's pockets—and his shoes—before you deep-six him."

The pirates swept through the *Yorkshire Lady* like a plague of ravenous locusts. They ripped open every compartment, box, sea chest and drawer. They took everything that could be torn loose and carried—even the ship's cheap cutlery and the straight razor that

Captain Humphrey Harwood had inherited from his father.

They pressed the captured crew into service to move the booty to their armed raider. When that task was completed at 2:35 p.m., the pirates herded them back to the *Yorkshire Lady* and roughly shoved them down into the hold.

"And don't forget *her*," the fat man ordered. He was pointing as the Chinese widow. Then he smiled craftily.

"No, bring her along. She'll keep the two kids quiet till we get to the island. Then you fellows can have her to play with."

"*Muchas gracias.* We could use another fresh woman," said Pepe Lopez, a former thief who'd served four years for robbing a church in Santo Domingo.

"Got to keep my crew happy, don't I?" the murderous captain chuckled smugly. They took the three frightened females back to the pirate craft, leaving behind four experienced arsonists to set the *Yorkshire Lady* ablaze.

The flames raced across the schooner swiftly. Then the captives trapped in the hold began to scream. Their agonized appeals were audible for several minutes as the raider pulled away. It would burn right down to the waterline, just like the others. No one would survive to describe what had happened or who had done it.

It was a good haul and a good life, the fat man told himself complacently. It hadn't been easy to convert the swift *Caroline* from a bloackade runner to a disguised and well-armed raider, but he'd done it. He'd bought the cannon in France and quietly recruited the tough new crew in various ports. Only three of his Confederate sailors remained; the others had lacked the stomach for this work—and the greed.

Now they'd hide out at their secret base for a few days before raiding further north. They were entitled to some pleasure after all this work. Bart Beecher looked at the two Chinese girls. One appeared to be fourteen, the other no more than fifteen. He had wondered about Asian females. These two seemed to promise a great deal of pleasure, perhaps as much as six or eight weeks of it. After that, he usually grew bored. Some women did not survive his brutal treatment that long, but this pair looked sturdy. They were also terrified, and that was fine with Beecher. A frightened woman would not dare to mock his huge body or spurn his advances.

They would obey, as slaves should. As *everyone* should.

In another year, Beecher would have amassed enough booty to retire to some pleasant country where he'd have a dozen slaves and a steady supply of girls. Anticipating that future, he turned for a final glance at the burning schooner. He watched the last flaming section of the mainmast slip beneath the waves.

No ship.

No survivors except for the three females in his power.

It was perfect.

Chapter Twenty-Two

Clean paved streets.

Neat whitewashed buildings and briskly efficient harbor officials.

Immaculate, disciplined police and the Union Jack on dozens of schools, public buildings and ships that filled the port.

The capital of Jamaica was all spit and polish as the center of a well-run British colony should be. Everything seemed correct and orderly as the *Sarah W. Lee* slowed to dock. There was no sign left of the popular discontent that had erupted in rebellion at Morant Bay ninety miles down the coast only a year earlier. It had been an uprising of free, but hungry men, Davis remembered. Slavery had officially ended in 1836.

"This isn't a rich island," the Georgian told Genevieve when the ship was tied up securely. "Nice people, but dirt poor in the main."

"Couldn't be poorer than Haiti," she replied.

She looked attractive in the sailor's attire. Her fear had long subsided and her pretty face was washed, and her blonde hair caught the afternoon sun.

"You'll be very popular with that hair here," Shelby Davis predicted good-humoredly.

"I don't intend to stay that long, *Capitain*. I think it's time to visit my parents in Paris. Six years in the Caribbean is enough, and they'll be glad to see me."

"Who wouldn't?" William Cicero Preston asked.

For a second, Davis wondered in which cabin she'd spent the previous night, but he decided not to question her. He had something else to ask the French woman.

"I have a favor to request," Davis told her. "There's a letter I'd like you to send from Paris. Take my word. There's a reason not to mail it here."

She smiled.

"A French *femme* who is, let's say, more than twenty-nine, does not ask questions, *Capitain,*" she assured. "Besides, I can deny *nothing* to a handsome *gentilhomme* who saved me from being eaten."

She was flirting, but ever so nicely.

It could well be to make Preston jealous, the Georgian speculated. From the look in the ship's physician's eyes, it seemed to be working.

"I'll remember that," Davis flirted back with a twinkle in his eyes. Then he asked Preston to escort her ashore to buy a dress or two while he supervised the unloading.

"We're not rich either," Davis said, "but I can contribute at least—"

"Don't worry about it, sir," the ship's physician broke in authoritatively. "*I* can take care of these minor purchases."

Then Preston took her arm firmly, while the captain strove to maintain a straight face, and guided the chic French woman ashore. Davis waited until the unloading was moving smoothly before he yielded supervision to his capable first mate.

"And when you're done, Paddy, there's one more thing," he announced.

"Yes, sir?"

"I noticed a Spanish ship at the next dock. Could be in from Cuba. Why don't you have a talk with some of their officers?"

"*Thanks*, Captain," Fitzgerald replied appreciatively. There wasn't much chance that there'd be any word of Isabella Garcia or the hunted Arias Brigade, but even the vaguest rumor or smallest possibility was worth pursuing.

Davis descended to the pier, made his way around the muscular longshoremen and decided to buy a cigar at the small shop at the end of the dock. There might be Cuban coronas or the flavorful Jamaican cheroots, both favorites of his. The Georgian didn't smoke cigars often, but he was in the mood for such relaxation now.

The storekeeper had both—as well as disturbing news. The weather was turning bad, and quickly. A storm was on the way from the Gulf of Mexico. The harbor master was advising all captains to remain in port for thirty-six hours or more. The Georgian wasn't eager to rush out to sea again anyway. He thanked the shopkeeper, paid for the two cigars and struck a match to light the cheroot.

"Shelby? Is that really you?"

The voice sounded Southern and friendly, but it could be a trick.

It wasn't. When he turned, he was startled to see the familiar face of Colonel Raymond Duval, the Louisiana plantation owner and gentleman soldier who'd been military aide to Robert E. Lee.

"Is it you?" Duval pressed.

He was tanned, well-dressed in civilian clothes that suggested a country life—and alone. Davis made certain that no one else was within earshot before he replied.

"It's me—but please speak my name softly. There's a Yankee price on my head, Colonel."

"I know," Duval answered and shook his hand warmly. "I heard before we left. Those damned Yankees have gone crazy, Shelby. Their carpetbaggers are ravaging the South, and I'm ashamed to say there are plenty of dirty scalawags helping."

The Georgian lit his cigar and puffed.

"What are scalawags?" he puzzled.

"Low-down Southerners working to line their pockets, crooked lawyers elected by illiterate ex-slaves to the new state legislatures, and gangs of slick thieves. They're giving fat contracts for so-called Reconstruction projects in exchange for big bribes and voting themselves huge salaries."

"I heard things were bad," Davis acknowledged.

"Worse than that. All the Southern banks went bust

when Confederate currency became worthless, and at the same time three and a half million Nigras were set free with no jobs, no money and no idea about how to get on. Some of them burned the cotton mills, it's said. Others just took up and left the farms. It was *chaos*."

"Things might be better by now, Colonel."

"Couldn't be worse. All our shipping halted. Factories closed. No food coming from the plantations. Nobody to take care of our wounded and crippled, and gangs of hungry ex-soldiers wandering the hills and roads. Some poor devils are robbing and killing, but the scalawags and their Yankee cronies just don't give a damn. Too much for decent folks to take, so we all pulled out in April of '66."

"Your whole family?" the Georgian asked.

"Lot more'n that, Shelby. How about fifty-one families—two hundred and eight people from New Orleans and nearby! We ran farms up there, and we're doing the same down here. It's a whole Confederate community. We're building from the ground up."

But the Confederacy was now history, Davis thought.

"Land's cheap here, and so is labor. We pooled our women's jewelry, our family silver—everything—to raise Yankee money. It was enough to buy two big farms from an old English lady about twenty-five miles from here. We're not beaten yet, if you know what I mean."

The Georgian squinted uncertainly.

Duval couldn't mean what he was hinting.

"I'm not sure, Colonel."

"The South will rise again! We'll build a new Confederacy *here*. Doesn't matter that much if the blacks who tend the fields are legally slaves or not. Let them be as free as jaybirds on paper, so long as they take orders and work cheap. Feeding and clothing those slaves back home cost almost as much as the wages on this island. We've got six hundred and eighty acres and plans to buy more. Probably be hiring more of those folks the British brought in from India after slavery ended here. They do fine work on plantations.''

It all sounded like the dispassionate analysis of a military staff officer—which, in fact, Duval had been.

Maybe they could do it.

The notion of building a new Confederate world in Jamaica was odd, but hardly impossible. Davis had already heard of another group of Confederate exiles starting a big settlement down in Brazil. Was it pride or principle that had driven more than one thousand Southerners to the jungles of South America, the Georgian wondered.

''Another seventeen families coming in next week, Shelby. Maybe your mother'll be with them.''

The Georgian's heart leaped.

''My *mother?*''

''You knew that she moved to your aunt's place near Baton Rouge right after Sherman burned Atlanta, didn't you?''

Davis shook his head.

''She's all right,'' Duval told him. ''Had some problems on the roads to Louisiana, and she picked up a touch of fever. She was over it—well, *just about*—when we left.''

She probably hadn't received his letter.

He'd send another from Paris via Genevieve Carpentier.

''And how's my father?''

"Walking again."

"What does that mean?"

"Some damnfool deserters shot him. They wanted his horse. I told you it was chaos."

Shelby Davis tensed under the impact. His face clouded in anger.

"Somebody's got to stop this, Colonel."

"Tell the Yankees and their boot-lickin' friends. They're running everything. Listen, four families arrived last week. One's from near your aunt's place. They might have fresh news, and we'd all be mighty proud to have a famous hero visit New Dixie. My daughter'd be 'specially pleased."

"Annette's with you?" Davis asked as he recalled his romance seven years earlier with Duval's voluptuous daughter.

Duval shook his head and smiled.

"No, she's gone to ranch in Texas with her husband. Major Phil Sweetwater, served with Nathan Forrest's cavalry. I'm talking about my baby girl—Louise. She's read all about you."

Coping with a starry-eyed adolescent wasn't very appealing, but the chance of word about his father convinced the Georgian. They had no cargo, and the ship couldn't go out anyway, not into a major storm.

"I've got a few errands, Shelby," the ex-colonel reported, "but those won't take more than an hour."

That was perfect. It gave Davis time to write the two letters, leave them with Fitzgerald for the French woman and instruct the first mate that he'd be back from the Southern settlement by nightfall the next day.

As the two former Confederate officers rode west

along the winding coastal road, Davis got his first good look at the scenic beauties of Jamaica. Before this, he'd seen only the ports of Kingston on the south coast and Montego Bay on the sandy northern shore. This fertile island was dressed with a wide variety of trees—poinciana, mahoe, mahogany, cedar, logwood and the rock-hard lignum vitae. Scattered between them was a dazzling assortment of colorful bougainvillea, poinsettia, hibiscus, allamandia and orchids.

There were ferns and flowers everywhere. It was even lovelier than the countryside near Savannah where Shelby Davis had been raised, and he could see—with both his eyes and his mind—why the Southern self-exiles would want to begin again here. The parrots, doves, nightingales and cling-cling birds filled the afternoon with a music that anyone would enjoy.

They were singing as the Americans cantered past the sugar, cotton, coffee, tobacco and cocoa fields. Their sweet sounds were everywhere when Davis and Duval reached the plantation house that was the headquarters of New Dixie.

The first person to greet them as they dismounted was Duval's younger daughter.

She wasn't a baby at all.

Louise Duval had the body of a woman and the face of a great beauty. Her figure was even more breathtaking than the Georgian's recollection of her sister, and her perfect features and masses of jet black hair were the stuff of sailors' dreams. Her face had the elegance of a cameo. Her eyes were dark and warm, and the French part of her ancestry was visible and appealing.

She was almost the exact opposite of Sarah Warren.

In complexion, in hair coloring, in bones and hips, in eyes—even in height.

She was smaller, more delicate and jewel-like.

Both were big-breasted women who stood straight and looked you directly in the eye. Those were the only similarities, so how could he, and why did he, find this just-bloomed patrician nymphet so attractive?

"I have a surprise for you," Duval told her with the grin of an adoring father.

She looked at his saddle for some box or package.

"I don't see it, Papa," she pouted prettily.

There was just the barest trace of a Gallic accent in her honey-and-cream drawl. Yes, her sister had spoken like that too.

"*He* is your *cadeau*, my dear," Duval explained. "Louise, I have the honor to present to you one of the greatest warriors and gentlemen of the Confederacy—our finest and bravest naval commander, Captain Shelby Davis!"

For a moment the Georgian thought that she was about to faint. She looked stunned, almost overwhelmed. Her face flushed and her eyes stared and her angel's bow of a mouth opened in something akin to awe.

"I'm not sure your father's being just to my friend, Admiral Semmes," the Georgian observed, "but it's a pleasure to meet you, Miss Duval."

It took her several seconds to speak.

"Shelby Davis of the *Georgia*?" she whispered.

"At your service, Ma'am."

She was glowing as she turned to her father.

"The most wonderful present I could ever imagine!

Oh, thank you, Papa. Imagine—me meeting Shelby Davis! The most daring hero of them all!"

"We have met before, Ma'am," Davis reminded her pleasantly. "You were ten, as I recall."

"I'm not ten now, Captain," she declared proudly and braced her shoulders. Splendid bosoms must run in the family, Davis guessed.

"I can see that," he acknowledged wryly. "If you don't mind my saying so, you've grown up to be just as pretty as—"

"My *sister*?" she challenged.

"No, your mother—a most beautiful and charming lady."

Duval chuckled, amused at the way the Georgian had nimbly avoided her trap. Aware that she'd be furious if he didn't, the former Confederate colonel invited his excited daughter to join them as he showed Davis around the settlement. Wherever they rode—in homes or warehouses or blacksmith shop, in the compact hospital or sugar mill or the school—Southerners hailed Shelby Davis as a hero.

"You're very flattering," he told the teacher.

"No, but I guess you don't understand," she answered cheerfully. "You're back among *your own* now, Captain."

And Louise Duval beamed.

It was important that he realized that, and that he come to believe that his place was here.

If he were here, he'd be respected and safe.

If he were here, she'd be fulfilled and happy.

She had to be careful not to scare him off, the hot-eyed eighteen-year-old told herself. This was no ordinary man. He was as sensitive as a person as he was daring as a naval hero. She couldn't be too bold. She had wanted him for years—first as a dreamy schoolgirl and now as a hungering, healthy woman. Lots of high-born girls were married by eighteen in Louisiana, but she'd been waiting for this myth of a man to come for her.

Now he was beside her.

Now it was all possible.

He was even better looking, more modest and smarter than she'd recalled—and so very strong and quietly male. Though she remained a well-protected and virtuous virgin, she was sure—in her womb—that this man would be a magnificent lover. She was glad that she'd waited for him. He would ask for her hand in a few months—perhaps in five or six, if all went well. She would bear him strong sons and the most lovely of daughters, just as in her dreams.

She was going to marry him.

It was all coming true.

Even as he listened to her father's account of New Dixie, Shelby Davis was thinking of her too. No man who wasn't sick or troubled could avoid that if he were so close to this nubile and glowing young beauty. She had a freshness and openness that made him forget about ugliness and brutality, and that was good. He could not help but be pleased that so lovely a female admired him, and that she seemed so content and comfortable with him. There was no strain, no tension.

Of course, she was somewhat young.

It could be another adolescent's crush on a well-publicized combat hero.

Even though he recognized that his restlessness was probably loneliness at bottom, it wouldn't be fair to take advantage of this eighteen-year-old's infatuation. She could do better—find someone more suitable than a man twelve years her senior who'd been through hell and was still running for his life.

Meanwhile, they could play at flirting. That was an acceptable form of behavior for young Southern gentry and one basically free of either meaning or danger. They played the game effortlessly until dinner, when Colonel Duval raised other issues. He spoke of the great possibilities for building estates and wealth in these expanding farms, and then turned to the transport problem.

"If we had our own ship we could move our crops for much less, and we could bring in supplies and equipment a lot cheaper," Duval declared over dessert.

"Trouble sending things by land?" Davis asked.

"There could be, Shelby. There's a whole herd of people up in the hills near here who worry me. Children and grandchildren of slaves who ran away years ago. They've got guns, and they're dangerous."

It was the old memories and fears of slave rebellions—the nightmare that had haunted Southern whites for so many decades, Davis thought silently. How long would this distrust and suspicion go on?

"We could use you and your ship, Shelby," Duval continued. "And there's also a need for your men. We're short of young men here. So many of our brave boys died fighting those dirty Yanks that we've got at least forty unmarried women who could use husbands—maybe more."

The Georgian nodded compassionately.

He knew what it was like to be alone.

"I'll tell them, Colonel," he said.

"Lot safer here than wandering the Caribbean where some Yankee warship might attack you if those damn pirates don't."

"We don't intend to stay out forever," the Georgian told him as the maid poured coffee into his cup. "I think my crew means to return to their families and homes and friends—to the life they had."

"They won't find that life in the U.S.A., Shelby. But it's here in New Dixie for anyone who wants it."

At that moment Duval's wife saw that Davis was growing uncomfortable, and—as a gracious hostess should—moved to change the subject. Had he enjoyed the fruit she'd served? She apologized for the wine. It was difficult to secure the better French vintages. They were on order, and she hoped to have them when he returned.

After dinner, Shelby Davis strolled in the gardens with Louise Duval. The night was balmy and the moon bright, and the masses of tropical flowers reminded him of other blossoms long ago and far away.

"Brings back memories of our place near Savannah," he told her. "It's hard to accept that I'll probably never see that house again."

"You can build a fine new house here, Shelby. A man like you can do anything."

He nodded noncommittally. She'd watched his reactions to her father's rhetoric during dinner. She'd noticed his silent lack of enthusiasm. Now was the time to let him know where she stood.

"You could make a great life here—be a great leader and help others rebuild their lives, too," she said earnestly. "Forget all that political talk about the Yankees and such. They're terrible, but there's nothing we can do about it. But we can do everything we want *here*. You and I are young and this is a young place—still growing."

She looked straight into his eyes.

"Your father says the South will rise again."

"And I respect him. He's a wonderful man, Shelby. Maybe it will in forty or fifty years, but we're too young to wait. It would be a crime to waste our youth waiting and hating. Why, we'd be no better than those damn Yankees if we did!"

"Do the others here share you views, Louise?"

"What do *you* care about the others?" she challenged. "*You're* Shelby Davis. You're *the best*."

Then, without warning, she stepped forward and took his hands.

"Don't worry, Captain. I'm not going to kiss you."

She looked very attractive, petite—and mischievous.

"A Southern lady *nevair*, no, *nevair*, throws herself at a strange gentleman. It would be unthinkable, suh. It would be *forward*."

She was teasing him, and rather stylishly.

"No, she waits for him to proceed at a discreet pace. Perhaps the third or fourth time they meet. Back in proper circles in Louisiana, suh, it was the sixth time. Are you *discreet* and *proper*, Captain?"

"More discreet than proper," he fenced with a smile.

"That's a wonderful balance, suh. Well-suited to this informal island, I'd say. I hear that men are forward out here—even gentlemen from good families. I understand they sometimes just grab innocent girls and—you won't believe this, Captain—kiss them the very first time they go walking!"

She moved closer and her lips parted in invitation.

"I wouldn't do anything like that," Davis told her.

Then he kissed her gently on the lips—for several seconds. He stepped back to look down into her fiery black eyes.

"Your father'd shoot me if he knew I did that," Davis told her.

"No, he wouldn't," she denied passionately and Davis had to laugh.

"I didn't know you were as witty as you are pretty," he admitted.

"There's a lot about me that you don't know—*yet*."

"I'll bet."

Then they started back towards the big house. She stopped him just outside the door.

"When are you leaving?" she asked.

"In the morning. A ship's captain is like a woman. His work is never done," he joked.

"When are you returning?"

"What makes you so sure I will?" he tested.

"Because you're an extremely intelligent and sensible man—and because I want you to. You've *got* to, Shelby."

This time *she* kissed *him*—hard.

"You're so forward, Captain," she teased again.

And he laughed once more.

"I'll be back as soon as I can," he promised, and they were both smiling as they entered the house.

Chapter Twenty-Three

At every port that the *Sarah W. Lee* visited during the next nine weeks there were fresh reports of new sinkings by the unknown pirates. They struck again and again, moving up and down the Caribbean at great speed.

"Steam," Shelby Davis told the commandant of a French frigate in Martinique. "Their ship must be steam-powered and well-disguised. You might want to spread the word."

"*Absolument*. I'll do it immediately."

So the warning moved from harbor to harbor, from Trinidad in the southern Caribbean all the way up to Bermuda. The European powers that had colonies in the area recognized the threat of steam-powered pirates, and each decided to send additional warships—in the near future. Unfortunately, there were no vessels available for dispatch to the Caribbean now, since other parts of the world had higher priorities—but by September that would be remedied.

So Bart Beecher and his savage brigands went on robbing, raping, killing—and mocking their victims. In fact, they grew bolder and attacked even larger ships. Now the bodies of murdered sailors floated in bigger clusters. Fear spread like fever across the islands.

On August 16, Shelby Davis got his first glimpse of the pirates' work. The *Sarah W. Lee* was ninety miles south of the Puerto Rican port of Ponce and heading west in the early morning sun. The ship was steaming slowly. It was Paddy Fitzgerald who saw them first.

Corpses.

A full dozen.

Men, women and children. One girl no more than nine or ten. And a priest—in full clerical garb—floating face up.

The fish had been at work on these bodies for some time. Attracted by the blood from the wounds in each corpse, a swarm of silver-blue barracuda was still tearing at the ruined bodies.

The Georgian ordered the ship to stop, then put over two boats to collect the dead. They were entitled to a decent burial. The *Sarah W. Lee* would bring them to Santo Domingo and turn them over to the church authorities there. As the bodies were carried on deck, he saw the bloody holes made by blade and bullet.

There could be no doubt.

They'd all been murdered—almost surely by the pirates.

The first mate saw the wrath in Davis' face.

"Somebody's bound to catch those bastards soon, Captain," he predicted.

"Not soon enough."

The ship steamed west for another five hours before the mustachioed ensign from Texas called Shelby Davis' attention to the dark pillar on the horizon. It was too much smoke for the normal emissions of a stack. A vessel was ablaze—only five or six miles away.

Fire at sea was a terrible thing.

It was the unwritten law that no mariner could ignore a burning ship, and every man on the *Sarah W. Lee* knew it.

"Full speed ahead!" Davis ordered.

Within five minutes, the former raider was hurrying across the Caribbean with every knot that her engines could muster. The whole ship was vibrating as the heavy machinery responded to the call. Everyone but the engine-room crew was on deck, straining and peering ahead.

Davis too was eyeing the black smoke—and thinking.

It was quite automatic.

A captain always had to plan ahead, to prepare for various contingencies.

Perhaps it was a fire.

Maybe it was something more dangerous.

"Paddy."

"Yes, sir."

"Please sound battle stations."

The first mate's brow furrowed for several seconds before he understood.

"You think it's *them*, Captain?"

"We'll know soon enough."

The gun crew ran to their cannons, and word spread across the ship almost as quickly.

It might be the butchers.

The ex-raider might be going back to war again. It was a risky thing to do, for such a battle could expose the real identity of the hunted ship. If the bloody pirates were there, however, there could be no turning back. They had to be stopped. The killing must end.

Now the men on the *Sarah W. Lee* saw two ships about a mile and a half ahead. One was an inter-island schooner, embraced by flame from bow to stern. Her canvas sails were all ablaze, giving her the look of an ancient Viking craft torched for some ritual funeral.

The other vessel was a three-stacker steamship flying the Spanish flag. Cannon peered from several gunports. It was cruising slowly away from the burning craft.

This *had* to be the pirates.

"So that's how they do it," Davis thought aloud. "They loot the cargo and burn the ships to sink them."

Then he studied the armed steamer more carefully.

There was something familiar about that silhouette, those rakish lines. She was built for speed. He'd seen her before.

Where?

She was a blockade runner.

"The *Caroline!*" Shelby Davis identified triumphantly.

"You sure, Captain?" Fitzgerald asked.

"Dead sure. It's Bart Beecher, the biggest bastard of them all. So he's been sinking unarmed schooners for years. Let's see how he does with a warship."

The first mate shook his head.

"Terrible that a Confederate ship's turned pirate," he lamented.

"The *Caroline* never really served the Confederacy," Davis corrected angrily. "Bart Beecher ran her for his own profit. *This* ship served the Confederacy!"

"And well, sir," Fitzgerald agreed.

"Run up the flag!" the Georgian ordered. "Let that animal know who's blowing him out of the water. Run up our flag *NOW!*"

So it was that more than two years after Lee surrendered at Appomattox and the last Southern vessel yielded, the banner of the Confederate States of America flew once again.

When the men on the deck saw the long-hidden Stars and Bars fluttering defiantly in the trade winds one thousand miles from home, they cheered. They shouted and roared and pointed. For a full minute they went wild.

They didn't care where they were or how briefly that banner would fly.

They had stopped hiding and fearing.

They were fighting men on a Confederate warship again, sailing under their flag and a captain they loved.

By some miracle their time of glory had returned.

Now the pirates celebrating on the *Caroline* saw them approaching, and Beecher raised his telescope to examine the vessel that would be his next victim.

He was stunned by the sight of the Confederate flag.

He was shaken by the sight of the cannon. The rapidly closing steamer was showing her teeth. Davis had ordered every gun to be ready, even those long masked.

It couldn't be the *Georgia*, Beecher told himself.

It couldn't be.

The *Georgia* and her crew were long dead. No one had seen them for years. They had to be at the bottom of the sea.

Suddenly Beecher remembered the handsome young captain of the *Georgia* who'd humiliated him that afternoon three years earlier.

Shelby Davis, an arrogant, meddling aristocrat.

A fake "hero" with the right family connections.

This was Beecher's chance for vengeance.

He ordered his gunners to halt the carousing and man their weapons. The ship that couldn't be the *Georgia* was barely a mile away. For a few moments Beecher wondered whether to flee. His blockade runner was a bit faster than the *Georgia*. It was built expressly for speed. The cautious move would be to run.

Beecher decided to fight. He'd teach that snotty Davis a lesson. He'd pay him back at last.

"Fire!" the beefy pirate bellowed. His cannon boomed. Two shells fell short. One whistled between the *Georgia's* smokestacks and another tore a hole in the prow.

"Fire!" Davis ordered.

Three hits in the first salvo. The *Caroline* shuddered under the impact. She'd never taken cannon fire before, never fought a foe who was equally armed.

The pirates reloaded quickly. Their gun crews were experienced at that, if not in fair combat. The *Caroline's* cannon roared again. But Davis swung the wheel of his ship sharply five seconds before they fired.

No hits at all this time.

He turned the *Georgia* so the guns on her other side

faced the pirate ship. Another salvo. Four square hits. One destroyed a pirate cannon and gun crew. Another started a fire in the aft hold. The third tore into the engine room, gouging a hole in the main boiler. Scalding steam spouted in a terrible gush, killing two men and burning four others horribly.

And the steam pressure started to fall.

The *Caroline* was slowing.

Beecher felt it. He shouted obscenities, screamed at his gunners to keep shooting and howled a command that speed be maintained.

Two shells struck the *Georgia* amidships as she turned again. She shuddered, but her batteries thundered back defiantly. Three more hits. Then another four. The pirate craft reeled under the battering. Three separate fires were burning, and panicky brigands fled their cannon in screaming fear.

The shells stacked by one gun exploded with a roar, and seven men perished. Both boilers were knocked out now. There were nine dead stokers and engineers sprawled in the searing steam, scalded and half-skinned by the intensely hot and fatal fog. Only three of the pirate craft's cannon were still firing—and these intermittently.

The *Caroline* was dead in the water, lurching as the *Georgia's* inspired gunners pounded her with hit after hit. The two ships were barely half a mile apart, with the crippled pirate vessel motionless, as Davis skillfully zigzagged to offer a minimum target.

The fires were spreading on the pirate ship. Some of the crew were struggling to launch lifeboats. Others were simply jumping into the sea. Anything was better than being burned alive. The murderers who had cheerfully cremated so many innocent people had no stomach for such a fate. Another explosion jarred the *Caroline*. The mast with the fake Spanish flag crashed down onto the deck, crushing one pirate gunner like a bug.

Pepe Lopez was screaming. Beecher's second mate had not been afraid to rob and stab in his native Santo Domingo, to shoot and rape and kill again and again at sea in the past two years. He had not been afraid of committing unspeakable acts of cruelty and degradation, but now he was totally terrified.

The *Caroline* was doomed.

He had to get into a lifeboat.

Two of them had been shattered by shells. A third was burning. The davits to lower another were jammed. There was but one boat left—one chance to survive. Lopez saw Beecher lumbering towards it through the flames and bodies. Yes, his *capitano* would save him!

There were already eight men in the small boat as Beecher began to lift himself laboriously over the side.

"Save me, *Capitano!*" Lopez pleaded, and lunged for the boat.

"Certainly," Beecher replied with a sneer and drew a derringer. His second mate opened his lips to plead. Beecher shot him in the head twice, shoved him aside and got into the dinghy. Ignoring the dying squeals of his second mate, he tugged at the line that would lower the small craft. The lifeboat was afloat seventy seconds later, with eight sailors rowing hard to escape the undertow that would accompany the sinking of the *Caroline*.

Another explosion tore at the once sleek blockade runner. The entire deck was a sheet of flickering yellow flame. Three of the crew had hesitated, but now, seeing that they had no choice, they jumped into the water. They cried out for the lifeboat to pick them up. Beecher ignored their desperate appeals.

There was still one man alive on the *Caroline*. He was a stoker who'd been blinded by the blast of steam. He'd somehow found his way to the deck, and now he was wandering through the bodies and the burning debris, calling out for someone to help him. But there was no one to hear. He was still shouting in pain and rage as the *Caroline* began to slip beneath the waves.

Davis looked carefully through his telescope at the lifeboat.

There he was—the monster.

It was Bart Beecher, the man who'd sworn to kill him. Now he'd pick Beecher and his survivors from the sea and deliver them ashore for trial and execution. It hardly mattered at which port he gave them to the police. These killers were wanted everywhere within a thousand miles.

There was no trace of the ship that the pirates had just sunk. It was already at the bottom of the Caribbean, and this time no corpses bobbed on the waves. The *Caroline* was almost gone too. As the last of the pirate craft vanished into the sea, Davis' crew cheered again.

Then he pointed at the boat in which Beecher was trying to get away.

"Let's fish that garbage out of the sea, Paddy," the Georgian ordered.

Steaming at one-third speed, the former Confederate raider moved closer to the lifeboat. When the gap was reduced to some sixty yards, three sailors on the deck tossed down lines to save the men in the small craft.

"Why don't we just forget about them?" one crewman grumbled. "They're not worth the trouble to rescue."

And two of the gunners agreed, but no one would defy Shelby Davis' plan—except the men in the lifeboat.

They had pistols, and they were shooting at those who meant to save them. It was pointless, suicidal and insane.

"I mean to bring those butchers in for the gallows," Davis announced, then commanded the helmsman to guide the ship in a slow circle just out of pistol range. Then a grim-faced Shelby Davis ordered two gun crews to blow the lifeboat into kindling.

They did.

It was not easy to hit such a small bobbing target, but on the third salvo one shell scored a direct hit that killed two pirates and pitched the others into the water. Screaming from the hurt of a gash in his left leg, Bart Beecher paddled frantically. The others swimming beside him were also crying out in panic, begging for help.

"Oh my God!" William Cicero Preston said, pointing.

Big dorsal fins cutting through the water.

Sharks!

At least a dozen of them.

Moving in for the kill.

The pirates saw the sharks now, and began to thrash in the water hysterically as they howled for rescue. Their flailing-about seemed to attract the sharks as much as the blood seeping from several of the wounded pirates. Sharks weren't that common in this part of the Caribbean.

"Divine retribution," Fitzgerald judged solemnly.

Davis ordered his crew to grab rifles and shoot at the huge-jawed creatures, and commanded that the ship race to where the pirates swam.

Seconds later, a shark took off one man's leg at the knee and another brigand simply vanished, dragged down by an unseen predator. Beecher started to swim away from the others. He didn't get very far. His paddling was halted when a ten-foot-long shark snapped off his right foot. He screamed and screamed and screamed as blood gushed from the stump.

Then three sharks finished him in big bites.

The other pirates didn't last much longer. Though two sharks were hit by the riflemen, the others kept attacking savagely until not one of the vicious thugs survived.

The killers had been killed.

There was no reason to linger here.

Shelby Davis ordered the Confederate flag to be lowered, and the whole crew stood at attention as the Stars and Bars came down. Some wept. As the mustachioed ensign folded the banner tenderly for storage, Davis realized he'd probably never fly that flag again.

That was the past.

Now he had to face the future.

Chapter Twenty-Four

When he saw the entrance to Kingston harbor ahead, Davis warned his crew again.

No matter how proud they were, no matter how tempting it might be, whether stone sober or half tipsy and even if the girl they were trying to impress was the greatest beauty in the Caribbean, they could not tell anyone that they'd sunk the pirate craft.

It was too risky. It could cost them their lives.

It would draw dangerous attention to their own vessel. People would wonder how a half-armed merchantman could defeat the scourge of the Caribbean. Someone, perhaps a naval officer or a journalist, would speculate on how a tramp steamer could prevail in such a fight.

There was no point in winning the battle if they lost the war. Safety was more important than glory. Who got the credit didn't matter. Someday they could speak of their victory, but not until it was safe to go home. Any man who even hinted at what had happened would be risking the necks of the entire crew.

The stood listening in the morning sun, nodding silently in understanding. Then he sent them back to their posts, and thought of Louise Duval. She was young, but very attractive. She had spirit and an appetite for living. Both her beauty and her personality made her the most appealing woman he'd met in a long time. She had grace and fire. Yes, he would return to see her at New Dixie.

They entered the harbor. He thought again of his decision not to tell his crew of Colonel Duval's invitation—not yet. He'd put it off because he hadn't made up his own mind. Had that been a mistake? Was he being unfair to them? Was it a captain's sound caution or a man's selfishness that had guided him?

He would go to the Confederate settlement again. He had to feel it out completely before he offered them the choice. They'd surely ask him what *he* was going to do, and he wouldn't be able to answer until he'd seen her and New Dixie once more. It wouldn't be right to put it off much longer. A captain was supposed to be able to make decisions—and so was a grown man.

Fitzgerald would surely say no. His heart was in Cuba. Preston was also unlikely to stay in Jamaica. His family waited in Carolina, and despite the doctor's fling with the passionate young Haitian beauty, Preston was basically a family man. So was the chief engineer as was burly Israel Diamond, the master gunner who presided over the ship's cannon. He couldn't be that certain about the others. Some of the younger ones with no ties back in the States might say yes, and that might leave the ship without a full crew.

The ship had always come first.

Now he wondered about the crew. They had a claim on him that was just as great. A crew was made up of individuals. Individuals had rights too—rights that a compassionate captain such as Shelby Davis could not ignore. If some of them preferred the peace and opportunity of New Dixie to the chaos and punishment of Yankee misrule back in the conquered Southern states, who was he to deny them? A captain wasn't God, even though he often had to act as if he were.

He watched impassively as Fitzgerald directed the docking. Paddy did his work well, the Georgian observed. He was certainly capable of running this ship if Davis left it for Duval's offer. He could carry on in command for another year or so until the senseless Yankee hatred subsided and this ship could go home safely.

When the lines were all secure, Davis went ashore to find the offices of Jamaica Sundries Ltd. and tell the importers that their cargo had arrived. Following directions supplied by an efficient and crisply dignified black police constable, he had no difficulty in locating the two-story building. The red-faced Welshman named Jenkins who headed the firm was delighted that his shipment was in, and offered Davis another cargo to be moved north to Nassau on Wednesday.

That gave Davis forty-eight hours to visit New Dixie.

The cargo was locally brewed beer, which Mr. Richard Jenkins recommended highly. Declining a glass, the Georgian accepted the assignment and left to find transportation to New Dixie. Davis was fifty yards from

Jamaica Sundries Ltd. when he walked by a distinguished-looking man. He stopped in his tracks.

He knew that man.

Calloway. John T. Calloway, the pharmacist who'd served the Davis family and others in Savannah.

They shook hands, and the pharmacist told him that he'd only arrived the previous day en route to the Southern settlement down the coast.

"How are things in Savannah?" Davis asked.

"Couldn't say. I've been in Louisiana for the past fifteen months, and things are terrible there."

"Louisiana? Did you see my parents?"

Calloway's face showed distress.

He nodded.

"What is it?"

"Sorry about your mother, Shelby. A fine woman."

Then he saw the shock in the mariner's eyes.

"You didn't know?" The pharmacist questioned.

"Know what? What's wong?"

"Fever—bad fever. Took a lot of people."

"Is she . . . dead?"

"Not yet, but mighty sick. Didn't look good when I left. By now? Well, I'm sorry I brought the bad news, son. I was always real fond of your . . ."

But Davis was hurrying away. His mother was sick—perhaps terminally. He had to go to her. He couldn't risk the ship or the lives of the others, so he'd go alone. Nobody knew him in Louisiana—no Yankees anyway. He'd never been in that state.

He rushed to the harbormaster's office. There was a British vessel named the Dover Star leaving for the

U.S.A. on the evening tide. She was at Pier Four, and her skipper was Captain Greenwood.

At ten minutes after noon, Shelby Davis returned to his ship to tell Fitzgerald what he was doing and to put him in command until the Georgian came back. They'd rendezvous here in six weeks. That should be plenty of time for the round trip.

Neither of them spoke of the danger.

It was implicit that if Davis didn't get back, Fitzgerald was to carry on.

"May the road rise with you," Fitzgerald said, quoting the traditional Irish wish for good luck.

"Thanks, Paddy."

They shook hands, and Shelby Davis packed his clothes quickly. He left his ship at half past one. By five p.m. he was at sea on a strange and foreign vessel—a passenger for the first time in as long as he could remember.

She couldn't be dead, he told himself as he watched the Jamaican shore disappear.

She'd weathered fever before.

She was a strong-willed and majestic woman who'd fight for her life as she'd battled for her principles for so many years.

She'd be there when he arrived.

She had to be. She wouldn't leave without bidding her favorite son good-by.

There were U.S. gunboats in New Orleans harbor.

There were U.S. troops in the great port's streets.

The city looked as if it were under military occupation.

It was. It had been since 1862 when a flotilla of warships led by Admiral David Farragut had blasted through Southern defenses and the Confederate forces retreated northward up the Mississippi.

Then ''Beast'' Butler arrived. Major General Benjamin Butler, a Massachusetts lawyer who got his commission in May 1861 as a political payoff, soon became the most hated Union officer in the South. Commander of the U.S. garrison, Butler was furious when proud Confederate women showed their disdain for the army of occupation in a dozen ways. In retaliation, this angry man issued an official order that any female who did not exhibit proper respect for the Union flag or uniform should be treated as ''a woman of the town, plying her trade,'' i.e., a common whore. This and his other brutal tactics had won him both the nickname ''Beast'' and the undying hatred of the entire South.

Now Butler had left to serve as a ''make Dixie pay'' congressman, but the occupation of New Orleans was still extremely stern and punitive. Shelby Davis could see the resentment in a hundred faces as he rode from the dock on his way to his dying mother. First French, then Spanish and later French again before the U.S. bought Louisiana from Napoleon, New Orleans had been a cheery and exuberant town with a lively and cosmopolitan population. Now it had a grim quality. The bitterness of both the occupiers and the occupied hung as thick as the humid August air. You could almost touch it.

From the moment he'd disembarked with the forged papers that identified him as Peter Norris of Baltimore, Davis had pretended to be unaware of or indifferent to this atmosphere. As he passed the second cavalry patrol in sixteen miles, he nodded politely as a loyal resident of Maryland should. He had resolved to speak as little as possible, for his Georgia drawl could be dangerous.

Anything could be dangerous.

Everything could be dangerous.

He must do nothing to attract attention. He'd said only a few words when he bought his seat on the coach, and he remained equally taciturn as it moved northwest past the fields of sugar and cotton en route to Reserve, a small farming community in Saint John the Baptist Parish. Long ruled by devout French Catholics, Louisiana still called its counties parishes.

Fortunately, the other passengers were not very loquacious either. The August heat discouraged small talk. At half past three, the man who called himself Peter Norris climbed down from the coach on the dusty main street and nodded farewell to the driver. Then he found Reserve's small post office. The clerk on duty spoke with a lush French accent, and that was good. It meant he wasn't a Yankee official who might report a stranger.

"Ah, *oui*. Dah-veess? But there are two *familles* with that *nom*. *Les Jeunes*—the young ones with five *enfants* or the older *peuple* who came last year?"

Shelby Davis had the location a minute later, and twenty-five minutes after that he faced the house where his parents now lived. It was a neat little residence of four rooms, minute in comparison to the eleven-room establishment in which he'd grown up in Georgia. He tied the rented horse to the fence post and knocked on the door.

Then he saw his father.

"Shelby!" John Howell Davis cried out in joy.

He was fifty-seven, the mariner recalled, but he looked a lot older. Still ramrod-straight and lean, he showed the effects of the long years of war and Reconstruction. His hair was grey, and he radiated weariness. But there was something else in this man's eyes. He was worn, but he wasn't defeated.

They embraced.

Then John Davis took his son to the bedroom to see his mother. She was thin and exhausted, but she sat up immediately when she saw her son. Tears flooded her eyes.

"Don't cry, Mom. I'm all right. I've come a long way to see you. Please don't cry."

She dabbed at her eyes with a crumpled lace handkerchief. Shelby Davis recognized the design. This was one of four that he'd given her on her birthday, a week before the war began.

"I'm not crying . . . Oh, Shelby . . . *Shelby,*" she rejoiced.

He sat on the edge of the bed and held her close, feeling the muffled sobs she was choking back.

"They said you were dead. Oh, Shelby, they said you were dead!"

"We knew you weren't, son," John Davis assured.

"In a sense I am," the former raider captain joked, "and so's the *Georgia*. We've both got new names. We had to."

"And where've you been?" his father asked.

"Out in the Caribbean. I came straight from there when I heard how sick this Georgia lady was."

"I was sick," she admitted.

"Very sick. For weeks. It looked bad," John Davis reported. "Fact is, her fever only broke last night."

"Just in time for my homecoming. It's a nice little place."

It was nothing like the estate they'd had in Georgia, and they all knew it. Now that they were together, nobody cared.

"Is it safe for you to come back now?" Lucinda Davis asked.

"I think so. Can't be sure, but I can hardly imagine that anybody in Washington even remembers me or the ship."

His father shook his head.

"I think they were watching the house a few months ago," he said.

"Now, John. That was back before Christmas. It's all right now, isn't it?"

"Sure, Ma," Shelby Davis assured the frail woman. "It's fine."

Then he saw the head and shoulders of a man in the window.

It was a U.S. soldier, and he was pointing a rifle directly at the mariner.

Shelby Davis' eyes turned to the next window.

Another trooper's rifle.

He stood up and moved away from the bed.

If they were going to shoot, he didn't want to risk a bullet hitting his mother.

He'd find an excuse to leave the house. That way the soldiers would have no reason to fire in. They could seize him outside.

"I've got a present for you, Ma," he lied. "I'll go out and get it."

At that moment the front door crashed open. At the same instant the troopers rammed their gun muzzles through the panes, scattering glass across the room. A Yankee lieutenant and three soldiers charged across the threshold.

They pointed their weapons at their famous enemy.

"Don't move!" the officer with the heavy pistol roared. "One move and I'll kill you!"

Shelby Davis stood absolutely still.

"We've been waiting for you, Reb," the lieutenant taunted. "I told them you'd come back to see yore poor sick mammy, and danged if you didn't!"

Now his mother slumped back onto the pillow. She was numb with guilt. Her only son's love for her would cost him his life.

"We been waiting for ten or eleven weeks, Mr. Shelby Davis, and you danced right into our trap. Next week you'll be dancing on a rope, mister!"

"Not if I get a fair trial. I did nothing wrong," the former Confederate captain said calmly.

The lieutenant grinned.

"You'll get a fair trial, pirate. And a fair hanging," he promised. He gestured, and two troopers stepped forward.

"And you'll tell us where your murdering friends are," he predicted. "Come on, Johnny Reb. There's a cell waiting for you in New Orleans."

The soldiers hustled him out of the house.

A minute later, John and Lucinda Davis saw him through the broken window—just a glimpse—as the

Federal troops took him away. In a moment the soldiers and their prisoner were out of sight.

Only then did Shelby's mother allow herself to weep. She cried for a long time.

Chapter Twenty-Five

If the trial would be anything like the newspaper reports of his arrest, it would be anything but fair. Thoroughly intimidated by the military government or else owned by scalawags indebted to the Yankees, every daily in the state denounced Shelby Davis in blaring headlines. His "heinous crimes" were emblazoned on all the front pages.

"It isn't going to be a trial," sighed defense attorney Henry Rosamond. "It'll be a circus."

"I'm sure you'll do your best. Since my parents chose you, that must be pretty good," Davis answered.

He sounded more confident than he was. The Georgian didn't really expect justice in this super-heated atmosphere of hate. Thousands of decent Yankee lads had died in the war, and the generous surrender terms that Grant had given to Lee at Appomattox had cheated their friends and families of the chance to punish the battered Confederate soldiers who'd slain them.

This was a chance for mass revenge.

So this one man would symbolize all the deep, stomach-turning and irrational hurt and hatred.

Shelby Davis would pay for all of them.

And there was anger among the former Confederates in Louisiana, too. In their eyes, this handsome and almost legendary Georgian had been a white knight on a charger—a gallant hero of historic proportion. He reminded them of all their ruined dreams and tattered fantasies about dashing and invincible Southern warriors—gentleman soldiers who could do anything. It was outrageous that this famous and well-bred sea captain should be slandered and reviled as a vicious murderer by press and public officials alike. It was intolerable that Captain Shelby Davis of the *Georgia* should be dragged to court each day in chains like some common criminal.

The indignation grew. The fury of the ex-Confederates spread, and soon there were rumors that a mob of thousands would storm the U.S. courthouse to set him free. Fearful Federal authorities appealed for troops to protect them and their prisoner. From the first day of the trial, three hundred Union soldiers with fixed bayonets ringed the courthouse while another strong detachment guarded the prison at night.

Defense lawyer Henry Rosamond had been right.

It was a circus, and an ugly one.

The judge assigned was the harshest man on the Federal bench in Louisiana, T. Rowland Edwards—known for imposing the maximum sentence the law allowed. Judge Edwards made it clear where he stood from the outset. He denied the request for a jury trial on grounds that so many local residents were Rebel sympathizers that no jury here would convict Davis. He rushed the case to trial at a speed unheard of in Louisiana legal history.

In cases where a death penalty was possible, the defense usually got three or four months to prepare. Davis' lawyer was given three weeks. Once the trial began, a parade of government witnesses, including a U.S. Navy admiral, testified that the *Georgia* had ruthlessly sunk various U.S. merchant ships after the Confederacy had formally surrendered and all hostilities had ceased. There had been great loss of life. Since the *Georgia* no longer had any status as a warship, these vicious deeds were a blatant violation of international law and U.S. statutes.

Shelby Davis and his crew were pirates and murderers.

The penalty for either was death.

Then the Georgian testified that he'd had no way of knowing that the war was over and that he had not known it until his ship docked at Liverpool.

"That's one man's unsubstantiated statement," the judge challenged. "A criminal can say anything to save his neck. Where are the corroborating witnesses?"

Davis glanced at his attorney and shook his head. The only people who could confirm this were his crew, and he would not betray them.

The trial lasted only four and a half days, and that included the lengthy summations and rhetoric of the lawyers on both sides. Then the judge announced that he'd make his decision overnight and read it in court at two the next afternoon.

It was, of course, a foregone conclusion.

Everyone knew that he'd order Shelby Davis hanged.

The crowds outside were even bigger that following afternoon. The troops on guard were reinforced. Cannon were brought up—three on each side of the courthouse. If the wild Rebels charged, there'd be grapeshot to scythe them down.

Judge Edwards was a punctual man. He entered the courtroom precisely at two p.m. and began to read a summary of the evidence. He was done at 2:07. Then he went on to review the provisions of U.S. law that governed piracy and murder at sea. At 2:13 he was ready to read his decision.

Edwards was a dry and punctilious graduate of the noted Harvard Law School, and he had to dot each "i" and cross every "t" meticulously. Whatever he was as a human, this proper Bostonian was a careful lawyer. He had spent hours drafting his decision, for he knew that it would be quoted in papers and law journals across the country—maybe even aboard. Yes, Judge T. Rowland Evans had an appetite for fame, and this was his big chance. Another might never come his way.

"I have considered both the evidence—the facts—and the law *very* carefully," he intoned majestically. "This is an extremely important case, one that has understandably attracted national attention."

He paused for a moment to relish the situation.

Then his sense of judicial manners moved him ahead.

"Before I go on to issue my decision and sentence, I will give the defendant one more opportunity to atone for his atrocious deeds by telling us where his fellow criminals are hiding. That could be a factor—a *possible* factor—in mitigating the sentence.''

''They are outside the United States and beyond the jurisdiction of this court,'' Davis announced. ''That's all I can tell you, Your Honor.''

Edwards' head bobbed in disdain.

''I'll proceed to the decision. It seems obvious to me, as it must to everyone here, that but one decision is possible.''

A stir swept across the room.

This was *the* moment.

The judge would sentence the Johnny Reb killer to swing.

''I hereby find the defendant, Shelby Davis—formerly a captain in the navy of the so-called Confederate State of America—''

Just then the rear door to the courtroom opened and Judge Edwards stopped in mid-sentence. He looked at the two people who'd entered. He didn't know the woman, but he certainly recognized the well-dressed man.

''We have a distinguished public servant with us,'' Edwards boasted. ''The Governor of this great state and my classmate at Harvard.''

''And we have another witness, Judge Edwards,'' the barrel-chested governor declared. ''An important witness with vital testimony.''

The judge looked uneasy. The case was over.

''She happens to be my sister,'' the governor announced loudly in a voice that bordered on being threatening.

T. Rowland Edwards swallowed hard. Even though a Federal judge was appointed for life, it might be foolhardy to make an enemy of a governor who had excellent connections in Washington.

"Why, of course, Governor. Bring your sister down so she may be sworn in to testify."

Shelby Davis turned to look at this unexpected witness, wondering who she might be and what she could add.

He saw a full-figured beauty with masses of extraordinary red hair.

It was the Yankee whaling captain's daughter.

It was Sarah Warren.

Chapter Twenty-Six

She wasn't dead.

His heart leaped, and he stood up instantly to see her better—to see all of her.

"Sarah!" he whispered.

The guards jerked him down roughly, gouging his wrists by pulling on the chains. He felt no pain. It was a miracle. She was alive. Nothing else mattered. Even if they hanged him, he had seen his love again.

She was sworn in immediately, and began to testify without a moment's delay. She looked directly at him as she spoke.

"My name is Sarah Warren. I live in New Bedford, Massachusetts, with my father. His name is Joshua Warren. Captain Joshua Warren. He's the master of a whaling ship named the *Exeter*. In 1864, he was in command of another whaler. That was the *Simon Grundy*.

I was with him on the North Atlantic when it was sunk."

"By whom?" the judge asked.

"By the Confederate warship *Georgia*—commanded by Captain Shelby Davis."

"We've heard about other ships he sank," Judge Edwards told her.

"May I go on?"

"Of course."

"First, I understand that he's accused of being indifferent to the loss of life and of abandoning survivors. That's a lie!"

A gasp ran through the room.

"That's a flat-out lie. I was raised to tell the truth, and I'm saying right now—under oath on this Holy Bible—that it's a lie! He and his crew rescued every single man—and woman—from the *Simon Grundy*. We were taken aboard his vessel and treated well."

Now Edwards was eyeing her curiously.

Did she have some personal interest in this handsome Rebel?

Could Edwards really believe her?

"He sank your father's ship after the war was over, didn't he?" the judge accused.

"He didn't know the war was over. Neither did we. Both ships had been at sea for weeks. None of us was aware of the surrender until the *Georgia* docked in Liverpool—ten weeks after Appomattox."

The judge was visibly stunned.

"Go on."

"A fortnight after the *Georgia* left Liverpool, my father and I and two of his officers boarded a ship to return to the United States. It went down in a storm, but I was lucky again. A French vessel picked up a dozen survivors and took us to Bordeaux. We didn't get home until the middle of July. I've been living in New Bedford since."

"This is most unusual testimony, Miss Warren . . . Ah . . . I'm confident that the sister of our distinguished governor would not . . . *tamper* with the truth, but I can't help noting how you're looking at the defendant. Please forgive me, but I must ask how you feel about him."

"I respect him . . . and *I love him*."

Another gasp spread through the courtroom.

Edwards shrugged.

"I'll have to consider that in evaluating your testimony. I mean no discourtesy, but it *is* uncorroborated."

"No, it isn't."

Now her brother came forward with a sheaf of papers. He gave them to Edwards.

"These are sworm affidavits taken by a U.S. magistrate in Boston. Five are by members of the *Simon Grundy's* crew, the governor of Louisiana announced firmly, "and another is by my father. They all confirm exactly what my sister has just told you. Six affidavits by Yankees who *don't* love Captain Davis but who believe in truth and justice, as I do—and as I'm sure *you* do."

There was a threat buried in the words.

"Of course," T. Rowland Edwards stalled.

"My . . . father . . . doesn't . . . lie."

"I wouldn't . . . There's no question . . ." the judge

fumbled. "A surprise witness at the last minute . . . Why wasn't she here with the affidavits earlier?"

"I came as soon as I heard, Your Honor," she told him.

The judge slowly folded the sheet of paper on which he'd written his decision and sentence.

"For the record, Your Honor," Governor Ezra Warren said with his eyes on the many journalists in the room, "I happen to despise Rebels—all of them. I despise injustice *more*."

Edwards' stomach knotted in anger beneath his impressive judicial robes. The damn governor was showing off his virtue to the press and simultaneously protecting his political future, leaving the dirty and dangerous work for Edwards to clean up. No matter what the judge did, it would be messy.

Morality—that was it.

T. Rowland Edwards would show him who could be more noble and pious.

Even if it cost Edwards that promotion to the higher court, he'd have the satisfaction of impressing other judges and lawyers with his intellectual integrity. It would certainly win the approval of his professors back at Harvard, who'd never taken Edwards too seriously as a legal thinker. Yes, he'd show them all!

It didn't *have* to wreck his career either, Edwards calculated shrewdly. The bitterness towards the Southerners had to subside sooner or later. A judge who'd been tough, but fair might move up quickly then—maybe even to the Supreme Court. Sure, the President was already battling to ease the harshness of Reconstruction—

and it was the President who picked Supreme Court justices.

There was something else working deep inside the judge. He had his pride. He couldn't possibly send an innocent man to the gallows—even a Rebel. As much as he resented the indifference of his law school teachers, they had instilled a respect for right in him. It was still there within him like a boulder, hard and unbreakable.

"We'll have to adjourn this proceeding until I've studied these affidavits and telegraphed to the U.S. magistrate in Boston as well as the men who signed these papers."

The sweating federal prosecutor rose to object.

"Your Honor, I can't see—"

"Please, Mr. Lester. You wouldn't want to hang an innocent man, would you?" Edwards asked virtuously.

The prosecutor sat down.

The nation was stunned. New Orleans went wild. When Edwards found Shelby Davis innocent five days later, there were celebrations all over the city—and in the town of Reserve in Saint John the Baptist Parish.

And there was a wedding.

Up until the last minute, the governor of Louisiana insisted that he wouldn't attend. But he did.

His love for his sister and grudging respect for the man who'd saved her and his father made him.

It was a small wedding and a brief ceremony.

When it was over, the bride and groom kissed for a very long time. His mother wept openly and unashamedly.

It was then that Shelby Davis told them.

"We'll be leaving in a few days," he said, holding

tight to the hand of the woman for whom he'd waited so long.

"Why? Where?" his father asked.

"Why? Because there's still too much hate here. We don't want to raise children in a country torn by bitterness, and we're planning on a lot of children."

"A *lot*," Sarah Warren Davis confirmed happily.

"We're going to Jamaica first," her beaming husband announced. "I've got to tell my crew—my friends—that they're not hunted men anymore. They'll be coming home too."

Except Paddy Fitzgerald.

He had business in Cuba.

"And there are some other people I've got to talk to in Jamaica," the former raider captain continued.

Colonel Raymond Duval.

His beautiful young daughter, Louise.

He had to let them know that he would not join them in New Dixie. There was too much looking back, too much anger there too.

"And after Jamaica?" Governor Warren asked.

"I'll try to find a new command—a ship that needs a captain. That's what I am, and what I want to be. Maybe we'll be able to buy the . . . the *Sarah W. Lee*. Nice name for a ship, isn't it?"

The redheaded bride glowed.

Even her brother smiled.

"We'll settle down on some peaceful island, build a house and a family. We'll find a place where the War Between the States is just dim foreign history."

Then Mr. and Mrs. Shelby Davis said their good-bys to family and friends.

"Won't you ever come back, son?" his father asked.

"In time. *This* is our country, you know. But for now, we're Caribbeans."

Eleven months and four days later, Sarah Warren Davis gave birth to twins of stunning good looks. They named the boy Joshua after a certain New Bedford whaling captain. They called the redheaded girl Roberta in honor of the South's greatest general.

They were quite sure he wouldn't mind.